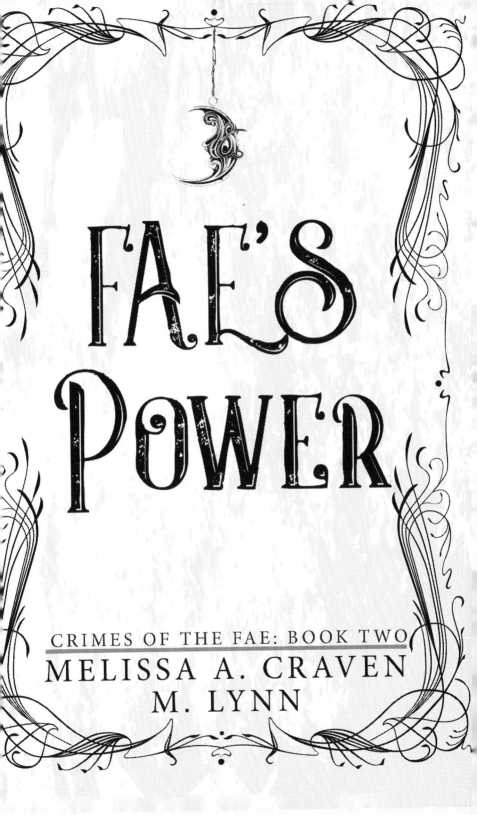

FAE'S POWER

CRIMES OF THE FAE: BOOK TWO

MELISSA A. CRAVEN
M. LYNN

Edited by Cindy Ray Hale
Cover by Covers by Combs

For those who gave Griff a second chance. And for those who didn't, but you aren't seeing this anyway.

PRISON REALM

NORTHERN VATLA

LOCH VILLANDI

FARGELSI KINGDOM

SOUTHERN VATLA

⊛DRAGUR FOREST

⊛VINDUR CITY

ISKALT KINGDOM

EASTERN VATLANDS

ELDFAL

SANDUR

SOL LOCH

UR KINGDOM

TEOTANN OASIS

ELDUR DESERT

CH LANGT

RADUR CITY

CHAPTER ONE

Riona

I'm losing my patience.

Riona read the words as they appeared in front of her, wishing she could wipe them from her mind as easily as she could from the spelled journal.

I'm losing my patience.

She knew what would happen to her and Griffin if they didn't return to Myrkur soon.

King Egan. He was the only king she'd ever known until stepping foot outside what the Light Fae called the prison realm. Egan raised her from a small child. He'd given her a purpose, a calling. And at one time, she'd loved him for it.

Maybe not in the way a normal fae loves. She'd watched how Queen Brea looked at her children, the heartbreaking agony she'd felt when Callum O'Shea tore them from her. Riona had never felt that way about anyone. With Egan, she'd appreciated all he'd done for her and let herself be blinded, unable to see the cruelty.

His words sent a shiver down her spine.

Glancing toward the door of the bedroom she shared with Gulliver, she watched for any activity in the hall. She couldn't afford an interruption now. Riona pulled out the inkless quill and began to write. Living her life without magic had left her vulnerable to awe. Like the first time Egan showed her the set of books that could communicate with each other.

Despite the lack of ink, black words appeared as she wrote.

This is not an easy task, sire. But we will not let you down.

She'd written to Egan every chance she got, telling him stories of the world beyond their borders where beauty was more than the stars in the perpetually dark sky.

She stared out her window overlooking the Iskalt fields. Children chased each other through the snowy courtyard, reminding Riona why she was still here. She cared—which was a new sensation for her.

Two months ago, the twins of Iskalt were stolen away. In the aftermath, it was like Iskalt lost its soul. The entire kingdom mourned two royal children they most likely had never met.

It was a far cry from Myrkur where citizens stole from each other, only caring about themselves.

Riona wiped a hand over her words, and they disappeared. A knock sounded on her door, and she shoved the book under her pillow and stood, smoothing out the dress the queen had given her. The woman had even been nice enough to have it altered for Riona's wings.

Where did such kindness come from?

Stepping into the hall, she found a grim looking Griffin waiting for her. He'd changed since the kids were taken. Even if no one here remembered him, he was still their uncle.

"Have you been in there all morning?" He tried to peek around her, but she moved to shut the door behind her.

"I needed a rest."

He ran a hand through his unkempt auburn hair and pushed out a sigh. "I know what you mean. I'm exhausted."

"Then why don't you take a rest as well?" She studied him closer, examining the signs of his weariness that grew each day. Dark circles under his eyes. Pale, ashy cheeks.

He leaned against the wall as if he needed it to hold him up. "I can't. Not until we find Tia and Toby."

"You'll be no good to them half-dead."

He closed his eyes and leaned his head back against the wall. "That's what Brea keeps saying. She's become the voice of reason for the O'Shea men. Never would have seen her as the reasonable one."

Riona wasn't sure what to make of the Iskaltian queen. She was kind and thoughtful, but there was a layer of distrust beneath everything else. Life had made her wary, like it did for most fae, and losing two of her children exacerbated the feeling.

"Griff." Riona nudged his arm. "Was there a reason you came to get me?"

"Yes." His eyes slid open. "I wanted to make sure you were okay."

Over the last two months, they'd made the jump to the human realm ten times, following leads that never panned out. It was hard on all of them, but they couldn't stop. "I'm fine, but you look like you're about to keel over."

"That's because I am." He stumbled, and she caught him around the waist.

"Come, you need sleep." She tried to lead him back into her room, but he pulled away.

"No, they need us in council chambers."

Riona sighed. Another meeting discussing leads and trying not to give in to the hopelessness of their task. The twins could be anywhere, and it wasn't like the human realm was small.

Taking Griffin's arm to steady him, Riona led him down the long hall. And then another. And another. The palace of Iskalt was a labyrinth of never-ending stone walls, colorful tapestries, and elaborate carved doors and statues. Torches burned in brackets, lighting the way, and braziers smoldered in corners, warming the hallways. There were no windows this deep in the palace aside from the bed chamber that abutted the outer wall, and Riona had started longing to see the sun everywhere she went. As soon as their mission was complete, they'd return to the darkness of Myrkur, and the sun would be just another memory of her time here.

When they reached council chambers, the magnificent carved doors stood open, and voices poured out into the hall.

Lochlan, sounding just as tired as Griffin, argued with a man Riona hadn't seen in months as he'd chased his own leads. Finn, King Consort of Eldur, had refused to return to Iskalt until he had something to tell his friends. Brea stood across the table, staring down at a set of maps.

"Lochlan," she snapped. "You aren't making any sense. You'll be no good to the twins if you die trying to find them. Go."

"Did she just give a king orders?" Riona whispered.

Griffin nodded, the first hint of a grin appearing on his

face. It dropped when Lochlan stalked toward them. He sent an icy glare Riona's way, and she felt it all the way down to her toes. The distrust. The King of Iskalt did not like her much.

If only he knew how right that instinct was.

Magic flooded Riona as she watched Lochlan walk away. Not her magic—that would require her to have some. No, this was by Egan's design. A powerful spell. She'd seen him recite it once from a scrap of ancient looking paper he kept under lock and key. It allowed him to steal magic from the barrier, but as Dark Fae, she never understood how he wielded it.

She held back the cry trying to push past her lips as the magic pulled at her, sending a searing pain into her chest. She dropped Griffin's arm and backed away until her butt hit the wall.

What would Griffin say if he knew?

She betrayed him with every breath she took.

Because Riona would always belong to the king of Myrkur, and the magic he'd placed around her like a noose reminded her of that at every turn.

Brea spoke about something, but Riona couldn't concentrate with Egan's magic squeezing the life out of her. He wasn't happy with her response in the journal. She closed her eyes, counting backward from ten. The magic loosened and faded. Egan never went too far to remind her she was his, at least not yet.

Riona searched the room to make sure no one noticed her distress. Griffin gave her a worried frown, and she averted her eyes.

"Finn." Brea sighed. "You saw him. He can't keep going on like this."

Finn scratched his chin. "Do you think he'll actually rest?"

"He needs to." She shot Griffin a pointed look. "As do you."

"Not a chance. I'm ready to go back into the human realm when we have a new lead."

Brea rolled her eyes to the ceiling and grunted a word that sounded way too much like "Men!"

Riona moved closer to the table where maps were strewn over the surface. "This is the human realm?"

"Part of it." Brea ran a finger over a land mass. "The problem is they could be anywhere. Callum is an O'Shea, he can open portals anywhere in the human world so long as he's been there before. We don't know where in Iskalt he left from. If we did, we could wait for him to return."

"Do we know how he escaped yet?" The investigation had been going on since he left.

Brea nodded, her hand curling around the edge of the table. "My girl..." She sucked in a breath. "We think Tia released him. It may not have been on purpose, but there are traces of her magic in the cells. It's the only logical answer."

Tia released her own kidnapper?

Riona never wanted to feel for these people. She didn't want to worry about Griffin or find herself thankful Gulliver hadn't been taken along with the twins.

Yet, here she was.

"Do we have another lead?"

Finn stepped forward. "Of a sort." He scratched the top of his head where Riona knew a crown sat when he was in his home kingdom of Eldur. He'd married Queen Alona, but apparently these Light Fae royals just dropped everything to help each other. Who did that?

"Finn." Brea sighed.

"Right, Lochlan dropped me in the human realm a few days ago after you all came back—in Ireland again. My time there was more enlightening this time. Humans chronicle every bit of history, including strange happenings. If Sorcha's book has been in the human realm for a while, there would be evidence in the form of things humans couldn't explain, a power they didn't understand."

Griffin dropped into a chair near the table. He gave Finn a wary look. Was he another fae who'd forgotten Griffin? "What did you find?"

At first, they'd tried to search for the kids in the human realm, but they'd eventually realized it was a futile search. There was only one thing Callum would truly want—Sorcha's book. If they found that, they'd find the kids.

"I'm not really sure." Finn rubbed his eyes before reaching into his pocket and pulling out a folded piece of odd-looking parchment.

Riona stepped closer. "What's that?"

Finn unfolded it. "It's what the humans call paper." He slapped it down on the table, making Griffin jump.

A series of numbers stretched across the lined page. "I don't understand."

"There's a story most humans don't believe to be true, yet they still documented it in the Irish archives. There is a local legend that tells about a small village that disappeared three hundred years ago."

"What do you mean disappeared?"

Finn fixed his eyes on her. "It's just gone. Archeologists from all across the human realm have studied the location intensely, trying to figure out what happened. They never did. But stuck in between pages of an old book recounting the story of this village, I found these numbers. I don't know what they mean, or really if they have any meaning at all, but right now, they're the only clue we have. I think it could be a coded message."

Brea wrapped an arm around Finn's waist and leaned into him. "Thank you for coming when we needed you."

Riona studied them, wondering how this queen could be so open with her affections. It didn't make a lot of sense. Emotions were something to be contained and controlled. Egan had taught her that. Show someone your emotions, and you showed them your weakness.

"You should go home to Eldur and my sister, Finn. You've done enough here, and she needs you."

No one argued with Brea, it seemed. She took careful care of many grown men—kings even—as well as small children. There was something so … human about that, at least what Riona had heard of humans. She didn't possess an ounce of fae cruelty or wicked tendencies. She wasn't cold like her husband.

Riona looked down at Griffin, whose eyes hadn't left Brea and Finn. He stared at them with a longing that tugged at her —this time without magic.

Griffin wanted them to remember him, but she'd seen a reluctance in that as well. He'd told her enough for her to know he'd supported the wrong queen on the wrong side of a war. If the people he loved remembered him, they'd also remember everything he'd done.

"I don't think there's anything more we can do today." Riona gave Brea a pointed look before flicking her eyes to Griffin.

Brea nodded. "We'll come back at this with fresh minds tomorrow. Griffin, you have to rest." She rounded the table and put a hand on Griffin's shoulder without saying anything.

Riona helped him from the chair, and together they went back the way they'd come.

Riona pushed open the door to their sitting room to find Gulliver asleep on the settee.

Griffin sort-of smiled when he looked at the boy, his tail curled around his legs. "He has the right idea."

Riona led Griffin to his room before dumping him on the bed. His hand shot out to snatch her wrist.

"Griff…"

"Please, Riona. Don't leave."

She'd never heard such desperation in Griffin's voice before.

"I have so many images running through my mind every time I close my eyes." He turned glassy eyes on her. "I can't sleep in the human realm. I can't sleep here. There's so much at stake, and all I can see are Shauna and Nessa. We've been gone too long. What do you think he's doing to them?"

Riona couldn't leave him, not with a question like that hanging over him. Bending down, she unlaced her boots and kicked them off before climbing on to the oversized bed. Her wings curled in against her back, letting her settle on her side.

"You're afraid," she whispered.

He nodded. "I'm supposed to be finding Sorcha's book, and we keep coming to dead ends. What if Egan decides enough is enough? What if he assumes we aren't coming back, that we've escaped?"

The truth was on the tip of her tongue. She could never truly escape Egan, not with his magic in her veins.

But she couldn't tell him.

"Shauna and Nessa are survivors, Griff."

He nodded. "That won't stop Egan. And now Callum has my niece and nephew. You don't know the man. He is everything that is wrong with this world. I'm scared for them, Riona." He didn't mention the dream they'd all come to a silent agreement not to speak about. What brought Griffin to Iskalt so quickly months ago was news that Brea's daughter was dreaming of him, of the prison realm.

Of the fact he was supposed to save her. Griffin didn't say it, but Riona knew it drove him.

She reached forward and put her hand over his heart. "Fear is the biggest motivator. We'll find the children, and then we'll bring Egan the book and save your family."

His eyes slid shut. "But what if bringing Egan the book ends up killing us all?"

A chill raced through her from the tips of her wings to her toes. She knew so little about magic, about this book, but what if Egan used it to start a war?

The man sleeping beside her had done a lot of evil, and he was paying for it now.

But for the first time, she wondered if they weren't playing on the same side.

Griffin would complete Egan's mission, he'd find the book. She was sure of it.

But would he hand it over to Egan? Or would he get them all killed?

CHAPTER TWO

Griffin

A crack reverberated around the room as Griffin slammed his fist into the table. "I can't break it."

It was the middle of the night, and they'd had the sequence of numbers since Finn returned days ago. Most of the palace slept—including Gulliver and Riona.

Lochlan looked up from where he was dripping wax onto the numbers for some unknown reason. "Maybe if you helped me, this would go quicker."

Griffin eyed the tomes surrounding him. He had every book on magic in Iskalt surrounding him, and Lochlan thought the solution was playing with wax?

Standing to stretch his stiff limbs, Griffin joined Lochlan at the table. "I don't really understand what you're doing."

Lochlan didn't look up. "A couple years ago, we found how Callum and Regan were passing messages. There were two ways. They had a set of books she'd spelled. Write in one, and it would show up in the other. For anything official that would need a paper trail, Regan sent messages on parchment spelled to react to hot wax."

Griffin stared at his brother, wondering how many discoveries they'd made in the last ten years. Regan didn't tell Griffin about her secret communications, and for reasons he couldn't understand, the thought burned.

He'd always clung to the fact that one fae had trusted him completely, one fae had loved him.

He leaned forward to peer at the paper. "Is it working?"

Lochlan sighed. "No." He put the candle back on the table. "But something has to. It's just code. We've broken plenty such codes before."

"Yes, but if this is a human code, magic won't decipher it."

Lochlan leaned back in his chair. "How do humans live such frustrating lives?"

"They aren't frustrating to them because they never knew any different."

"Stop trying to make me feel bad about being mad at the humans for this." Lochlan darted a glare at him, but his lip turned up into a wry smile.

Griffin chuckled and rubbed his eyes. "We need to get creative."

"My wax idea was creative."

"Maybe we need more eyes. I can wake Riona. There's only a seventy-five percent chance she'll punch me for it."

"No." Lochlan shook his head and leaned forward. "Griffin, I may not remember you, but you *feel* like my brother—if that makes sense. And brothers always have each other's backs, so I know I can trust you."

Griffin squirmed, stepping away. In his world, brothers stood on opposite sides of a war. But he couldn't tell

Lochlan. This was the first time his brother had ever trusted him, and Griffin didn't want to give that up. "So ... you don't trust Riona?"

"You told us yourself she's an agent of the king we're supposed to hate in Myrkur."

He thought back on the journey he'd shared with Riona, where he could almost forget who she was beholden to. She'd kissed him, making him realize he wasn't truly in love with Brea. It was the biggest revelation of his life. And yet, here was Lochlan voicing the exact concerns he'd once had about Riona himself.

"I don't know if I can trust her. Did I ever tell you how we met?"

Lochlan shook his head.

"It was in the fighting pits."

"Fighting pits?" Lochlan swallowed.

"I was fighting to free Nessa—the first time she was captured. Such things are a common occurrence in Myrkur. I won, but it was close. The rules dictated one of us had to die, but I refused to kill her. In return, she later let me go when I broke into a stronghold to save Gulliver. But then she led men to destroy my entire village."

Lochlan rubbed a tired hand over his face. "The prison realm ... it's a very different kind of place, isn't it?"

"Well, first, there's no sun, only constant night. The king's men roam the countryside capturing people to become indentured servants to work in the king's mines." One corner of his mouth turned up. "But there's a place—or used to be—where the villagers worked together to keep everyone alive. We were a family. And now Egan has two members of that family and the rest are homeless and likely starving. So we will try everything, Loch. We will break this code, so that one day I can return to free my family and rebuild my home."

"I wish I remembered you, Griffin. I wish I knew our history, because something tells me you're someone I cared about deeply."

Griffin didn't tell him the truth, he couldn't. Lochlan had never cared for him as brothers should.

And that had been Griffin's fault.

Griffin crawled into bed as the sun rose on the horizon. He didn't bother to change his clothing before his eyes slid shut.

Almost immediately, he could see them. Shauna and Nessa. His family. As much as he loved being around Lochlan and Brea, even when they barely knew him, they weren't the people he worried for most.

He was killing himself trying to find the twins because that book was his way back to the people he loved most.

As he drifted off to sleep, he could hear Egan's voice calling to Shauna, his best friend, the girl who'd saved him in the prison realm. She hadn't asked what he'd done or if he was dangerous. The day she found him, she'd only asked if he was hungry before bringing him to the village that had served as his sanctuary for nearly a decade.

Not everything was bad in the prison realm. It was the first time he truly understood what it was to fight for other people, to care for them.

If he was going to be fatalistic, he could almost say the prison realm saved him. It allowed him to become a better version of himself. One Lochlan could respect.

Egan's words drowned out every other thought in his sleepy mind.

"Stay away from her," Griffin groaned.

A warm hand slipped into his. "Griff?"

His eyes popped open. "Egan, he's going to kill them."

"Why? He has no reason to." Riona climbed over him to get to the other side of the bed. Her silky soft wings brushed his arm.

"We have to find this book, Riona. And these kids."

She sat still for a long moment, her breath the only sound in the room. Pulling back the covers, she slipped underneath. "You won't find anything if you're half-dead from sleep deprivation."

Griffin's entire body relaxed. She was right. Her presence should remind him of what they had to do, of who she worked for, but instead, it calmed him. "I'm going to save them."

Riona's tattoos moved and swirled as if they wanted to tell him everything Riona held back. "Sleep, Griff."

He closed his eyes once again, and this time, he didn't see Shauna and Nessa in their cells at Egan's palace. He saw the villagers he loved like family, the ones left behind to rebuild what was taken from them.

———

Griffin didn't know what time it was when he woke. Riona and Gulliver were nowhere to be found, so he took his time shaving with the blade Lochlan had given him. He bathed and changed into a pair of thick black woolen pants and a vest over a long-sleeved white linen shirt.

His stomach growled as he yanked his boots on. When

had he last eaten? It wasn't yesterday afternoon. Maybe the morning? He was starting to lose track of the days in Iskalt and in the human realm. Every action bled together to create a nonstop quest.

When he reached the dining room, only Brea sat at the high table. The sight of her made his breath hitch. Even if he knew he wasn't in love with her anymore, he never wanted to stop feeling confident in her presence. She'd always given him strength, and he needed it now more than ever.

"Good morning, Griffin." She smiled, but he'd always been able to spot her false expressions.

"Good?" He lowered himself into a chair next to her. "Maybe we should stick with morning."

"Well, it's almost lunch, but the kitchens know to keep breakfast running late for me each morning."

"Because you're lazy?" He forgot for a moment that he couldn't joke with Brea like that anymore.

Brea lifted one brow. "Because I'm a mother who spends most of the morning with my children."

"That too." Griffin nodded to the man who set a water goblet in front of him. He took a long drink before setting it down. Neither of them mentioned she had two fewer kids to prepare for the day.

Brea called a servant over and whispered something in his ear. The servant nodded and walked away.

"There was a time, your Majesty—"

"Don't call me that."

"—where you'd have laughed at the idea of servants catering to your every whim."

"There was also a time I thought I was human."

Griffin searched the hall, his eyes landing on all the

servants waiting to be given an order. "You told me it was a flaw to like you."

"That sounds … yes, I can see that." She chewed on a lip. "I wish I remembered, Griff."

"Sometimes I wish I'd forgotten it all."

A servant placed a plate in front of each of them. Griffin surveyed their fare. Salted fish, berry pastries, poached eggs.

Brea chewed on a bite of egg before looking toward him once more. "I don't think you really want that. It hurts, Griff, to know someone was so intwined in our lives, and yet we don't even recognize them. You brought me from the human realm. You changed my life, and I've wracked my brain trying to see your face in any of my memories."

"If you remembered me, you wouldn't have invited me to your table."

"No. You can't believe that. Everything inside me is screaming to trust you. I don't understand it, but it's like I know you're the only fae who can repair my family. We aren't whole without Tia and Toby. And now, I'm wondering if a part of us has been missing this entire time. Maybe we aren't whole without you either."

"Please don't say that." He scooted his chair back and stood, his appetite suddenly gone.

Brea ran after him. "Griffin? What did I say? Is it so wrong to want to love you? To want you in our family?"

He turned on his heel so quickly she almost slammed into his chest. "Yes."

"Why? Why can't I trust you?"

"I'm not a good man, Brea." Or at least he didn't use to be. "Regan was like a mother to me, and I chose her over you again and again. I tricked you into a fae marriage you didn't want. I didn't just bring you from the human realm, I abducted you on Regan's orders." He leaned down, staring into her wide eyes. "I abducted Myles after making you believe he was dead." That was the deal breaker for the Brea he knew. She could take everything else, but the lies about Myles hurt her the most.

Brea's eyes hardened, and Griffin waited for her to throw him against the wall with her magic, or at the very least, yell at him. Instead, she stepped forward, sliding her arms around his waist.

He stiffened, figuring she was going to crush him with her power. There were so many things she could do to him.

After a long moment, he realized it was the worst kind of punishment of all.

A hug.

There was no pain to satisfy him, nothing that could serve as his penance.

After a while, his arms threaded around her as a tear leaked from the corner of his eye.

"I don't know who you were, Griff," she whispered, gazing up at him. "But I'm beginning to see who you *are*. We are all capable of so much bad. Bad is easy. It's the good that's hard, change is even harder."

Her voice tapered off, but she didn't end the hug. Silence stretched between them as the image of Brea shifted in his mind. Could he really be part of two families? Was it possible to get Lochlan and Brea back?

No.

Not while they were still without their memories.

Brea released him and stepped away. "You're going to save them. I know it. And those kids will get to love you too. I refuse to believe I'll never see them again. Promise me you won't give up, Griff. Promise you'll find them? They need to know their uncle Griff."

It would be a false promise, they both knew that. But he needed to say it just as much as she needed to hear it.

"I will bring your children back to you."

Her face brightened the slightest bit. "Good, now come and eat."

He shook his head. "There's someone I need to see."

She gave him an understanding nod before he sprinted down the hall, backtracking to his room. When he slammed open the door, he found Gulliver and Riona sitting on the floor playing some game with marbles.

Riona was mesmerizing with her moving tattoos and dark eyes. Her white wings made her a contradiction, and it fit her. The light and the dark. The good and the bad.

This time, he was hoping for a little of the bad. Only Riona would have the information he needed.

Gulliver smiled up at him. "Griff! You want to play? All you have to do is pick up marbles in a sequence, creating your own pattern. I can show you."

Griff knew the game. It was how they taught kids to break codes in Fargelsi.

"I'm sorry, Gullie. Maybe later. I need to speak with Riona."

Gulliver shrugged and went back to playing.

Riona gave him a quizzical look as she pushed herself off the floor. Griffin led her into his bedroom and shut the door before turning on her. "How much do you know about Sorcha's book?"

Riona's stern look fell away into surprise. "Just as much as you—"

"Don't lie to me. You were Egan's champion. Before we

met, I remember every time I saw you sitting atop your steed next to the king, bowing to his every whim."

"You don't understand." She sidestepped him and sat on the bed.

"Then make me." He took a seat beside her. This wasn't supposed to be an argument. The accusations fell past his lips before he could stop them. But he knew Riona, he understood her like few others could.

Because she was just like him.

Riona rested her elbows on her knees and hunched forward. "I don't know anything about the book, but he has a spell that allows him to wield magic from the barrier."

Griffin knew there was a reason Egan was able to return his portal magic to him. This wasn't news, and there was no proof the spell was from the book.

"What about you?" Riona's eyes pinned him with her glare. "Regan never told you about the book while you were subjugating the Fargelsian people?"

She hadn't. But she also hadn't had him turning the human realm upside down for it. Which meant Brandon might be right. Regan knew where it was. She'd studied it, had spells from it. He tried to recall the memories he'd pushed to the back of his mind, realizing how much she had kept from him.

He hadn't been her son or her champion. Not her partner —that was Callum. So, what was he?

Gullible.

He sighed. "She didn't mention it or where it could be."

Riona lifted her face to his. "A book with so much power wouldn't be in the human realm without protections. We don't even know what this book can do, how much power it can wield."

"Riona," he whispered.

Her eyes locked onto his, her voice softening as she nodded. "If it's truly as powerful as we've been told, what if it can not only bring the magical barrier around the prison realm down, but this book ... have you ever wondered if it can make the world remember?"

His heart thundered in his chest whether from Riona's nearness or the questions that rolled through his mind. What if he could restore memories and cease being the forgotten prince, the one everyone felt like they knew but never would without their memories?

He flopped back on the bed. "Why is it that every choice feels like another set of chains?" Lies wrapped around him like steel tightening until he gasped for breath.

If they found this book, the truth would be right at his fingertips.

Riona lay beside him, her thigh brushing his. "I don't have all the answers, Griff. But we'll find this book. We'll save the twins and return to free Shauna and Nessa." She sat up, letting her eyes meet his before she stood. "We won't fail, because you won't let us."

He stared after her as she left him behind. She was right, they'd find it. But Griffin knew they couldn't give it to Egan.

He only wished Riona agreed.

He needed to talk to someone—someone who preferably couldn't talk back. Ruffling Gulliver's hair on his way past, Griffin stepped into the hall and turned the opposite way of the main hall. He'd rarely spent much time in this palace, but it still felt familiar. It called to his roots.

The library wasn't far. Griffin ducked into the stone archway to see solid oak bookshelves lining the walls. He skimmed the dusty leather spines on his way to the back corner where a forgotten portrait hung.

There were many paintings of his parents around the palace grounds, but none were like this, so lifelike it stirred memories he couldn't possibly have. Neither he nor Lochlan hung on these walls. A royal child in Iskalt got their first portrait done on their sixth birthday. They'd both been gone by then, living in separate kingdoms.

He sat on the arm of a nearby couch and studied them. His father had auburn hair just like Griff's, but Lochlan favored their mother.

"What would you two think of me now?" he asked. It would have broken their hearts to see him choose Regan's side against his brother. But if they were here, they'd have forgotten him too.

"I want my family back. But the moment I have them, they're going to abandon me. I'm sorry. For everything. I'm just ... sorry." He buried his face in his hands.

Words failed him as his back shook. His parents were the only ones who got to see him cry. He had to be strong. For Riona and Gulliver, for his brother and his children. For Shauna and Nessa. Brea.

For everyone who'd end up hurt or dead if Egan got his hands on the book.

"I'm going to save them all." And then he'd disappear into the prison realm again to let his first family live their lives without him. Even if he could return their memories with Sorcha's book, these people ... they'd never forgive him.

CHAPTER THREE

Griffin

Griffin stared at the rumpled and stained page with a series of numbers he couldn't make sense of. They'd tried every magical solution known to them. They'd applied all of their combined knowledge—which was considerable—to crack the code, but were still missing something vital. He could feel it, right on the tip of his fingers if he could just grasp it.

The numbers started to blend together, and Griffin wiped a weary hand across his bleary eyes, hoping for a moment of clarity that never came.

5 4 1 6 2 0 1 7 2 1 0 1 5 4 7 6 8

In all likelihood, the numbers were just numbers, and they were chasing a dead end, but it was the only solid lead they had. It had to yield something. Some clue to the whereabouts of the book or the twins, or both. Something to make the last weeks of research fruitful.

When Finn returned from the human realm with the code, they were all excited, convinced they had the information they were looking for. But that excitement quickly yielded to frustration. They'd sent copies of the code with trusted messengers to the Fargelsian and Eldurian queens who were also hard at work trying to interpret the numbers themselves. Alona and Finn stumbled upon a source in the Eldurian palace library that confirmed a possible name for the vanished village in Ireland. *Aghadoon.* It could hold the secrets to Sorcha's spell book, or it could be another false lead. If Aghadoon once existed somewhere in Ireland, and if Callum knew of the village and its connection to the book, then it was likely he'd be somewhere in Ireland as well.

"It's useless." Lochlan balled up the sheet of parchment he'd spent the last hours poring over and tossed it into the fireplace. "It's time we search elsewhere. We've lost too much time as it is." He tugged a hand through his tangled blond hair, looking exactly like a desperate father. "Brea is inconsolable today, and I'm worried for her health. We've had to call in a wet-nurse for Ciara. Brea's under so much stress she is struggling to feed her enough."

"Maybe you're right. We should send two parties and continue our search of the human realm." Griffin leaned back in his chair, his limbs stiff from too much time bent over parchment. It was like looking for a needle in a haystack the size of the palace. Impossible. But he'd made a promise to Brea he intended to keep. He would bring her children home.

"We can each lead a search party. I'll take Finn, and you can take Myles. We'll cover more ground that way." Lochlan flipped through pages of research and files containing copies of everything they'd discovered. His end of the dining table was covered in the intel they'd collected.

"Loch, you know you have to stay here. You have a kingdom to—"

Lochlan's fist slammed against the table. "I don't care about the kingdom. My children are missing. I have advisors who can handle the day to day business of Iskalt."

"A king must keep his people first and foremost in his mind. I know that's not what you want to hear, but Iskalt needs you."

"My children need me too."

"You will serve them better here while those you trust do everything in their power to find Tia and Toby and bring them home. With Callum on the loose, you cannot be seen as a weak king or he will take your throne when you're not looking, and then where will Iskalt be?"

"Spoken like a true prince of the realm." Lochlan sighed. "You are right, brother. My resources are at your disposal. You will lead the next excursion into the human realm. But you will keep a close eye on Riona. Her interest does not lie with ours."

Something tugged at Griffin's cold heart at the strength of Lochlan's trust in him. With everything he had, Griffin did not want to betray that trust.

"Myles, stop dragging me." Brea's voice echoed in the hall. "At least let me take Ciara back to the nursery."

Lochlan was already out of his seat when the human came barging into the dining hall turned study, Brea, clutching a sleeping Ciara, trailing along behind him.

"Bring her with you, she'll want to hear this too." Myles

rushed across the room, looking half crazed and as sleep deprived as the rest of them.

"You realize she's just eight months old, right?" Brea followed him, catching his sense of urgency.

"You reek of horses, human." Lochlan took in Myles' travel-stained clothes.

"I figured it out." Myles beamed at them.

"Figured what out?" Brea tried to shove him into a seat. He looked near collapse from what was likely a mad dash across two kingdoms to bring whatever news he had for them.

Lochlan poured him a glass of wine, but Myles waved it away.

"It's in Ireland like we thought." He slammed a human map onto the table, a grid of red lines drawn with a careful hand across the Irish island. "It's coordinates."

"What?" Lochlan and Griffin asked as Brea gasped in surprise.

"Location coordinates." Myles reached for the parchment Griffin had been staring at for hours. "It's not a code or a random series of numbers." Myles sat down in Griffin's chair, scribbling the numbers into a formula.

"5 4 1 6 2 0 1 7 2 1 0 1 5 4 7 6 8 is actually 54° 16' 20.172" North by 10° 1' 54.768" West." Myles sat back with a triumphant grin.

"Of course." Brea snatched the map to study the area circled in red ink. "What's there?"

"The question is what's not there," Myles said.

"Aghadoon?" Brea gasped.

"There's a castle ruin at these coordinates."

"And you think we can find it? The real Aghadoon?"

"It has to be there. We'll find it, Brea. I promise."

"If you two are done speaking in code, do you think you could share it with the rest of us?" Lochlan's fists rested at his sides, but his body was tensed like a mountain cat ready to pounce.

"Map coordinates, Loch." Myles stood, placing his hands on the king's shoulders. "The numbers lead to an exact latitude and longitude location in Ireland. It's a lead. A good one."

"You leave now." Lochlan took the map to study the location. "You said there was an old castle?"

"It's a ruin." Myles nodded. "But it should be a good place to look for our next lead. It can't be a coincidence that we're looking for the vanishing village of Aghadoon, and these coordinates lead where they do. Someone wanted it found. There's no other reason the coordinates would have been left in that old book."

"Myles needs to rest," Brea interjected. "He's dead on his feet, and it's noon, anyway. No one is going anywhere until the moon rises. Go find a bed, Myles—and a bath, you reek. We'll be ready for you when you wake."

"Thank you, Brea." He seemed to wilt before their eyes now that his message was delivered.

"Thank *you*." Brea passed Ciara off to Lochlan and pulled her best friend into her arms. "I don't know what I'd do without you."

"Good thing you'll never have to figure it out." He wrapped his arms around her.

After he'd gone, Lochlan glared at his wife. "We?"

"Yes *we*." Brea took in a deep breath, a sign she was preparing to win an argument. Griffin knew that look all too well. They were in for a fight.

"I'm going with Myles and Griffin this time."

"No, you aren't." Lochlan passed Ciara back to her. "Our youngest children still need you."

"We have a wet nurse now, you'll manage without me." She passed the baby back to him. "Ciara will adjust to the wet-nurse."

"And Kayleigh? Will she understand when her mother leaves? She's not handling the absence of Tierney and Tobias at all."

The little Iskalt princess was beside herself with the missing twins. She stuck to Lochlan and Brea like glue and wouldn't leave her remaining sister's side. The nanny had her hands full with keeping Kayleigh in the nursery when her parents weren't there.

"I know." Brea's shoulders fell in defeat, taking her daughter back from Lochlan's arms. "They're my babies, Loch. I feel so useless staying here and doing nothing."

"Join the freaking club." Lochlan growled, the human phrase sounding odd on his lips. "We have to trust our friends to do this, Brea. I know you're capable of storming the human world and taking on Callum all by yourself, but we don't have that luxury this time."

"I know." Brea's brow furrowed in disappointment and anger.

"Will you watch over Gulliver while I'm away?" Griffin asked her. "He's awfully fond of you," he teased. It was no secret the lad had a bit of a crush on the Iskalt queen. Not that Griffin could blame him. But Gulliver had several crushes these days.

"No way, Griff. I'm coming with you." Gulliver marched into the room with a pastry in each hand and berry filling smeared on his face. Gulliver spent a lot of his free time in the kitchens, and from what Griffin had heard, the cooks loved the boy with the tail.

"You're staying here." Griffin folded his arms across his chest, quite sick of this argument he'd had three times in the span of an hour. "You don't belong in the human world."

"Haven't we already figured out I'm an automatic glamourer—is that a word? Being Dark Fae does have some benefits, you know. Like humans being too blind to see the tail attached to my butt." Gulliver crammed half a pastry in his mouth.

Griffin bent down to pluck the second pastry from his hands. "I was referring to your penchant for saying things humans don't understand. We can't glamour your mouth shut, though that is an intriguing idea."

"I'm going." Gulliver mimicked Griffin's pose. "We're in this together, Griff, and the twins are my friends. I want to help you and Riona."

"Go pack." Griffin sighed.

"Perhaps you can leave before she realizes..." Lochlan suggested.

"She'll be more suspicious if I leave her behind." Griffin turned back to Brea. "Am I a bad parent for wanting to keep him with me so I can know he's safe even if we end up in a dangerous situation?"

"In my book that makes you a good parent." Brea kissed him on the cheek and turned to go.

Griffin made his way back to his rooms, eager for a nap before they traveled after moonrise. It felt good to have a plan again. To be doing something that would take him another step closer to freeing Shauna and Nessa from Eagan's grasp.

"Packed already?" Griffin peeked into Riona's room. She was resting on her bed, writing in her journal. She did that a lot.

"Ready to go." She ran a hand across her page and closed the cover. "Gullie caught me up to speed."

"I wish I could make him stay here where it's safe." He lingered in the doorway, feeling anxious for her company. "But I'm also relieved he'll be with me."

"Come inside, Griff." She laughed at his transparency. "I have a question for you." She patted the bed beside her.

He left the door cracked but welcomed a moment alone with Riona. He enjoyed moments like this when she was in a good mood. It happened so rarely.

Griffin dropped down onto the bed beside her, toeing off his boots and letting them slide to the floor. "What's your question?"

Riona glanced at the hallway. "You didn't see our little eavesdropper out there did you?"

"No, I made him go take a nap, but he's probably out waiting in the moon garden so he can be sure we don't leave without him. Or he's out hunting for things to steal before we leave." Griffin massaged his temples. "What's on your mind, Riona?"

"Are we still working on the same side?" she blurted.

"What? Of course, we are." Griffin moved to grab her hand, but they weren't hand-holding, reassuring kinds of friends. At least not yet. "I'm with you, Riona. My mind is always on Nessa and Shauna. They are my family."

"It's just a little confusing seeing you bond with your

brother and his wife. They're your family too, and I can imagine it's difficult to choose between them."

"I'm not choosing Shauna and Nessa over my brother's family." Griffin sighed. "I want to help bring the twins back, but I'm not losing sight of our mission."

"Even if it means betraying your brother and Brea?" Her voice took on a hard edge.

Griffin heaved a weary sigh. "I'd like to think there's a way to do what we came here to do and help my brother at the same time." He was walking a dangerous line with Riona. He could never forget she was Egan's envoy in this venture. He wanted to trust her, but at the same time, he couldn't divulge all his intentions to her.

"It's just ... if you screw this up, he will blame me, and I can't ... won't allow that."

"I won't let that happen. No matter what."

Griffin would do whatever it took to save Nessa and Shauna and every innocent inside the magical walls of Myrkur. But he would not allow Egan to bring his army into this realm or open the floodgates for every criminal sent to the prison realm to come back for their revenge.

He just had to figure out how to do all of that, save the twins, free Shauna and Nessa from Egan's clutches before he could figure out what Griffin was up to, and keep the book out of the wrong hands. And hopefully not lose Riona in the process.

CHAPTER FOUR

Griffin

Myles was the last person to stumble through the portal before Griff closed it. He groaned as he pitched forward, landing on his knees. "Griff, why is it so much smoother when Lochlan opens portals?"

Griffin smirked down at him. "Your human body can't take it?"

Myles pushed himself up from the grass and crossed his arms, but the guy couldn't be menacing if he tried.

Griffin shielded his eyes with his hand and stared into the bright sky, not taking his eyes from the faint outline of the moon. Before being sent to the prison realm, his Iskalt magic rejoiced in the light of the moon. That was when it could play. His fingers curled into his palm as the buzz from opening the portal wore off, leaving Griffin weak. Like a human. No strength pulsed through his veins, but he could still remember how it had felt.

Like he could do anything.

Griffin turned to make sure Riona and Gulliver were okay and watched them pick themselves up off the crunchy grass. If he'd had his way, they'd go directly to the coordinates Finn found. But when did he ever get his way?

Lochlan didn't want his brother walking into a trap, even with his kids at stake.

And this woman they'd come to see, this Ashlin, she was the only fae any of them had met who knew anything about Sorcha's book. She had to know of the secret village. He thought back to the last time they visited her, the way she'd lied to them and then disappeared. Griffin wouldn't let that happen again.

"Surprised you listened to Loch and brought us here." Myles brushed grass from his butt. "We've been trying to catch Ashlin at home for months."

Exhaustion wound through Griffin, and he had no comeback for Myles. The portals used to be easy. Griffin could open them with a flick of his wrist. But that was before his magic had been taken from him.

"Is this how humans feel?" He directed the question to Myles. "Tired and weak all the time."

Myles shrugged. "Pretty much. Maybe the vampire king took too much from you?"

Griffin wasn't sure what a vampire was, but he could guess who Myles meant. Egan. The Dark Fae King hadn't really taken Griffin's magic, but the prison realm had robbed it of him nonetheless, leaving their group unprotected in the human realm.

Myles circled Gulliver.

"It's gone again, right?" Gulliver's eyes followed him.

Riona knocked into Myles' shoulder on her way by. "Just like my wings have been every time we've come."

Griffin had trouble trusting something he didn't understand, and it seemed he wasn't the only one because Myles shot him a suspicious look. The Dark Fae features were invisible to humans in the human realm.

How was that possible when Griffin had to rely on Lochlan's glamour to hide his ears?

Myles' face softened when he met Gulliver's gaze. "Yes, you look normal. Like me."

Griffin snorted. "Human is not normal."

"Well." Myles started forward. "Let's go forward on our vampire king/ice king mission. Hey, they should meet. That would be epic."

"What's a vampire?" Gulliver whispered to Myles as they walked toward the village.

"They're this wicked cool creature who drinks blood and can only come out at night."

"Drinks blood?" Riona shook her head in disbelief. "And humans find this entertaining?"

"Oh, totally." Myles grinned but there was fear behind it.

"We need to move faster." The ruins of Bealadannan looked as desolate as Griffin remembered it from the first time they'd come in search of the twins, when they'd learned about the lineage of O'Rourke twins—Sorcha's lineage.

Griffin kept his hands clenched, his jaw firm, as they walked through the dirt streets of the village. Crumbling buildings stood on either side, and the people who lived in them didn't peek out their windows like they had before.

At the other end of the village sat a single house on the cliff's edge.

They reached the stone cottage. Smoke curled up toward

the sky, billowing out of a chimney. Someone was home. But when they got closer, they realized the door stood open.

A foreboding feeling wound through Griffin, and he picked up his pace, running the rest of the way. When he reached the cottage, he peered inside. Ashlin's belongings were scattered around the cottage, spilling out through the door. A fire raged in the hearth, the tea kettle hanging over it, this time not piercing the air with its song.

It held a similarity to how they'd found the place two months ago when they'd returned. Since then, each time they came looking for Ashlin, everything had been tidied, but she was never home.

Riona, Gulliver, and Myles joined him.

"Do you think..." Myles didn't finish the sentence as he covered his mouth with his hand.

Griffin examined every part of the cottage, looking for clues. "Did someone ... take her? Everyone, get inside."

They hadn't expected much from the old woman after she'd sent them on a fool's errand to an empty grave, but Griffin had hoped she'd give them more information when he presented the numbers to her. He couldn't storm a disappearing village if he knew nothing about it.

Griffin surveyed the cottage, wondering who could want to abduct an old woman. A folded parchment sat atop the bed. He bent to pick it up and unfolded it. One line of text stretched across the page. "Follow the numbers." He whispered the words again. "We're on the right path."

"Griff." Riona's tattoos spiraled fiercely, not sitting still on her skin. "I can't help feeling we needed her."

She was right. They'd just lost someone who could have been an ally.

He turned on his heel and walked to the door, hat in hand. "We need to leave." *Follow the numbers.*

They were trying.

Stepping outside, he gulped in fresh air, needing to remind himself they had real clues this time. He wasn't sure if he could take another dead end.

"Myles," he barked. "Bring the map."

Myles reached into his bag and retrieved the rolled-up map of Ireland. Griffin took it and spread it out on the ground, kneeling beside it.

"We're here." Myles pointed to a star that marked Ashlin's cottage.

"And where do we need to be?" Riona joined them.

"Here." Myles tapped the area that was circled. "Eastern Ireland, but lucky for us, I'm guessing it's only a three or four hour cab ride."

"Cab?" Riona gave him a confused look.

"Yes. We can't portal back to the fae realm and then the human realm again to get there faster because Griff has never been there. Plus, you all see him. He's barely standing."

"Not true." Griffin wobbled as he took a step forward.

Myles crossed his arms. "We don't have a choice. We have to take a cab that'll cost an absolute fortune." Myles shrugged. "And I listen to Loch. Well, sometimes. He told me to look out for you."

Griffin couldn't seem to process those words. Lochlan wanted to make sure he was safe? "I've seen cabs before." Griffin looked to Riona and Gulliver, needing anything to distract him from his self-pitying thoughts. "You are going to see a lot of things that scare you, but I promise they're safe. Myles, you brought human money, right?"

"Sure did. I had a feeling you were going to be an expensive date, Griff."

Griffin rubbed his chin. "We don't have time to figure out what happened to Ashlin, but we can assume it has something to do with us, with this book, so we must move along. We need to get as close to these coordinates as we can and find an inn. I don't feel comfortable checking out the village during the day. Even without my magic, the moon fortifies me."

Myles rolled up the map and pulled out another contraption Griffin had seen before.

"What's that?" Gulliver leaned closer.

"A cell phone." Myles hit a series of numbers and brought it to his ear. "Hello, I'm in need of a cab outside Bealadannan. Yes. Okay. Thank you."

He slipped the phone back into his bag before realizing they were all staring at him.

"Was he talking to himself just now?" Riona asked, turning her gaze to Griffin, like she worried for the human's sanity.

"What? I called the cab company to send a car." Myles shrugged.

"This is magic?"

"My phone?" He laughed. "No. But sometimes Lochlan takes me into the human realm so I can call my parents when we don't have time to visit. That's a kind of magic you could say."

Griffin wished he saw the world the way Myles did. He considered being able to talk to his family as good as magic. It had a purity to it, a purity that meant he was a good man.

Griffin didn't know what he was, but he'd never considered himself good.

They walked through the crumbling village to reach the other side where a paved road greeted them. He tried to remember his first time in the human realm. It seemed like a place where anything could happen. They didn't have fae magic, so they created magical objects instead.

Like the yellow cab pulling up in front of them.

A string of curses flew from Riona's mouth.

Gulliver stared on in awe.

Griffin only shrugged and opened the door as he greeted the Irishman in front. "Good afternoon." He always resorted to formal speak, the words of a prince, when talking to humans he didn't know.

The man smiled. "Dinna just stand there, lad. Tell me where I can take ye."

Griffin ushered the rest of the group in and gestured to Myles. Myles leaned forward between the seats. "We're headed for Dublin."

"Ah, Americans. Knew ye looked funny. Kidding. Kidding. Dublin ye say? That's quite the drive."

Myles pulled out a wad of human bills. "Got anything better to do today?"

The man's eyebrows shot up. "No, sir. Guess I'm headin' to Dublin with a load of Yanks."

Myles patted his shoulder and relaxed back into his seat, squished between Riona and Griffin. Gulliver sat up front, a giant grin on his face as his eyes darted to each of the human surroundings they passed.

When the cab started moving, Gulliver squealed and clapped his hands together.

Riona remained quiet, a green pallor to her cheeks.

Griffin had an acute awareness of his companions. Their

mission rested on them being able to blend into the human world.

Myles stretched his arms along the back of Griffin and Riona's seats, oblivious to the venomous looks sent his way. "Griff," he whispered. "When you first abducted me in the human world, did you ever think I'd be so integral to your future?"

Griffin grunted. "You are not integral."

"Sure I am. Tell him, Riona."

Riona's jaw clenched. "Get your arm off the back of my seat, or I'll fly you into the sky and drop you."

The driver looked at them in the rear-view mirror.

"Riona." Griffin raised a brow.

She crossed her arms but didn't respond.

Myles smiled as he started humming a song Griffin hadn't heard before. It was all a grand adventure to him. The king consort of Fargelsi hadn't changed a bit in ten years. He was still the boy with too much laughter in his eyes, too much joy that didn't belong in a fae world that could cause such pain.

Griffin settled back in his seat, preparing for the long drive to Dublin—wherever that was.

Riona and Gulliver stared at the cab as it drove away like it was the last lifeline they had.

Griffin had spent a lot of time in the human world, but he'd never seen one of their big cities. They'd driven through dusk, reaching their destination as the moon claimed the sky. Even in the dark, this place put fae cities to shame.

Maybe if the book truly could restore memories, he could

live in the human realm, at least until Lochlan stopped trying to kill him.

Though, the Lochlan he knew now, the king of Iskalt and father of four was so very different from the cold, hard brother who'd only had scorn for Griffin.

"What do we do now?" To Riona's credit, she didn't seem scared of the cars driving down narrow streets. Tall buildings lined the sidewalks, giving the city a closed in feel.

Yet … it was beautiful in a way so completely different from the fae kingdoms.

"We get ourselves a room. Myles, what time is it?"

Myles pulled out his phone. "Eight PM."

"Okay, let's rest tonight and do more tomorrow. We should find a room at one of the inns." The driver had dropped them off in front of a building called the Holiday Inn. "This one may be appropriate." It had inn right in the name, but the huge building looked nothing like any inn Griffin had ever seen.

No one argued, so Griffin went inside. They walked across white tile to where a human sat behind a desk.

"I'll handle this." Myles and the woman at the desk struck up a conversation Griffin couldn't understand. Bed sizes? Smoking?

The human world was always overwhelming, and Griffin wasn't sure how much more he could handle tonight.

To his surprise, Gulliver clutched Riona's hand.

Myles returned to them and held out a small piece of plastic to Griff.

"Do I look like a dust bin?" Griffin eyed the plastic card.

"It's your room key. I got us two, because I am *not* sharing a bed with you. Come on. We're on the eighth floor."

Myles led them to a set of silver doors. He pressed a

button on the wall and then waited. When the doors slid open, Gulliver jumped back.

Even Griffin stayed where he was.

Myles stood on the threshold. "Come on. It's just an elevator. It's safe. I promise." He urged them inside the closet-like room.

Griffin looked back at the woman who was watching them. They had to do this. "Myles is the human. We need to trust him." Words he'd never imagined himself saying.

Once the four of them were inside, the doors slid shut, and Myles pressed a button on the wall.

Gulliver screamed as the elevator moved. Riona pressed herself back against the wall, barely breathing until the doors slid open again. The rooms outside the magic closet were different this time. Griffin and Riona peered into the hallway.

Myles walked out first. "I choose Gulliver as my sleeping buddy. He's more tolerable than you two." He stopped at a door. "This is us. You guys are next door."

Griffin watched the way Myles slid the plastic into the slot to open the door, so he followed suit. It took him a few times to get the door open. Riona reluctantly followed him inside.

"I don't like this place." Riona set her small sack on one of the beds as her eyes scanned the foreign place. "I don't like it at all. There's too much magic everywhere." She fanned her hands out, gesturing at all the human gadgets around the room.

"I keep telling you it's not magic. Humans would call it science or engineering."

"I don't care what they call it. I don't like it."

Griffin sighed, having no energy for all the human things

in this room. "Let's just get some rest. Tomorrow, maybe it won't look so daunting."

She didn't look like she believed him.

Riona's scream jolted Griffin from his restless sleep. At first, he'd thought it was Shauna screaming in his dreams. It took him a moment to wake up. A sound came from the bathroom, the reason for the scream.

Griffin kicked the blankets off his legs and heaved himself from the bed. He rubbed his eyes as he approached the closed washroom door. He knocked, not sure she could hear him over the noise inside.

The door opened, revealing Riona sitting on the closed toilet—he knew that one from previous visits—in a fluffy white robe with a contraption blowing hot air.

Griffin leaned against the door frame, and she turned off the air blaster, putting it on a hook on the wall. "You okay?"

She nodded. "I couldn't sleep so I decided to examine the human magic. Did you know they can make water fall from the sky just by turning a handle?"

He did know that. "It's called a shower."

"Their chamber pot cleans itself."

"A toilet."

"But the most miraculous item is this contraption that blows hot air. Do they use it to dry their bodies, do you think?"

Griffin chuckled. "I haven't seen one of those before." He sighed. "I've been to the human realm countless times, but..." It had lost the awe for him. How did he admit that to someone who still only saw magic?

Riona bound her long braids on top of her head and smiled. It was such a rare sight, Griffin wanted to savor it. How could Lochlan not trust this woman? All she needed was someone to give her the chance to be good, the chance to fight on the right side.

Griffin had watched her change over the last few months. She talked more now and had become protective of Gulliver.

"What's that smile for?" she asked.

He shrugged, guilt gnawing at him for spending a single moment not thinking of Shauna and Nessa and how Riona had played a part in destroying his village.

Leaving the bathroom behind, he crawled back into his bed, wanting the conflicting emotions to disappear. If he closed his eyes, he saw them, the two girls in the prison realm he had to save. But … it wasn't only about them anymore.

Riona emerged and climbed into her bed, her eyes closed.

"Riona?" he whispered.

"Yes?" She turned onto her side, the back of the robe bulging with her wings.

"What do you see when you close your eyes?" He needed to know, to believe in her, to know she believed in him.

Riona didn't answer for a long time. "Long ago, before you came to Myrkur, there were rumors. I was a child at the time, but I remember everything so clearly. My people lived near the water as we were children of the sea and sky, feared for our ancient ways but also revered. You ask what I see at night? I see fire and blood. I see my people on their knees as the wings were ripped from their backs. Griff, I see the moment I should have died."

"But you didn't."

"No. Instead, I got to live with the memories as an indentured servant to Egan. Some say it was a fate worse than death. To be the last of my kind—or at least to think I was the last." None of them had forgotten Nihal.

"Yet, you're loyal to him."

She closed her eyes, but he knew she wasn't sleeping.

"Do you want to know what I see?"

She didn't respond to his question.

"I see destruction and ruin. I see a scared people huddling together, unable to even find enough food to eat. I see you sitting atop your horse."

Her eyes blinked open.

"But then I see you saving Gulliver, saving me. And I see Shauna and Nessa, my family brought to the king's palace. I have so many conflicting images in my dreams. I understand you, Riona, because I have been there. But I have changed. I won't serve another tyrant with my eyes shut. Can you say the same?"

She rolled over, her back to him. "I do not know."

It would have to be enough for now.

An incessant knocking sounded on their door way too early in the morning. Griffin grumbled to himself as he pulled it open.

Gulliver darted past him with a plate piled with food. "Griff, did you know this inn has *free* food in the morning? That means you don't have to pay for it."

"I know what free means." Griffin rubbed the sleep from his eyes.

"They let you have as much as you want."

Myles walked in after him. "I knew the kid would like

that."

Gulliver climbed onto Riona's bed, offering her a plate of eggs and toast. She shook her head.

Their conversation from hours before stuck in Griffin's mind, but he needed to trust her.

"Riona." Gulliver beamed. "I like your dress. It looks soft. I had one like that in my room, but there were no trousers with it."

Myles held back a laugh. "Gullie, that's not a dress."

"It's not?" Riona looked to him.

Myles bit his fist until he had his laughter under control. "It's called a bathrobe. No one goes into public in those."

She frowned as if she didn't believe him.

Griffin flopped back onto his bed, and Gulliver threw him a pastry.

"Humans have the best food." Gulliver crammed long thin pastries into his mouth.

"Those are called French toast sticks." Myles perched on the end of Griffin's bed. "What's the plan for today?"

Not for the first time, Griffin wished he had use of his magic. "We have to stay in our rooms until nightfall when I can hide my fae features more easily."

"What about me?" Myles asked. "I'm the normal looking one—"

"Yes." Sarcasm dripped from Riona's words. "Humans are the normal ones."

"No, Myles is right." An idea formed in Griffin's mind. "The coordinates are outside Dublin, probably an hour's cab ride. You could go see what's there. We know the village has disappeared but look for clues. Ask around about the local legends. Anything."

"Can I go?" Gulliver's eyes lit up. "No one can see I'm not

human." Griffin frowned, and Gulliver answered his own question for Griffin. "No, Gullie. It's too dangerous for little old you."

"I'm sorry, kiddo." Myles offered Griffin a salute. "Human at your service." He stole a pastry from Gulliver and practically skipped from the room.

Riona groaned as she lay her head back. "Your human is odd."

"Very."

"And you trust him with this task? I could fly to Aghadoon and make sure no one saw me." She sat up, the tops of her wings poking from the collar of the loose robe.

"Have your wings always been dark?" Gulliver asked through a mouth of food.

"Dark? They're white." She frowned at him.

"Not the tips."

Griffin's eyes widened as he noticed what Gulliver had pointed out. Black shadows speckled the top of her otherwise pure white wings.

Riona shot to her feet and ran into the bathroom. A scream echoed from her. When she returned, she had a shirt on that fit around her wings in the back. "Griff, what do you think it is?" She sounded scared.

Griffin stood and walked toward her. He ran a finger over the black tips, and she shivered.

"Griff," she whispered. "This isn't supposed to happen. The darkness ... I don't know what's caused it."

Griffin pulled her into a hug. "We'll figure this out. I promise."

He'd have to add it to the growing list of promises he'd already made. But what if, at the end of the day, he couldn't keep a single one of them?

CHAPTER FIVE

Griffin

"There's nothing there? What do you mean there's nothing there?" Griffin stared at Myles wanting to throttle him for wasting the whole day.

"Just what I said. There is *nothing* with a capital "N" at these coordinates." He tossed a worn piece of paper onto the table. The numbers carefully written in his human codes of latitude and longitude.

"No village or town?" Griffin frowned.

"Not even a house."

"Are you sure you looked everywhere?" Riona asked.

"Trust me. There is nothing there but a lot of grass, a hill, and some old ruins that used to be a castle."

"What about around the area? Did you check in the nearby towns?" Griffin asked.

"Listen, guys." Myles gave a patient sigh. "We can go back tonight, but I'm telling you, there is nothing anywhere near these coordinates. It's miles and miles of just ... Ireland. Craggy hills, stumpy grass, some rocks and the occasional goat. That's it. So unless some of the human tales were right and the Fair Folk actually do live under the hills, then we're at a dead end."

"What is he rambling about?" Riona turned to Griffin for a translation.

"What's a Fair Folk?" Gulliver looked up from playing with the bedside lamp. He was fascinated with the on/off switch.

"You're a Fair Folk," Myles answered absently, sinking down to the bed beside Gulliver and kicking off his shoes.

"She said to follow the numbers." Griffin paced the hotel room. After a full day inside, he was climbing the walls, eager to do something. Anything other than waste more time.

"It's almost sunset." Riona bent to look out the window for the millionth time. "We'll go to this place and see if we find something the human overlooked."

"I'm right here, you know." Myles glared at her.

"I see you." She stared blankly back at him.

"You do know I am the king of Fargelsi, right?"

"Yes, but you are not my king." Riona returned to her bed to rummage through Gulliver's bag. He'd taken everything from his room that wasn't nailed down.

"Really, Gullie, do you need to take the clicky box?" Riona tossed a long black rectangular device back onto the bed.

"I like the buttons."

"That's a remote control." Myles ran a hand through his hair and rolled his eyes to the ceiling.

"Which is why I want it." Gulliver snatched it up. "It controls things."

"It doesn't control *things*." Myles wrestled the remote

out of Gulliver's hands. "It controls a television. That television in our room specifically. Without the TV, it's useless."

"It's not magic?" Gulliver frowned.

"Nothing here is magic. Truly." Myles seemed like he wanted to beat that knowledge into their heads.

"I don't care what you call it, it seems like magic to me," Riona said stubbornly. "And I've decided I don't much care for it."

"Just because you don't understand something, doesn't mean it's magic," Myles said. "You two would do well to remember that."

"Then how will we know when something really is magic?" Gulliver asked.

"I will tell you. And if I'm not around, then Griffin will tell you."

"Like right away?" Gulliver gave him a pleading look.

"The moment I see real magic, you'll be the first to know."

"Let's go." Griffin finally said. "By the time we get there, it will be dark."

Myles gave him a long look. "You look less exhausted than this morning at least."

Griffin only shrugged in answer. He didn't want to admit how the moon strengthened him, how he'd never fully recovered from opening the portal the day before, and the day seemed to drain the life right out of him.

"Is that wise, to risk you being seen without a glamour?" Myles asked. "We should wait for dark before we leave this room."

"I have a hat." Griffin yanked a hat over his head. The wide brim provided cover for his ears.

"And that looks ridiculous. People are going to stare at

you for the dorky hat and catch sight of the ears." Myles pushed him back down onto the bed. "We wait."

"Fine." He'd liked Myles better when he wasn't a king. He'd gotten bossy in his old age.

For the next hour, Griffin watched Myles teach Gulliver and Riona about the science and technology behind the things they perceived as human magic. He was only half listening, trying to call on his strength in the fading twilight.

"I get what you're saying, Myles, but it still seems like a form of magic, this technology," Riona said. "I understand the bat-ery makes the clicky box work and the sensor-ma-gig in the box tells the tele-thing what to do. But that's just like the way Griffin's magic is powered by the moon, and he tells it to open a portal."

"No." Myles shook his head, clearly aggravated. "That's not the same thing at all."

"I'm pretty sure it is." Riona relaxed against the head-board on her bed. "Humans have magic, it's just a little different. But fae magic is all different too. Iskalt magic is not the same as Eldur, and Fargelsi magic is even more different. So is human magic. Myrkur is the real land without magic." She shrugged like it was all that simple.

"No, no." Myles stood. "That's so not it, Riona."

"As entertaining as this debate is," Griffin interrupted before Myles was moved to tears. "The moon has risen." He could feel his strength returning with the fading of the light. In a matter of moments, the weariness left him.

Myles dug an article of clothing out of his bag and threw it to Griffin. "Wear my sweatshirt. It has a hood."

Griffin slipped it on. "How do I look?"

"Handsomely human." Myles grinned. "And a stylish one at that."

Griffin turned to Riona and Gulliver. "Are their features still hidden?"

Myles nodded. "We're good to go."

"This human is useful." Riona pursed her lips. "But I still don't like him."

"He'll grow on you." Griffin nodded. "Let's go."

It was still an event getting everyone down the elevator and into a cab without causing a stir among the humans passing by. Their elevator companions thought Riona was quite strange when she exclaimed, "It goes down too?" Not that Griffin liked the ride any more than she did.

"It might have been cheaper to buy a car than take cabs everywhere," Myles muttered as he paid the driver.

"You lot want me to wait for you?" the cabbie asked, staring down the empty road. "There's not much ter see 'ere at night. Not much ter see period," he muttered.

"Um, yes. Please. We just fancied a walk by the ruins tonight and don't want to get stuck." Myles closed the door.

"Bit odd of a place for a walk."

"Err, a friend said it was lovely. Just … wait here. But don't come closer. Please. We'll come right back to this spot."

"All right." The cabbie shook his head grumbling something about Americans as they walked away.

"See, there's nothing here." Myles turned to the roadside. "Just some goat paths that go up the hill through those crumbling pillars." He pointed to the tallest hill where the remains of a castle sat looking ready to collapse. "And more of the same on the other side of the road."

Riona turned around in a wide circle, her wings fluttering in the breeze. "How far did you go in each direction?"

"Several miles. I walked all day."

She nodded. "I will take to the skies and see what I can

find. You may not have looked far enough."

Griffin settled a hand on her arm to keep her from flying away.

"What is it, Griff?" Riona frowned at him. He stood, staring at the hillside Myles had spent the day exploring.

"What's wrong, man, you look like someone stepped on your grave."

"You don't see it?" Griffin turned toward them, hardly able to take his eyes away from the sight.

"See what?" Riona scowled. "It's as the human said before, there is nothing here."

"The human has a name. You may call me Myles, or your Highness, either works for me." Myles' tone took on a razor-sharp edge.

"As I've said before, you are not my king."

"Stop bickering, you two." Griffin's hand tightened on Riona's arm. "You really don't see it?"

"See what?" Gulliver asked.

"The village. It's right there." Griffin pointed to the hill-top. "Just beyond those old pillars."

"You can see it?" Myles turned around, peering into the darkness as if he could will himself to see what Griffin saw.

"The vanishing village." Griffin grinned. "It's not vanished at all. You just have to be Iskaltian to see it in the moonlight." Griffin stepped off the road to make his way up the hill.

"Gulliver, that's magic right there," Myles said.

"No, it's not, I can't see anything."

"That's why it's magic, because Griff sure sees something we don't."

"Wait, you're not going into an invisible village alone." Riona raced after him.

"It's not invisible to me." Griffin kept moving.

"You've lost your mind." Riona ran ahead, squinting for all she was worth. "Nothing is there, Griffin."

"There is a quaint little village at the top of that hill. I can see it clear as day."

"I don't like this."

"She doesn't like much, does she?" Myles muttered.

"Just wait here and let me investigate. Ashlin said to follow the numbers, and those coordinates led us right here. I have to look."

"Be careful, Griff," Myles said. "We'll wait here for you."

"I won't be long."

"Take me with you, Griff," Gulliver begged. "I want to see the magic village."

"I need to go in alone this time, buddy." Griffin bent to meet his gaze. "Stay here with Riona and keep an eye on her and Myles for me. Make sure they don't kill each other. I'll take you next time if it proves to be safe."

"I never get to do the fun stuff." Gulliver kicked at the ground.

"And don't steal anything while I'm gone," Griffin called over his shoulder.

"What am I going to steal, Griff? Rocks?" Gulliver's voice rang out in the quiet night.

"Are we sure he hasn't gone mad?" Riona whispered, watching him make his way up the hill.

But Griffin was as sane as he'd ever been.

The village was old to be sure, and he couldn't see anyone out and about, but the place was well cared for. Lights flickered in windows all around the town center. It had a distinct Fargelsi aura about the town. As if a Gelsi village had been lifted up and transplanted in the human realm. But for what reason?

The goat path turned to cobblestone streets with tufts of grass growing between the stones here and there.

"Hello?" Griffin called, startled to see a young man driving a mule-drawn cart right toward him. "Good evening, sir. Might I have a word?" Griffin asked. The driver seemed to look right through him as he passed. "I was wondering if you could tell me about this place?" Griff raised his voice.

The man gave him a horrified look and flicked the reins, driving his mule into a trot.

"Please, just a moment of your time?" Griffin tried to follow him, but the man turned down another street, driving his cart as fast as he dared.

"Get to yer chores, lads, or there'll be no pie for you come supper." A woman's voice sounded behind him, and Griffin turned to find a fae woman sweeping the front steps of her cottage. Her three young boys scampered to the rear of the house where a barn leaned precariously to the left.

"Madam, might I have a word?" Griffin took a step toward her, and she screamed, running into the house and slamming the door behind her.

The reception was the same wherever he went. Few were out and about, most likely preferring to be inside with their families. He was beginning to think no one would speak to him and worried the village would fade with the sunrise, and he would have to come back tomorrow evening.

"You have caused quite a stir, young man." An elderly fae gentleman walked along the cobblestone street toward Griffin. He walked with a cane and a slight limp as he approached warily. "My people are frightened."

"I can't say I blame them," Griffin said. "I'm a little frightened myself."

"Where do you hail from?"

"Iskalt." Griffin didn't see a reason to hide that fact.

"You should return." The man turned to leave.

"Wait, please. I've come a long way to this place."

"What you seek can't be found, young man. You should leave at once, you and your friends on the hillside."

"Tell me what this place is, please?" He needed to get this man talking. "Ashlin sent me here."

"Ashlin?" The wiry fae peered into his eyes, searching for something Griffin couldn't fathom.

"She told me I would find what I'm looking for here." Well, she'd told him to follow the numbers. That was close enough to the truth.

"She should know better than to send strangers into our midst. There hasn't been an unknown descendant in generations. Not in this world or any other."

"Descendants? Descendants of whom?" Griffin asked. "I am of Iskalt, I can see your village in the moonlight."

"Only the descendants can see through the magic that shields this village—day or night. You must go, young sir. We do not trust outsiders here. And Ashlin is no friend of ours. Not any longer."

"What descendants? Tell me that, and I will leave," Griffin begged.

"The direct descendants of the O'Rourke."

"Which O'Rourke? Sorcha?" Griffin took a step closer.

"Do not speak that blasphemous name here, lad. The O'Rourke was her twin. The lady Herself was our ancestress. If you can see this place, you must carry at least a drop of her blood. But it is of no matter. You must leave and forget you ever saw or heard the name of Aghadoon." The man tapped his cane against the cobblestones, and he and the village faded into the rising mist.

CHAPTER SIX

Riona

"What the heck is he doing?" Riona sat in the field, letting the high grasses obscure her from view. Griffin was a small figure at the top of the hill. He used his hands like he was talking to someone, but there was no one there with him.

"I always knew something wasn't right with Griff." Myles threw himself down beside her. "Maybe he's finally lost it, seeing villages and people no one else can see."

"Don't say that." Gulliver picked at the grass. "I'm sure there's an explanation for his behavior."

Riona snorted. "You, boy, are too young and too naïve."

"Griff doesn't think so." His eyes narrowed. "He trusts me more than he trusts you. At least I never followed King Egan."

"The vampire king?" Myles looked to Riona, excitement in his eyes.

"Why do you keep calling him that?" She was sure she'd

regret the question just like she regretted every question that spurred Myles' incessant talking.

"There's no sun in the prison realm, right?"

Riona's jaw clenched. "In *Myrkur* we live in perpetual darkness, but we have mornings and evenings just like you do. You just have to look close enough to see the subtle changes as our day fades to night."

"Well, Vampires can only come out at night. Hence the vampire king. When I lived in Ohio, Brea and I spent a lot of time watching shows on Netflix. Her absolute favorite was called *Buffy the Vampire Slayer*." He smiled and laid back to stare up at the stars. "She used to hide from her parents at my house." He rolled onto his side and propped his head up with one hand. "And now we're both fae royalty." A laugh burst out of him. "You should have seen my parents' faces when I told them I was basically living out my own fairytale."

Riona had never given much thought to humans or the secret fae world they knew little about. Yet, curiosity now warred with her distaste for the human. "How did they react?"

"Well, at first they didn't believe me. They're Ohio stock, you know."

No, she didn't know.

"What's an Ohio?" Gulliver asked, still not taking his eyes from Griffin up on the hill.

Myles waited a moment before answering. "It's home. Where Brea and I grew up. My parents still live there. Lochlan brings me home occasionally—if I catch him in a good mood. He has a soft spot for me."

Riona doubted that. The icy king had nothing soft about him. "So, they believe you now?"

He nodded. "It's been ten years, and I still look like I'm an eighteen-year-old senior in high school with the slower aging in the fae world. I still don't totally understand it, but my wife tells me I'll live much longer than I would have in the human world, so it's cool. Over the years, my parents were sort of forced to imagine the fae world did exist. But they refuse to come visit."

"I never knew my parents." Gulliver pulled his knees in to his chest.

"Let me ask you something, Gullie." Myles sat up. "Who makes you feel safe? Who helps you when you're hurt or makes sure you have food to eat? Who loves you?"

Gulliver glanced back at Myles before fixating on the top of that hill once more. "Griff."

Myles patted his back. "Then I'd say you know your father at least."

Riona's brow creased. "We can't just choose who our parents are." If all of what Myles claimed was true, didn't that make Egan a sort of parent to her? He'd taken her to the palace after her people were destroyed. He'd made sure she was safe and cared for. In his way.

Myles shrugged. "Sure, we can."

"It's that simple for you, isn't it?"

"Everything is simple if we try to make it so."

Riona shook her head but didn't respond. Her life was anything but simple.

Gulliver rested his chin on his knees. "I want it to be that simple."

In those words, Riona heard herself. She didn't want to be the indentured servant who couldn't escape the king. She didn't want the prison magic to fall, thrusting the Dark Fae into the realm of the Light only for them to be persecuted for their physical differences.

"Griff will change the world so everything can be simple."

Riona met Myles' gaze. She'd rarely heard the human say anything without a joking tone. Until now. "How do you have so much faith in him? Unlike the rest of your people, you know who he is, what he's done."

"I don't have faith in *him*. I have faith in *people*. Anyone can change if they try hard enough."

Riona tore her eyes away from him. "I don't believe that."

"Then I'm sorry for you." He drew in a deep breath. "I don't like what Griff did to me. I don't like how he hurt people I love, but that was ten years ago. And from what I hear, that was ten years of Griffin protecting the people he cared about, fighting for the ones who couldn't fight for themselves. I want him to deserve my faith, but for that, I need to give him a chance."

In the distance, Griffin started down the hill. Riona watched his every movement. "Your human ideals could be the thing that breaks you."

Myles shook his head. "No. My human ideals keep me grounded in a world so unlike my own. If I break, it will be because of fae duplicity. If you don't believe the best in people—or fae—it'll be a very lonely existence."

Gulliver jumped to his feet and ran toward Griffin. "Are you okay? Did you find it? What happens next?"

Griffin's face told Riona all she needed to know. He hadn't learned anything new. "The village wasn't really there, was it?" She crossed her arms.

Griffin put one hand on Gulliver's shoulder and rubbed his eyes with the other. "No, it was."

Riona climbed to her feet, wiping the grass from her trousers. "So, you were right? Your Iskalt magic allowed you to see it?"

Griffin sighed. "I don't know. They kept speaking of descendants of *the O'Rourke* being able to see it, but that's the thing. I don't have any Fargelsian blood in me, let alone Fargelsian royal blood."

"But you served a Fargelsian queen." Myles pushed himself off the ground to join the others. "Could that have something to do with it?"

He shook his head. "Regan raised me, but I had no real relation to her." He turned his gaze on Riona. "Before we leave, could you do a sweep of the area. Just to make sure we haven't missed anything."

"Yes." Her wings stretched to their full size, the night contrasting against the white brilliance of the wings, except for the dark shadows that crept along the edges. She thought there might be more darkness there now than there was earlier in the day, but she tried not to think about it. With a powerful flap, she jumped into the air, her entire body relaxing into the movement. Flying was a rare pleasure for her since she'd left Myrkur, and she'd missed it.

The damp air grew thinner the higher she went. She breathed it in as she changed direction and spiraled down toward the hill seeing nothing of the village Griffin claimed was there.

A light from something on the ground caught her eye, and she hovered over the hill, lowering slowly until her feet touched the grassy knoll. The light faded as if it was a dying magic, but Riona inched closer. Below where the light had been there was an odd-looking envelope. Wasting no time, she picked up the envelope and jumped into the air, letting her wings do most of the work.

Griffin looked up at her as she hovered above them.

Myles grinned. "I don't think I could ever get used to watching someone fly."

Griffin issued a quiet "me either" but she was probably imagining the awe in his voice. Her face flushed as she set one foot on the ground and then the other. Her wings folded in naturally at her back.

"Did anyone see you?" Griffin asked.

"There would have to be people here to see me." She held out the envelope. "I found this."

Griffin took it and turned it over, having what seemed like the same thoughts as Riona. "It's clean."

Riona nodded. "Which means it was just recently left. There was a bit of light magic making sure I saw it."

"Open it." Gulliver bounced eagerly on his toes.

Riona couldn't blame him. They'd reached so many dead ends over the months that they were due for something helpful.

Griffin opened the envelope and pulled out a single square of colorful paper. "It's sticky on the back."

"That's because it's a Post-It." Myles smiled in excitement over a piece of paper. "On one of my trips to the human realm, Lochlan and I went shopping so Brea could have her human comforts. I bought a ton of Post-Its, and now my wife is obsessed with them."

"A queen is obsessed with a tiny piece of paper?"

Griffin's eyes focused on the odd little paper. "What does this mean?"

Riona took it from his hands and read it aloud. "Ashlin sends her regards. Come find us again to get the answers you seek."

"The old woman?" Myles rubbed the back of his neck. "The one who was abducted?"

"What if she wasn't?" Riona thought back to the cottage on the cliffs. "What if she only left in a hurry when she saw us coming?" Riona turned the paper over and froze. "More numbers."

"How many?" Griff asked. "Like the ones before? Myles, do you have your maps?"

Myles crossed his arms. "Yes, Griff. I brought them out into this field where we weren't supposed to have use for them."

"What about your phone? You said it could find things, information from someone named Google."

Myles tipped his head back, like he was searching the sky for patience. "Google is not a person, but we're in the middle of nowhere, an hour away from the city. I don't have service." He checked the time on the phone. "Let's go before the cab waiting for us leaves, and we really do get stuck."

Riona scowled, but there was no malice behind it, only a bone-deep weariness from chasing the smallest leads and still finding no trace of the book or the Iskalt kids.

They crossed the fields to get back to the road, and relief wound through Riona as she saw the yellow ... cab ... waiting for them. "If we had horses, they'd wait for us too." Sure, the cab was faster, but she couldn't shake the eerie feeling of sitting in something that didn't need a horse or water to move.

"Riona." Griffin released a weary sigh. "The human realm is different from ours, and we'll be here a while. I refuse to go back again without the twins or a way to save Shauna and Nessa. So, just get used to the idea that you won't understand most things here, and you need to trust me to know what I'm doing."

She climbed into the cab, not giving Griffin an answer.

She wanted to trust him, everything inside her was begging her to tell him the truth. The problem was, once she did, he'd never trust her again. Once he learned of the book she used to communicate with Egan. When he knew of the magic tying her to the king.

He thought they were the same because they both served evil rulers, but it wasn't the same at all. By Griffin's own admission, Regan trusted him. Sort of. She let him go into the human world regularly or even to the other fae kingdoms.

But Egan … Riona never got to be separated from him, she didn't get his trust, only his control.

Griffin would open his eyes to it one day and realize Riona didn't belong here with these people who would do anything to find the Iskalt twins. She didn't belong among the queens who'd defeated Regan. They were good, truly good. To their people, their friends, even those they didn't trust, like her.

Riona never got the chance to be good.

"You're quiet." Griffin nudged her as the cab bumped down the road. Her hand shot out to grab the door handle.

"These cabs give me stomach pains."

Myles leaned over. "If you puke, make sure it's on Griff, not me."

Griffin shot him a scowl. "Are you okay, Riona? Do we need to stop?"

In truth, it wasn't the cab making her sick to her stomach. She'd come to the realization that nothing in her life was a choice. Everything had been set for her.

And she would have no chance at doing good. As much as she wanted to be on Griffin's side, she knew she would obey Egan in the end.

They reached the inn while the moon still hung high over the city. The ride was only an hour long, yet Riona could have kissed the ground as they spilled out of the cab.

Myles paid the driver and waved to him before he took off. It was so ingrained in the human to be polite, to follow the rules of society.

"Are all humans like you, Myles?"

Myles cocked his head. "Like me?"

"You didn't trick the man to take less money. You smile at every stranger you see. You're ... nice to your fellow humans."

Myles laughed. "No, not all humans are like that. You should see where I grew up. People are a lot less trusting there."

Griffin ushered them all through the double glass doors. Riona took Griff's advice and tried not to be amazed at everything she saw. She clamped her lips shut when they rode the elevator, though she would have preferred to scream. That thing was *not* fun.

The four of them filed into Myles' and Gulliver's room. Myles immediately went to his bed where he'd left the map of Ireland. He unrolled it on one of the beds. "This is where we are." He pointed to a star. "Here's the last coordinates." He tapped a circled location. "I'm guessing the village is still in Ireland. I mean, I've seen some powerful magic, but none that could move a village across an ocean."

"Ocean?" Gulliver leaned closer.

"Giant body of water. They separate the continents. Ireland is an island in itself, which means to leave, one would need to fly across the ocean."

"Fly?" Gulliver's eyes lit up. "I knew humans had magic."

Myles groaned. "Not this again. Humans can fly in things called airplanes. It's technology."

Gulliver sank down onto the bed, his shoulders slumped.

"Griff, hand me the coordinates." Myles pulled his phone free. "I'll plug them into Google."

Riona still wasn't convinced Google wasn't a person. Maybe the one providing magic to all their technology.

"That can't be right." Myles stared down at the screen, his brow creased.

"What is it?" Griffin tried to see what Myles saw, but Myles nudged him out of the way. "What's wrong?"

"Nothing ... necessarily." Myles pushed a hand through his hair, worry dancing across his features. "Maybe ... I'll try again." His fingers flew over the screen while the three fae around him watched in awe. Humans had every bit of information at their fingertips. The thought of such a thing had Riona feeling very small. That box could do more than her. Her only magic was in the wings on her back.

Myles eyebrows drew together. "Same place. Let me pull up a bigger map."

"You're going to pull a map out of that ... phone?" Gulliver couldn't contain his interest.

"No, but it will let me see a map on the screen." He said nothing more for a long moment before lifting his face to Griff. "Ohio."

"Let me see that." Griffin took the phone, his jaw tightening. "Is this Grafton?"

Myles sat on the edge of his bed. "Griff, those coordinates can't be right. How does an entire Irish village just move to Grafton, Ohio?"

"What's in Grafton?" Riona's eyes went from one to the other.

"My parents, for one." Myles shook his head in disbelief. "And also the farm Brea grew up on. Lochlan purchased it years ago."

Griffin's eyes widened. "They've been there." He turned to Riona. "The first place we came to in the human realm."

"Where the sun nearly blinded us?" she asked.

He nodded. "Myles, when I was in the village, they kept mentioning me being a descendant of Sorcha's or her sister's. But ... I don't have Fargelsian blood."

"That you know of," Myles interjected.

"Yes, that I know of. But do you know who does have royal Fargelsian blood?"

"Brea." The name was a whisper on Myles' lips. "There has to be a reason their next coordinates were Grafton." His eyes widened. "And the twins. If Callum is after the book, he won't be able to see the village, but Tia and Tobey…"

"We have to get to Grafton. Traveling like humans will take too long."

Riona caught on to what they were saying. "Griff, if we want to portal there, we have to portal to the fae realm and then to Grafton hours later. Are you strong enough?"

Griffin rubbed his face. "I don't have a choice. Collect your belongings. We leave in half an hour."

CHAPTER SEVEN

Griffin

Griffin was able to open a portal to the moon garden at the center of the Iskalt Palace, the last location he'd portaled from. They arrived back at the palace at mid-afternoon, and Griffin was grateful he had the excuse of daylight to avoid making another portal right away. There was something very wrong with his O'Shea magic. Without the full use of his Iskalt magic to fuel his O'Shea magic, it was somehow running out of steam. It was getting harder and harder to travel between the worlds, and the time skew grew more extreme each time.

They spent the afternoon in Lochlan's council chambers catching the king and queen up to speed on their findings, and after a hasty afternoon nap, it was time to leave for the human realm once more.

Griffin was beginning to think traveling the human way would have been much easier.

In the end, he couldn't open a portal large enough to pass through, so his brother had to step in and create one for them.

"Your magic is weak, brother," Lochlan said before Griffin stepped through the portal. "It is not your fault. This Dark Fae king will pay for what he's done to you and your people. We will get your magic back, and you will be strong again." Lochlan clapped him on the back, and with a wordless nod, Griffin stepped through the opening into the human realm to a fresh wave of sunlight, high in the sky. He wanted to weep at the sight. He was so tired, he couldn't count how many hours he'd been on his feet.

Gulliver stood on the back porch of Brea's childhood home, the door open, but neither he nor Riona seemed inclined to step inside.

"Did you break in?" Griffin asked, eager to make a bed in the barn and forget this day wasn't over yet. He had another invisible village to find. "And where is Myles?" He glanced around for their human chaperone.

"He ran off to see his family," Riona said absently. "Said he'd be back by sunset."

"Get to the part where you broke into Brea's old house, Gulliver."

"Key." Gulliver held up a silver keychain with a set of house keys as explanation.

"Did you steal them, or did Brea give them to you?"

"Brea gave them to us, said she has someone in the human realm to keep the house clean and stocked. Brea came here earlier to get us takeout—whatever that means—and said we should make ourselves at home."

"Then why are we out here and not in there?" Griffin asked.

"I'm not going in there." Riona backed away. "I think I'd rather sleep in the barn."

"What's wrong?"

Gulliver pointed into the dark entryway, and Griffin peeked inside, startled to see two human machines whirling and banging in the small mud room.

He had more experience with human machinery than these two, but household contraptions weren't his specialty. Particularly ones that made noise. Still, he knew enough not to fear them. "It's just a machine." He stepped inside, hoping he could figure out how to turn them off.

He touched the white front of the spinning machine to find it was quite hot. Something was inside, tumbling around and around. The machine made a loud beep, and Griffin jumped back. He turned to see Gulliver and Riona were halfway across the yard.

"It's okay, it stopped," Griffin called. He opened the hot door and stepped back, expecting steam or hot air to sweep out of the machine. Nothing happened, so he bent to look inside.

"Oh!" He stood up, checking the other machine filled with water. "I know what this is!" He waved Riona and Gulliver inside. "It's okay, come in."

"What is it?" Gulliver asked, clutching Riona's hand. Griffin wasn't sure if it was for his own comfort or for hers.

"This one washes clothes, and the other one dries them. Look." He reached into the dryer and pulled out three sets of clean sheets for the beds.

Riona touched the fabric and pulled it close when she felt the warmth. "The smell is like a field of wildflowers." She buried her face in the sheet. "What's it for?"

"The beds." Griffin peered into the machine that was still washing something.

"What's the wet one for?" Gulliver asked.

"Probably for the blankets, but we should leave that for Myles. I don't want to blow Brea's machine up."

Riona stepped back again, still clutching the sheet. "Do they make a habit of exploding?"

"Not if we don't mess with it." Griffin steered them both into the kitchen where Brea had left them a note to make themselves at home and help themselves to the takeout in the fridge and that only Myles was allowed to run the microwave or other appliances.

"What's takeout?" Gulliver asked.

"What's a fridge?" Riona scowled at all the human contraptions around the kitchen.

"I know two of these things." Griffin opened the refrigerator to find takeout boxes of Chinese food for their dinner later. "Gulliver, you're going to love this ... once Myles gets back."

"Aw that smells good. Why do we have to wait?"

"It's better hot. I know that's what the microwave is for." Griffin looked around the kitchen. "But I don't know which one that is, so we better not attempt it." Griffin put the food back in the fridge.

"I think we should try to sleep," Riona said. "My body thinks it's night." She swayed on her feet, holding her sheets like she wasn't about to give them up.

"Agreed." Griffin led them through the kitchen to the living room, feeling odd and a little uncomfortable in Brea's childhood home. "The bedrooms are probably upstairs." Griffin crept through the house like he shouldn't be there.

"Only one family lived here?" Riona shook her head in disbelief. "Brea's family must have been wealthy."

Griffin didn't have it in him to explain to her once again that what she saw was this world's version of borderline poverty.

"I get a bed to myself?" Gulliver's eyes widened at the queen size bed that used to belong to Brea's parents.

"You've been sleeping in a bed by yourself since we arrived in Iskalt," Griffin said.

"But that's in a palace," Riona said. "This is just a normal house, according to you."

"Make your beds and get some sleep." Griffin took a set of clean sheets from Riona and headed for the guest room, leaving Brea's old bedroom to Riona. He couldn't sleep there or in the room her parents once shared—a room she likely shared with Lochlan whenever they came here together. There were too many ghosts in this house already.

"What is this?" Riona stepped into his room holding a pink fluffy thing with a strap.

"Oh, Brea's note said she left you an eye mask on your pillow to help you sleep. Put it over your eyes, and it will block the sunlight."

Riona looked carefully at the sleep mask, nodding to herself. "I'm stealing this when we leave." She retreated across the hall to her room.

Griffin struggled with the sheets for much longer than necessary before he figured out how it worked. He hoped the others did better than he did. Collapsing in a heap under the cool, sweet smelling sheet, he fell asleep in moments.

Griffin woke to the sound of Myles' voice and the scent of something he didn't recognize.

His stomach growled at the memory of the Chinese food in the kitchen, and he rolled over, rubbing the sleep from his eyes. It was still light outside, but the sun was setting. He'd have his portal magic back soon, and he anticipated spending all night looking for the village somewhere around the rural areas near Brea's house. Possibly somewhere on the farm.

"Griff, you gotta try this 'umplin thing. It's so good." Gulliver's eyes lit with excitement when he joined them in the dining room.

"I think that's a dumpling, Gullie." Griffin took the seat beside him and grabbed the waxed carton with the spicy dumplings he liked.

"That's what I said." Gulliver slurped from a bowl of soup.

"Did you get to see your family?" Griffin asked Myles.

"Briefly." Myles yawned and patted his full stomach. "I fell asleep on Mom's couch, but it was good to see them."

Griffin helped himself to a little of everything, mixing the savory rice with the sweet red sauce he loved. Riona hadn't said much. She seemed to be focused on the food too.

Finally, she sat back and sighed, a contented smile on her face. "Gullie was right. Humans have the best food." She belched loudly and slapped a hand over her mouth, her cheeks flushing red before she burst out laughing.

Griffin laughed with her, happy to see her let her guard down. It happened so rarely, but he enjoyed the moments when he got to see glimpses of the real Riona.

His laughter froze as he looked past her through the window. He stood, shoving his empty plate aside as he paced to the window overlooking what was once a large pasture.

"What is it?" Riona leapt from her chair to join him. "What do you see?"

"It's here," Griffin whispered.

"What?" Gullie and Myles came to look at the yard bathed in moonlight.

"The village. It's right there in the pasture." Griffin pointed. "It looks just as it did in Ireland." The same crumbling pillars stood flanking a path through the tall grass, and he could just make out the cobblestone streets in the distance.

"Let's go then." Riona stepped toward the door.

"No need." Griffin's shoulders tensed. "Someone is coming here." A man made his way along the path through the pasture, looking over his shoulder as if he didn't want to be followed. "Stay inside." Griffin stepped through the kitchen and the mud room to the back porch. He wasn't too surprised when Riona ignored him and followed him into the yard. She stayed behind to watch as Griffin went to meet their mysterious visitor.

"You move across worlds quickly." It was the old man he'd met before. He came to a stop beneath the large oak tree at the edge of the pasture. A tire swing hung from the massive branches, and Griffin could imagine Brea playing there as a child.

"Someone was kind enough to leave directions." Griffin stood with his hands in his pockets, not sure how to proceed. He hadn't expected to find the village so quickly or to be confronted by the man who took it away before. His eyes flitted to the cane, preparing for the man to tap it and make the structures disappear, taking Griffin's hope with it.

"I told you to leave. You shouldna be here." The man's soft Irish burr took on a hard edge.

"Please, I don't know why I can see the village and my friends can't, but I'm supposed to be here."

"Yer a descendant. That much is plain." The man stepped forward, leaning heavily on his cane. "There was a time all descendants were friends." He held his hand out. "Seamas," he said simply.

"Griffin." Griffin shook his hand. "So, you're Fargelsian descendants?"

"I suppose we are at that." Seamas shrugged. "We're direct descendants of Grainne O'Rourke, Queen Sorcha's twin sister. And if you can see our village, then you are too."

"I can't imagine how. My blood is of Iskalt. I don't have Gelsi magic."

"Ye don't have to have the Gelsi power, but somewhere in your lineage yer linked with someone who does. Or did."

"What does it mean?"

"Ye know of the book?" Seamas asked.

Griffin nodded. "Though I'm starting to think I don't know nearly enough about it."

"Aye, that is true enough. The O'Rourke book of spells is powerful. Dangerous in the wrong hands. It is why I left ye in Ireland."

"Sorcha's book contains magic I desperately need." Griffin hoped this man would help him.

"It's na her book. She was keeper of it for a time, that is all. Its history reaches back further than just her or Grainne, though her descendants are the keepers now."

"You know where the book is?" Griffin glanced behind Seamas to the magical village he called home.

"Aye, it's there, and it's safe. That is all that matters. Ye canna have it. It's too dangerous and not mine to give."

"Can you show it to me?" Griffin asked. "I'd just like to

see if it contains information to break a certain kind of spell. If it doesn't, I will move on and look elsewhere for a solution."

He didn't respond for a long moment, and Griffin was sure he'd tell him to leave and never return. But he didn't. "Come wi' me." Seamas turned toward the pasture. "Leave yer lady to watch over ye from afar."

Griffin followed the strange old man, waving to Riona not to follow.

"Ye canna see the book, Griffin. It's hidden within the village. I don't even know where it is, so don't ye ask. But tell me about this spell, and I'll do my best to help ye if I can."

Griff shivered as they passed through the stone pillars into the village. The magic of this place seemed to affect him more this time than it had on his last visit.

Seamas led him to a large building at the center of the village. Griffin was startled to find the place was a library. Dimly lit by candlelight, the large room was filled with shelf after shelf of aged books. Some leather bound and cracked. Some were mere scrolls of parchment and some were modern notebooks.

"What is this place?" Griffin looked around in awe. He could hear a faint whisper among the aisles of books. A sound like pages rustling as someone flipped through an open book.

"We are the keepers of magic," Seamas explained, putting his cane across the doorway, drawing Griffin's attention away from the books. "Ye canna enter here. We don't know ye, young sir. Descendants who want to join us must first undergo a wee bit of testing of yer loyalties. After ye were seen in the village before, our elders gave me a talking to. I was not ter turn ye away without telling ye who we were."

Seamas sighed. "Apparently, you aren't the first to inquire of late."

"So, you're the keepers of the book's magic?"

"No, boy. We're the keepers of *all* magic."

Griffin felt uneasy as he put a hand on the wall to brace himself. The whispering sounds grew louder as Seamas spoke. It was as if the sound were intent on overpowering Seamas' voice.

"The ancient powers have been largely forgotten through the centuries as knowledge passed down through families. What most fae use today pales in comparison to what they once knew in the distant past. The O'Rourke ancestors have always kept a complete record of their Gelsi magic."

"The book?" Griffin asked, trying to focus on Seamas' words.

Seamas shook his head. "The Book holds many spells, aye, but it doesna hold all the secrets to the ancient powers. This room is that record, and the book is the key to accessing these records. I can try to help you, Griffin, but then ye need to go and na come back. The elders will try an convince ye to stay, but ye need to go. This is not the place for you."

Griffin had no intention of staying once he found what he needed to know. He crossed his arms over his chest as he explained the boundary magic Sorcha placed around Myrkur.

"Aye, we know of the prison realm. It isna wise to bring it down. That kind of magic changes over time. Becomes something else. It's best left alone."

"Unfortunately, that is not an option." Griffin's ears buzzed with the whispering sound growing louder, like an alarm trying to warn him of danger.

"Yer na the first to come asking about dangerous magic.

Another woman came looking for the book not too long ago. She was a descendant and knew of our village. We had to turn her away. Another man came looking. He wasna a descendent and couldna see our village. But the wee ones he had with him could."

"Children?" Griffin stood up straighter.

"Aye. Young ones. A boy and a girl."

"How long ago was this?" Griffin asked.

"A month or so ago." Seamas shrugged.

"Do you know where he went?"

"It doesna matter, the wee ones didn't tell him what they saw."

"It matters to me. To their parents!" Griffin slammed his fist against the rough wood of the door frame. "Did you speak to them like you spoke to me?"

"No, we let them pass from the village. There was no need to interfere since they posed no danger to the village." His eyes shifted away, and something about the tone of his voice made Griffin uneasy.

Griffin wasn't sure he believed him. "That man poses a threat to our whole world."

Seamas leaned forward his eyes narrowed to slits. "Yer contemplating magic that ought to be left alone. Can I not sway you to go home and not think of it again?"

"The lives of people I love are at risk if I do not find this book." The hair raised on the back of Griffin's neck, and he stood, backing away from Seamas toward the door. The whispering grew louder. He could almost make out a voice. A word.

Leave.

Griffin didn't need to be told twice. He turned and threw the door open.

"I'm afraid we canna allow you to leave now." Seamas followed him at a walk. Seemingly unconcerned with Griffin's quick departure from the library.

"I'm afraid you can't stop me." Griffin stumbled over the cobblestones.

"We are leaving this place. You will come with us." Seamas stood at the center of the street as an unnatural fog rolled in. "We must protect our knowledge, Griffin. The two worlds are at stake, and you're trying to play with dangerous magic."

Griffin panicked and did the only thing he could. He opened a portal to the moon garden at his brother's palace in Iskalt.

A hand gripped his shoulder at the last second and Griffin's heart thundered in his chest as he made the leap. Whoever grabbed him was coming to Iskalt with him.

CHAPTER EIGHT

Griffin

Griffin O'Shea had traveled by portal since he was a child. Traveling to and from the human realm was not supposed to be a difficult task for an O'Shea. But never before had he become stuck inside one.

The unfamiliar grip on his shoulder tightened as a long tunnel stretched out before him. Whispers echoed around him, beckoning him to follow. He moved slowly, as though engulfed in swamp water, the mud and muck making his movements sluggish.

Violet light flashed and flickered along the tunnel, like strikes of lightening from an angry sky just before a storm. A familiar, comforting sound filled his ears. Singing.

The whispering voices didn't like the song.

But this voice was sweet and melodic, drowning out the frightening whispers. He knew this voice as well as his own, but he couldn't recall how.

He could just make out her form in the distance, her blue dress billowing out behind her like watered silk. Her voice was angelic and powerful, as though it was the source of her fae magic. No creature of the human realm or of Myr could create such a sound. Such a sense of peace.

A lullaby.

One Griffin knew from his childhood.

Regan? He moved to follow her, but the hand on his shoulder held him back.

The woman turned to smile at him. She clutched a book in her arms, a tear coursed down her cheek like a fine drop of crystal.

Something pulled at Griffin's soul. The whispers chanted for him to follow her. To take back what was lost to him.

Dark clouds rolled in, and thunder shook the ground beneath him. She was gone, but her song lingered. Still the whispering called to him, begging him to find her among the swirling shapes and foreign sounds.

Tall buildings emerged from the clouds, their windows reflecting the brilliant light of the sun. Earthly sounds reached him now. Blaring horns, the odd human music he never seemed to understand no matter how often Brea had tried to explain it to him. Black city streets flashed by, the orange painted traffic lines as useless to him as ever. Flashing lights, too many people. Crosswalks. Odd human smells. Sirens. So much noise, Griffin would never make sense of it all.

Then he saw green grass. Trees. Birds. Familiar things, but it was only a flash of these things before the city returned. Loud and obnoxious, but somehow more pleasant. The aromas here were appealing, and the buildings less intimidating. The city streets flew past him in a grid pattern. Easy to remember, if only he could make sense of it.

The fae woman's song cut off abruptly, and the sounds of the city bombarded him. A scream chilled his blood, and the tunnel turned red.

The cloying scent of blood filled his senses just as Griffin stepped into Iskalt and his knees buckled beneath him. Unfamiliar arms lifted him from the ground and carried him inside the palace.

"Griffin?" Brea's voice called to him from the portal, urging him to come back.

Griffin's eyes fluttered open, and he sat up straight, making the room spin. "What happened?" He rubbed his eyes, trying to find his equilibrium.

"You made an unscheduled trip back to Iskalt," Lochlan said, peering over the edge of the settee with a frown at his younger brother. "You don't look so good."

Griffin took Brea's offered hand and moved to sit up. "I just arrived?" He shook his head, but the whispering still called to him.

"You arrived hours ago." Brea clutched his hand.

"And you didn't arrive alone," Lochlan added, his arms crossed over his chest.

Griffin grabbed his shoulder, remembering the moment before he leaped into his hastily made portal.

"Who is this ... creature you've brought back with you?"

"I am Dark Fae," the man said in a familiar voice. "The conduit."

"Nihal?" Griffin moved to stand up from the settee in Lochlan's study.

"It was time I left Aghadoon." Nihal shrugged.

"So it was you helping us? This whole time?" Griffin took a step toward the man, clutching Brea for support. "You gave us the coordinates?"

The big man nodded, his dark wings flexing. He reminded Griffin of Riona and the others he'd left behind.

"And you are?" Brea asked.

"I am Nihal, your Majesty." He gave a curt bow. "I am sorry I did not introduce myself before Griffin woke, but it was he I needed to speak with."

"And you have been helping my brother?" Lochlan asked.

"Several times," Griffin said with a shake of his head to clear the cobwebs from his mind. "We wouldn't have made it to Iskalt alive without Nihal's help." Griffin broke away from Brea and stumbled toward the Dark Fae to shake his hand. "Thank you. I think—no, I know—we would never have gotten this far without your aid." The whispering was fading from his mind, but the echo of the song was still with him.

"That was your music? In the portal? Did you do something?"

"That was all you, Griffin O'Shea. Something is very wrong with your magic. You are not well."

"We should let him rest," Brea said.

"No, Brea. He has them." Griffin shot her a look. "Callum was seen with Tia and Toby in the human world weeks ago. We cannot afford to slow down now."

"Are they okay? Who saw them? How are they?" Brea tugged on his shirtsleeve, demanding answers he didn't have.

"I don't know, Brea, but I think I know where we need to go next." He needed to find the woman he saw in the portal.

Myles would help him find the right city. Griffin headed toward the garden, thankful the sun had set when he was unconscious.

"And where do you think you're going?" Lochlan followed him.

"I have to go back." Griffin stumbled across the uneven stones into the moon garden, Brea and Lochlan following close on his heels.

"You're too sick to travel." Lochlan tried to pull him back inside.

"I can't leave them there alone." Griffin shivered in the cold, his ragged hot breath puffed out around him.

"Please, Griffin," Brea begged, her cheeks stained with tears for her children. "Just stay the night with us, and then Lochlan will open a portal for you tomorrow at moonrise. You're not well."

"Listen to your family, Griffin," Nihal said. "Tomorrow will be soon enough."

"No, I have to leave now." Griffin wiped the sweat from his forehead, not pausing long enough to think about how he shouldn't be sweating in the cold Iskalt night.

"I had to come here to escape the village. Now that I've given you an update on Tia and Toby's whereabouts, I have to get back to work." He wasn't sure where Callum would take them, only that they were with him in the human realm, and the woman he saw in the portal was the key to finding them and ending this for good.

"If you won't open a portal for us, then I will." Griffin turned to his brother, knowing full well if he tried to open a portal right now, it wouldn't happen.

"Will you rest when you get back?" Lochlan asked. "Or do I have to go with you and make you?"

"I'll rest for a little while if I must." Griffin couldn't get the song out of his head. Even now, his mind throbbed with the melody.

"I'll see he arrives safely." Nihal stepped to Griffin's side to take his arm.

"Be careful, brother." Lochlan took a deep breath and spread his arms wide to open a portal to their home in the human world.

Griffin nodded, clasping his brother's hand one last time. He leaned on Nihal's arm, and together they stepped into the early morning light under the large oak tree in the yard where he'd left Riona. She sat there now, awaiting his return.

"What are you doing here?" Riona gaped at Nihal.

Griffin's mind swirled with whispers and songs from his childhood, but he looked to the pasture to see the village was gone. With a deep breath, he shook his head. "How long was I gone?"

"A long time," Riona said. "I saw you run across the pasture, and then you disappeared into your portal."

"When was that?"

"Yesterday."

Griffin swayed on his feet, his head spinning as he sank to the ground in a boneless heap.

CHAPTER NINE

Riona

Riona couldn't remember worrying about anyone. She'd never experienced the fear that came with illness or the waiting because she'd never cared about anyone enough to fear their death. That was the worst part. She didn't want to care. "Griffin." She knocked on the door again. "Are you okay?" She heard the water running before the door to the washroom opened, revealing a sweating Griffin who could barely keep his head up.

"I'm fine." He tried to brush past her, but his steps faltered, and he slammed his shoulder into the wall.

"You are not fine." She took his arm and guided him down the hallway to the bed he'd claimed.

Something happened when he went into that village she couldn't see, but he never had the chance to tell them. As soon as he portaled back to the house—with Nihal—he'd collapsed into a heap on the grass. It took all of Riona and Nihal's strength to get him up the steps and into the house.

Kicking open the door, Riona helped Griffin to the bed. He collapsed onto it with a groan. Indecision warred within Riona. A part of her wanted to let Gulliver take care of Griffin. Or Myles because it seemed like a very human thing to get sick. Or at least, she assumed so. She'd kept her distance from those who fell ill at the palace of Myrkur. She'd heard of the things that could happen to the sick.

She sat on the corner of the bed, watching Griffin as if she'd never seen him before. The fae she'd met in Myrkur was strong, resilient—though she'd never admit those things to him. Riona had admired him from the moment he refused to kill her in the pits.

Myles appeared in the doorway, his eyes going wide. "He's still not well?"

Riona shook her head. They'd expected him to recover quickly once the portal magic settled down.

Myles set a cup of water on the table beside the bed. "Right now, we need to get him hydrated. Eventually, we'll have to get some food in him since he's puked acid the last two times he's thrown up."

"Acid? How does one puke acid?"

Myles pinned her with a look. "You fae could really benefit from some science lessons. Maybe I'll start a college when I get back to Fargelsi for Muggle Studies." He snorted out a laugh. "Your stomach has acid in it that helps break down the food you eat. So, once he was done throwing up everything else in his stomach, only acid was left."

Myles rubbed his eyes. "I've seen so few fae get sick."

"I've seen many." Gulliver stood in the doorway, his eyes on Griffin's sleeping form.

Riona stood. "That's not possible. If there was some sort of sickness, we'd have heard of it at the palace." *We.* Gulliver's scowl told her exactly how he felt about that *we.* Riona and Egan. Egan and Riona.

Myles looked from Gulliver to Riona. "From what I've gathered, the real pandemic in Myrkur is extreme poverty. I'm not surprised you two had different experiences with fae illnesses." He looked down at Griffin. "Let's let him rest. I brought some food back from my parents' place." He stalked from the room, expecting the two fae to follow him.

They reached the kitchen where Myles opened a bag of bread—Riona couldn't believe it came in bags—and slathered a brown substance on it. "Peanut butter and jelly. I figured it was time you two try the most human food there is." He finished the sandwiches with a red gelatinous substance that did not look appealing and put them on the table.

Gulliver picked one up and took a giant bite, his smile growing as he ate. Riona tried hers in nibbles, but she wasn't hungry, not with worry filling every part of her. Though, it was delicious, she had to admit.

"Gulliver." Myles leaned forward in his chair and rested his folded hands on the table. "I have lived in the fae realm for a long time, but at times like these, I feel more like my human self in my ignorance. You say many have fallen ill in the prison realm?"

Gulliver set his sandwich down and swallowed. "Before we left, there was a woman in our village, Sinead. She couldn't get out of bed without help. Most people wouldn't go near her, worried it was some Light Fae plague."

"So, she was a prisoner?" Riona asked.

Myles shot her a scowl. "Isn't everyone behind that magic a prisoner?"

Riona sighed and looked away. "No. Most of the Dark Fae living in Myrkur are there because it was once their kingdom. Generations of them were trapped once the magic was put in place. But Light Fae ... yes, they're there for a reason, some crime they committed—or they are descended from prisoners sent there."

"And their magic is taken?"

"Yes." Riona focused her gaze on the table. "That's the way the border magic works. No Light Fae who enters Myrkur keeps their magic. It is how we keep the peace within our borders."

Gulliver slammed his fist on the table, startling both Myles and Riona. "That's not true, and you know it. The way to keep the peace is to let us live in peace. But you and your king can't do that, can you? In Myrkur, you destroy everything you touch. We Dark Fae are just as much prisoners as the rest. And now Griff is sick just like Sinead. I blame you. I blame Egan. You took their magic. Light Fae are supposed to have power running through their veins."

Riona had nothing to say about his outburst. Gulliver wasn't wrong. There was no peace in Myrkur because Egan wanted to keep them weak so he remained strong. Maybe they didn't deserve peace. But the Dark Fae? The ones whose only magic lay in the features that made them different ... she'd helped him keep them in line too. Rising from her chair, Riona met Gulliver's angry, cat-like gaze. "I'm going to make sure Griff drinks that water."

When she reached the quiet of Griffin's room, she leaned against the door, letting her heart return to its natural rhythm. Lifting one arm, she watched the tattoos slither and change with no reason she'd ever been able to find. There was one fae she could ask, but she couldn't bring herself to go in search of Nihal quite yet. Gulliver was right about many things. Riona was a Dark Fae, one whose secrets were hidden, even from herself. She didn't know why she was the last of her kind. Well, she and Nihal were the last. Yet, she didn't even know the meaning of the messages etched into her very skin.

Riona reached the bed in two strides. She stared down at Griffin's calm expression. In sleep, he didn't have a haunted look about him. She couldn't imagine how it felt to walk around in a home where no one recognized him.

Her fingers brushed auburn hair away from his face. His lips moved as if he had something to say. The water had only been an excuse. She wouldn't wake Griffin when what he needed most was rest. "Please be okay," she whispered. "I can't do this without you." And what was *this*? Find the book? Get it to Egan?

Or discover a way to free themselves completely from Egan's hold?

"Riona," Myles whispered. She hadn't noticed him opening the door. "We need to talk."

"Where's Gulliver?"

"He went out with Nihal for a walk. The kid needed to blow off steam."

She wasn't sure what the odd phrase meant, but she understood the sincerity behind it. Myles was one of the few people from Griffin's life who had stopped looking at her with distrust in his eyes. Did that make him more perceptive or less?

She followed Myles to the backdoor. He slid it open, and they stepped onto the wooden deck. From there, they could see much of the surrounding lands. Fields that went unplanted, equipment that sat rusting in the sun. "This place is sad."

Myles rested his arms on the rail. "The Robinsons were pretty awful people. The day Griffin abducted Brea and took her to the fae realm, it changed her life for the better—ultimately, I mean. Finding out the Robinson's weren't Brea's parents made a lot of sense. She was always meant for better things than living with people who never treated her like a daughter."

"It is odd to me that a fae queen lived in the human world."

Myles shrugged, his expression turning serious. "I have a theory about Griff."

Riona leaned her back on the rail beside him. "Is it a theory that'll get us killed?"

"I honestly don't know. This entire mission reeks of death to me."

"Okay, I just wanted to know in advance. Go on."

"Fargelsi has the most extensive library in the fae realm—my wife's doing. She didn't grow up a royal. Instead, she was a servant who didn't know her father was the rightful king. The servants to Queen Regan weren't allowed to learn. Now, my wife makes sure everyone has the chance at schooling."

"An honorable endeavor."

"Yes. There are a number of books for children in particular. They use them to teach children to read. One such book is called *A Power to Understand*. It tells the story of a woman who loses her magic. She spends the entire book trying to do good works, hoping it will be returned to her. As she goes along, she becomes ill. It worsens and worsens, but she can't stop her altruistic way of living."

"Does the illness go away?"

He nodded. "At the end of the book, she does one last deed before dying. Saving the life of the king. He sees to it that her magic is restored. Within minutes, the illness is gone. She still dies, but it's her age that kills her."

"But it's just a story." Riona's brow furrowed. "Right?"

Myles looked over his shoulder at the house. "I thought so. But Gulliver told me more about Sinead in Myrkur. I think Griffin might have the same thing, and it's made worse every time he opens a portal."

Riona turned to look out over the fields that should be teeming with life. The same could be said for Griffin. "So, what do we need to do?"

"Not me." Myles met her gaze. "I cannot help. But the story says the illness is triggered in some people by losing and then regaining only a portion of their magic. You see, the bodies of Light Fae aren't meant to remain stable without the full use of their magic. The power strengthens every part of them. Without it, they start to crumble. I'm guessing it is Egan's doing."

"How am I supposed to help?"

Myles shrugged. "You'll find a way."

Riona watched him re-enter the house, her chest tight. She sucked in a deep breath. Did Myles know she communicated with Egan? Did Griffin?

Closing her eyes against the sun, she exhaled, letting it empty her out.

Back inside, Riona went directly to her room, which she'd been told was Brea's as a kid. She rummaged through her bag until her fingers found the familiar cracked leather. Would the journal work between worlds? She'd only ever contacted Egan in the fae realm when his magic tugged at her.

Her eyes widened as she realized she hadn't felt his power

since leaving Iskalt. The noose around her was gone. As long as she stayed in the human realm.

She opened the notebook and reached for the quill that would write her words without ink.

My King. Can you read this?

She waited with bated breath. Egan was the only fae who could save Griffin—if the children's story was true.

A few minutes passed before Egan's words appeared below hers.

You're late.

She was supposed to have contacted him yesterday.

I didn't know if the journal would work. And we've been busy following the village from Ireland to Ohio.

His response took so long she feared she'd angered him.

Have you located the book?

She stared at the words, not sure how he'd react if he learned they were still no closer to finding the book.

No. But we are close.

She could see his signature scowl in her mind.

Don't let me down.

This was her opening, she knew it.

There is something else, sire. Griffin has fallen ill. We think it's of a magical nature, and we know how to cure him. Without Griffin, we will not be able to bring the book to the fae realm.

Riona waited. And waited. Finally, a response came.

He needs his magic back.

How did he know? Were more fae in Myrkur ill?

Please, sire. We need him to accomplish our mission.

Egan didn't respond. After a few minutes staring at the journal for his words to appear, she slid a hand over their entire conversation, making it disappear with her touch the book recognized.

A throat clearing in the doorway had her shoving the book under a pillow. Gulliver stepped in, his arms crossed over his chest. "Riona."

She tried to erase the perpetual frown from her face, but Gulliver's words still wound through her mind. "Are you finished being a child?" He was young but youth did not excuse poor behavior. It was a policy they'd adapted in the prison realm.

He leaned against the doorframe. "Are you done betraying us?"

"Betraying you?" Riona sputtered. Her eyes flicked to where she'd hidden the book.

"We should be doing everything we can to help Griff, and you're in here writing in your journal. I don't know why Griff keeps insisting there's good in you. I see you in my dreams, Riona. Did you know that? I see the moment you almost killed Griff in the fighting pits. You didn't hesitate. Yet, he spared your life. I see you riding atop a dark horse— though, with wings, I have no clue why you'd need a horse— but you're destroying my village. You're what nightmares are made of."

His words shocked her, even though she knew the truth in them. She was not a fae to be trusted—she barely trusted herself—but she'd started thinking there was a bond building between her and Gulliver. The venom in his eyes was something she hadn't seen before. "Why do you say these things now?"

"Because Griff is going to die." Tears welled in his eyes. "He's going to die and leave me here with you until Lochlan finds us. You deserve to know that I will never hesitate in a fight. I won't let my opponent live. And those who betray me, betray Griff, will pay for it." With one final searing look, he pivoted on his heel and walked away, leaving Riona gaping behind him.

She was used to being hated by those in Myrkur. As the king's warrior, she knew what the other fae thought of her. She'd betrayed her race, the people slaughtered by Egan's men.

And yet, the hatred in Gulliver's eyes burned more painfully than any before.

She didn't want him to lose Griffin.

And her betrayal, her contact with Egan, just might be the thing that saved him in the end.

CHAPTER TEN

Griffin

Griffin found himself back in the fighting pits, waiting for the killing blow that would free him from the constant cycle of guilt and regret. Riona came at him, her wings stretching to the sky like she was an ethereal being, not mere fae. The tattoos along her arms spoke to him in a language he couldn't understand. He needed to find their true meaning.

But he wouldn't get the chance. He cowered as she raised a sword above her head. Before she brought it down, blackness crept along the edges of her wings, eventually spreading like spilled ink across blank parchment.

"Kill him," Egan commanded.

Nearby, a woman sang a familiar song, but Griffin couldn't quite make out the words. His surroundings changed, and he was back in Fela watching his people lose everything.

The lullaby strengthened, getting louder and louder until

it was all he heard as the horrors of the prison realm flashed across his mind.

Shauna and Nessa with the red roadmap of a whip across their backs.

Gulliver and his truncated tail.

"You're going to be too late." Griffin didn't know who whispered the words, but they had his eyes shooting open. His chest heaved with labored breaths, and sweat dripped down his face.

"Too late," he yelped.

"Griff?" Gulliver sat in a low chair beside the bed.

"Gullie." It was a dream, but it wasn't. Everything he saw had come to pass, and now he knew he'd be too late to prevent the worst of it. He lifted a weak hand to brush damp hair out of his face. "What are you sitting on?"

Gulliver grinned. "Myles says it's called a bean bag chair. It's quite comfortable. Though, I don't understand why anyone would waste perfectly good beans on a chair. Maybe it's a way of storing them to eat later on." He shrugged. "Humans are very strange, aren't they?"

Griffin rolled onto his side to stare down at Gulliver. "How long have I been out?"

"Two days." He shot him a pointed look. "Riona wanted to wake you yesterday, but Myles and I didn't let her. There's also another man here. Nihal, do you remember him? The guy who accidentally shipwrecked us on that island and then refused to tell us anything. Yeah, him and Riona are getting along great." There was too much sarcasm in that last sentence for it to be true. Riona didn't get along with anyone.

But Nihal wasn't just anyone. He and Riona were the last of their kind.

"Oh." Gulliver stood. "Also, the village is gone."

Griffin nodded, grabbing his head as pain stabbed through his skull. "That's why I portaled back to Iskalt at the last second, they tried to move the village while I was still in it. They didn't take anyone, did they? Gullie, help me up."

"No, we're all still here." Gulliver crossed his arms. "Myles thinks you should say please when asking me to do things. Human manners. I quite like the idea."

Griffin groaned. Gulliver had spent way too much time with Myles. "Fine. Gulliver, will you *please* help up the man who raised you? The one who kept you safe all these years without human manners getting in the way."

"Jesus H. Roosevelt Christ, don't get your panties in a bunch."

That was it. "Myles! Get your human self in here right this minute."

Footsteps sounded outside the door before Myles opened it. "You're awake. Good." He looked too Gulliver. "Did he say please?"

"Myles, what have you been watching with Gulliver?" It was the only explanation for his new human phrases.

"Oh." Myles laughed. "Well, Brea left her copy of the *Outlander* series. She always told me Jaime was the only human as beautiful as the fae, but I've got to say, I'm not seeing it. I mean, he's okay looking."

"It's the hair." Gulliver pursed his lips as if deep in thought. "It usually looks like it's in need of a wash."

"You know ... you're right."

Griffin sighed. "Will you two stop debating Jamie's attractiveness and help me get up?"

Myles lifted a brow. "What do you say, Griff?"

Griffin growled. "Please."

A smile tilted Myles' lips. "Just be glad I'm not making you call me Majesty. Because I am a king, you know."

Gulliver nodded. "He is." He held out a hand to help Griffin from the bed.

Griffin slid his legs over the side of the bed until his feet hit the carpet. "If we're ever going to find the twins and the book, I have to talk to Nihal." Griffin didn't understand why Nihal was still here if the village left.

"Okay." Myles took his other arm. "Do you want to hear my theory of you being sick?"

"Are you going to tell me, or just let this awkward silence continue?"

"Someone is grumpy." Myles led him out into the hall. "So, I think this is a magic illness. Light Fae bodies are made to hold magic. Without it, they can survive for a time—years even—before the illness is triggered."

"And how is it triggered?" Griffin focused on his feet so he didn't fall.

"By having only a part of your magic returned. Since that magic has nothing to latch on to, it sort of just floats in your body, causing harm every time you have to use it. Or even if you don't use it. It breaks down the magic wielder's cells."

Griffin didn't know what cells were or how Myles came to such a conclusion, but it made sense. Which also meant ... "The only way to cure me is getting my full power."

Myles nodded. "I think so."

But Griffin wasn't the only fae to fall ill. Sinead and who knew how many others had as well. "I need to talk to Riona."

Myles paused. "I thought you needed to talk to Nihal. He's outside. He won't come into the human house until you speak with him."

"I need them both." He looked to Gulliver. "Will you fetch Riona? Please."

Gulliver shared a smile with Myles. "I told you he could learn to be nice." He bounced away to find Riona.

Myles led him outside to where Nihal rested in the shade, his back leaning up against the trunk of a tree. He played his piccolo with his eyes closed.

As Griffin neared, the song grew louder, a familiar song. Griffin stopped moving.

"What's wrong?" Myles looked from Griffin to Nihal who'd stopped playing as he noticed them.

"Nothing." Griffin wasn't ready to share what had happened in his portal or the song and the whispers he'd heard.

Nihal stood, a smile gracing his young face. "Your Highness." He bowed.

Griffin had told him before not to address him as a prince. He didn't deserve that title. "Nihal." Griffin nodded.

"Sit, sit. We have many things to discuss now that you've returned to us."

Myles helped him sit and then backed away. "I'll leave you two to talk about the dangerous stuff. Plus, we found a ball. I'm going to teach Gulliver how to play football."

He walked away with only a single glance back. Griffin studied Nihal, looking for similarities to Riona. He didn't look as if he carried the weight of their ancestors on his shoulders. His blond hair fell into his bright green eyes. Where Riona's skin was dark, his was pale, almost white. Dark wings stretched out behind him. But it was the tattoos that provided the largest difference.

Riona's featured many colors that looked like they moved

along her skin. Nihal's black tattoos sat stationary on his skin.

Griffin snapped out of his thoughts as his eyes drifted to the field the village had occupied only days before. "You left the village."

Nihal shrugged. "It was time. As the only resident who wasn't a descendant of Grainne, I wasn't exactly wanted there."

"Then why were you allowed to enter? How did you even see it?"

"Those are good questions, but they aren't the right ones."

Griffin leaned forward, absently picking blades of grass. "What do you want me to ask?"

"It isn't about me. There are questions that will help you in your search, and others that will only hinder."

"How do I tell the difference?"

"Just ask what's in your heart, Griffin O'Shea."

Griffin waited a long moment. "The village ... if we find it again, will the outcome be any different?"

Nihal thought over his answer. "No. You will get no further information from the village."

"It's not only information I seek, but the book they protect."

Nihal scooted away from the tree and unfurled his wings. They weren't quite as large as Riona's, but their beauty was in their strength. "Is that really what is in your heart, or your head?"

Griffin had asked questions he thought were relevant, but were they really in his heart?

He drew in a deep breath. "Play it again."

Nihal stared at him. "Play what?"

"The song I heard, the lullaby. I need to hear it again.

Please." He needed to feel like he wasn't losing his mind hearing a song inside his portals and again in his dreams. A song he knew in his heart but had no memory of. Nothing made sense in this trek across the human realm.

The village was important, and then it wasn't.

His portals worked, and then they tried to trap him inside.

And now, he'd returned to the one place that held so much memory and none at all. He'd never spent much time at the Robinson farm, but it was the place that raised the girl who saved the fae realms from her own aunt, and from Griffin.

Nihal lifted the piccolo to his lips and started playing. As he did, Griffin's weakness fell away, carried by the rushing current of the song filling him in the way magic should, healing him—at least for the moment. "How is this possible?"

Nihal finished playing and lowered his piccolo. "Because the song is from the book of power. It grants temporary strength, but every page of that book comes at a cost. Many such pages have made their way into the fae realm by people like me—people granted portal magic by the book."

"Then you can open the next portal." Griffin sighed in relief, knowing the safety of his people didn't rest entirely on him.

Nihal shook his head.

"Don't do that," Griff pleaded. "Don't tell me I'm wrong. We need so desperately for something to work in our favor."

"My portal magic allows me to travel from Aghadoon to Talam only. That is why I had to tag along with you to Iskalt. It was from the island I dispersed various spells across the kingdoms with captains I trusted."

It sank into Griffin, the hopelessness. Without the village,

Nihal couldn't help, and the village was now lost to them, right along with the book. "Why have I heard that song before?"

"These questions, your Highness, are important, and I will give you answers. But first, ask me the thing your heart most desires to know."

"Riona," he whispered. "Why do her tattoos shift and dance while yours remain dormant?"

Nihal's lips twisted into a half smile. "Now, this is a question of the heart. Creatures like Riona, like me—fae of the sea and sky—who've long had their kin destroyed, we live for a purpose. There was a reason Riona did not die when her village was destroyed. There was a reason the book chose me as its conduit to the fae realm, able to carry spells through portals."

Riona crossed the yard toward them, picking up on the conversation. "A reason?" She stared down at the two of them. "Egan saved me."

Nihal's smile turned sad. "No, Riona, I'm sorry but that isn't accurate. Your magic saved you."

"I have no magic."

"Ah, you've been taught the great lie of the Dark Fae. You may not have magic pulsing at your fingertips like the Light Fae, but what do you call the figures dancing on your skin? What do you call the wings on your back? Or the fact that you appear human in this realm to human eyes in a way Light Fae cannot? So, yes, Riona Nieland, your magic is quite powerful."

He stroked the edges of his wings like he would a beloved pet. "To answer the prince's question, my tattoos no longer hold any magic."

"How is that possible?" Riona lowered herself to the grass.

Nihal surveyed them both. "Because their purpose has been fulfilled. The book of power holds the knowledge needed to interpret our markings, it can show us the purpose that has been chosen for us."

Griffin released a stream of curses. "And we just let the village disappear with the book. This time, we don't have an ally on the inside."

Nihal waited for all sound to cease, for Griffin to get ahold of his anger, for Riona to look at him with something other than disgust.

She lifted her face. "What did your tattoos reveal about you?"

"They marked me as a conduit, able to use certain spells in the book despite having no magic inside me. But that is not my only purpose." He looked to Griffin. "Don't worry, Highness. The village may be gone, but what they don't yet know is the book has already been stolen. I know this, because I helped steal it."

It made sense now—why Nihal let the village leave without him. He was a thief, one who'd stolen the most dangerous book in all the worlds.

"If you stole the book, where is it?" Griffin demanded.

Nihal shrugged. "I said I helped steal it, not that it was ever in my possession." He lifted his piccolo once more and played a new song, one that had the beat of Griffin's heart calming.

Griffin shook off the effect. "We need to go after the book."

"Yes." Nihal sighed, pulling the instrument away. "I suppose we do. You are not the only one looking."

"Callum," he breathed, meeting Riona's dark gaze. "Nihal, you must have seen the twins. How long has it been?"

"Three weeks, maybe four. I remember two children clinging to each other as they asked questions that obviously weren't for their benefit."

Griffin frowned. "Seamas told me they ignored the twins because they didn't pose a threat to the book. Callum eventually left because no one would respond to the twins' questions."

Nihal shook his head. "Seamas did not give you the full truth. He knew how dangerous the O'Rourke twins are to the book. The elders did refuse to acknowledge them, but they also cast them out of the village."

He wanted to ask why, but the book took precedence. If the book truly was no longer in the village, Griffin had to get to it before Callum could. He could save Shauna and Nessa.

Griffin stood, surprised by the strength the song gave him. He brushed off his pants. "We leave at nightfall. Nihal, you will lead us to the book." He was their only chance.

"Yes, your Highness. Ashlin took the book to protect it, but she can't continue to do it alone."

Ashlin? Griffin tried to recall where he'd heard the name. His eyes widened. "The old lady? She has the book?"

Nihal leaned his head back and closed his eyes. "When it comes to this book, this magic, not everything is as it seems. You'd be wise to remember that." He lifted his piccolo and Griffin walked back to the house, the music bolstering him.

Riona followed him down the long hall before a thought came to Griffin, the reason he'd wanted to see her earlier. He turned on his heel, and she almost slammed into him.

She didn't get mad or annoyed. Instead, she looked like she was trapped in her own thoughts.

"Riona." Griffin shook her shoulder. "Riona."

She snapped out of whatever daze she'd been in. "What?"

Griffin stepped away and rubbed the back of his neck. "Does Egan return parts of a fae's magic often?"

She shook her head. "You were the first. At least the first I knew of." But she wouldn't meet his eye.

That didn't make sense. Egan needed Griffin. He wouldn't risk doing something so volatile on him unless he knew it would work.

The truth sparked within him. Sinead. "He tested it." His jaw clenched. "How many?"

Riona looked like she was biting back a lie. "I really don't know, Griff. That's the truth. I know there were reports of sudden illness in seven villages, but I don't know if it has anything to do with … tampering with magic."

It had everything to do with Egan tampering with magic he knew nothing about. Griffin had never been so sure of anything. Egan must have experimented with returning small portions of power to Light Fae from different villages, seeing how far he could push them. He must have been counting on Griffin holding on until the book was back in Myrkur and he no longer needed Griffin.

"Myles," he called.

Myles appeared from the living room. "I'm sort of in the middle of the wedding scene right now."

"The what?" Griffin didn't take his eyes from Riona as he spoke to Myles.

"*Outlander.* Claire had to get really drunk to marry Jamie which is so totally not accurate. I mean, who wouldn't marry him? Well, I wouldn't. But plenty of others would want a piece of that? I'm definitely coming around on the hot knees thing."

"Myles." Griffin and Riona said it at the same time. "Shut up."

Myles shrugged. "Well, what did you want when you yelled my name?"

Griffin stepped away from Riona. "We leave at nightfall."

Myles' face sobered as he nodded. "We have another lead?"

Riona walked past them both. "You better be right to trust Nihal, Griff. I'm tired of dead ends."

Griffin sighed once she was no longer in sight. He couldn't quite figure Riona out. Sometimes she went out of her way to take care of him and others she wanted nothing to do with him. There was more pain inside her than he'd imagined.

Myles didn't move to go back to his show. "She's right, Griff. We can't keep chasing leads unless we find something soon. I'm a dad now as well as a king, and no matter how vital it is we get to this book, nothing is more important than my kids. They need me to come home."

Griffin stared at him as he walked back into the living room. He was right. They all had fae relying on them. Shauna and Nessa were never far from his mind.

But neither was the promise to Brea. He couldn't end this mission until Tia and Toby were safe at home where they belonged.

CHAPTER ELEVEN

Riona

My Lord, we have a new path. Though Griffin has grown ill and struggles to use his portal magic. I fear his illness could become a hindrance to your Majesty's goals.

Riona was familiar with the stabbing pains of guilt that plagued her whenever she communicated with Egan now. She was torn. Torn between doing what was right and what her king demanded. If she defied him … she was as good as dead.

She rested her head against Brea's old headboard. Her few belongings were packed, and it was time to move on. She likely wouldn't have privacy again for some time. Perhaps not until this was all over, and she was back in Myr where she belonged.

Riona didn't want to know what awaited her should she go against her king. Egan's reach was far, and his hold on her never failed to remind her whose creature she was. Even now, she absently rubbed her chest, just over her heart where Egan's grip tightened like a noose. His reply was a long time in coming. She stared at the page in front of her, her pulse pounding in her ears as she waited for his biting words.

So, the boy is ill. Let that be his motivation to end this once and for all.

The old Riona would have jumped to do his bidding, knowing that was the key to her survival. Egan had saved her and raised her in what she'd once thought was great wealth. In some twisted way, she'd felt a sense of loyalty to him for that. She'd learned a long time ago to harden her heart to the suffering of others, but she still saw it. Many times, she caused it. That was all she'd ever known in Myr. She'd never had anyone to care about other than herself.

As you command, my Lord. The magic you seek shall soon be within my grasp.

Finish the deed and return to me. I grow weary of waiting, and my patience runs thin at the news of yet another lead. See that this is the last one. Your place is at my side, Riona. I would have you near me once again.

Riona knew Egan fancied himself as her father. She'd used that to her advantage over the years. But she was just a possession to him. Something exotic and ferocious he could brandish like a weapon.

She knew better now. Her eyes were open to the possibilities that lay outside of Myr. Yet, she would never fit into the world of the Light Fae. And the human world frightened her. In a weird way, she was homesick. But Riona no longer knew where home was for her.

> *This creature of the night is tired of the sun. I look forward to giving you an update in person soon.*
>
> *Ever your servant,*
> *Riona*

She slammed the book shut, disgusted with herself. It was easy to follow Griffin and let herself forget she was the bad guy.

The sound of Nihal's song drifted up the stairs to her room. Even she could feel the boost in strength the sweet melody gave her. It chased away her sense of guilt, reminding her that the words she'd written were just words meant to pacify the king. She didn't really believe in them. Yet, she couldn't seem to decide how she would proceed in the end. Would she have the courage to stand with Griffin and let Egan's hold on her destroy her from the inside out? Or would she think only of herself and run back to the master who held her chains? Hoping he didn't kill Griffin or the others she'd grown to care about.

"Riona?" Gulliver peeked into the room. "Are you ready?"

"All set." Riona slipped her journal into her pack and scooted off the bed, turning to smooth the wrinkles from the quilt. She would leave the room as clean and orderly as she'd found it. In all her life, Riona had never had such a room like this. Not even growing up in Egan's castle. She'd lived with the other children who were wards of the king. And later, she'd moved into her stark cold room in the barracks. No matter what Griffin said, privacy and comfort like this was a luxury for the wealthy.

"I'm worried about Griff." Gulliver leaned against the door, waiting for her to finish tidying up. "He's too weak to open another portal."

"Nihal is helping him with that, giving him strength." Riona laid a comforting hand on his shoulder. "He will be fine, Gullie. We'll make sure of it."

"Can you get the king to give him his magic back?" Gulliver crossed his arms over his thin chest, looking between her and the book she'd just returned to her bag.

"If I could, I would." She sighed. "Our best bet is to help Griffin find this book and get him back to Lochlan and Brea." She shooed him out of the room, hoping the boy's endless questions had dried up for now.

"He's all I have, Riona." Gulliver's tail drooped lifelessly behind him.

Riona leaned down, gripping both of his shoulders. "I will not let anything happen to Griffin, you hear me?" She didn't know if it was a promise she could keep, but something inside her hoped it was.

Gulliver nodded, and they made their way down the stairs to the sound of Nihal's lullaby.

Riona gasped when she stepped into the living room to find Griffin sitting on the edge of the couch with rosy cheeks and a smile on his face. The glow of good health was a shock. It was such a contrast to his state from a few hours ago, she only now realized just how sick he'd really been.

"Griff!" Gulliver ran to his side, letting Griffin wrap his arms around him in a hug.

"I'm okay, buddy," Griffin murmured into his hair.

"How long will it last?" Riona turned to Nihal.

"Long enough," Nihal said. "We'd better leave now. We will have a chance to rest once we return to Iskalt for the day."

Traveling between worlds was an exhausting business, but Myles said the alternative was flying to their destination in a human metal contraption. No one here seemed to think that a viable option other than the human, and he was out voted.

Griffin was in a cheery mood as he led them across the yard into the moonlight, his arm draped across Gulliver's shoulders. Riona didn't miss the way Gulliver's tail wrapped around Griffin's wrist as they walked. The kid was really worried about Griffin.

"Everyone ready?" Griffin called to gather them close.

Riona watched him for signs that they were asking too much of his limited magic. It never failed to astound her the way his violet magic appeared in his hands, growing as he spread his arms to open a portal into Iskalt—where it seemed to be another cold, but sunny day.

Riona muttered as she shoved her sunglasses on and followed Gulliver through the portal. It really was as easy as stepping from one room to another. It just felt so wrong, foreign to her Dark Fae experience. She wondered if she'd ever get used to that kind of magic.

Myles and Nihal followed her through, filling the small moon garden with too many bodies. Lochlan and Brea came to greet them even before the portal closed behind Griffin, and he fell forward in a boneless heap.

"Griff!" Lochlan scrambled to his side. "What's wrong with my brother?" He looked up to Myles for answers.

"He's sick." Myles went to Brea's side as Lochlan scooped Griffin up in his arms. "The best we've been able to determine is that having use of only his portal magic is destroying him from the inside out."

"Then why did you let him make another portal?" Lochlan growled, marching into his study just off the garden.

"We were in dire need, your Majesty," Nihal said.

"And who do you think you are to make such choices?" Lochlan glared at the man with wings and tattoos so much like Riona's.

"Enough of that douchey-Loch. Nihal is our friend. So we'll dispense with the pleasantries that aren't really pleasant with you." Myles followed him from the study, leading them all toward the royal residence wing. "Let's just get Griffin somewhere quiet to rest, and I'll catch you up to speed."

Riona and the others followed the king to a room opposite the king's suite.

"The twins?" Brea turned pleading eyes on Myles for news of her children, even as she turned the blankets down for Griffin.

"Nihal has seen them recently."

"They are well enough, your Majesty." Nihal bowed. "I believe they are frightened, but well physically."

"Where are they now?" Riona heard Brea demand as she retreated into the hall with Gulliver.

"I want to sit with him," Gulliver insisted.

"Let's take care of you first." Riona steered him toward the kitchens, counting on his empty belly to distract him for a little while.

CHAPTER TWELVE

Griffin

The lullaby haunted Griffin. It called to him in the darkness of his dreams, giving him strength. But there was something else too. The song fortified him, yes, but he wondered what such magic cost, and in the end, would it be worth it?

Screams echoed around him, and the music stopped.

"Keep playing. It soothes him." A voice he couldn't identify reached him through the fog. "I think it reminds him of our childhood."

It did remind Griffin of when he was a small boy running through the gardens of the Gelsi palace with Regan chasing him, laughing and offering him hugs and sweets. Showering him with kisses and the love of a mother he so desperately needed. Those memories chased away the distressing sounds that called for his attention now.

Something about those sounds—and the voice that made them—tugged at his memory, but Griffin was so tired. Tired of running from his fears. Tired of the screams that haunted him. Tired of the blood that covered everything around him. He just wanted to sleep.

"He is not well, your Majesty. There is only so much the spelled music can do to help him."

"Keep playing. Rest now, brother." A comforting hand pressed against his shoulder and Griffin succumbed to the music, letting it send him into a peaceful slumber for a time.

———

The screams were louder now, and blood streamed down on Griffin like a torrent of icy rain.

She was in trouble. The woman he'd seen in the portal. The screams—the blood—belonged to her. Something was wrong. They needed to find her before it was too late.

Griffin sat up straight, his eyes open, but his surroundings made little sense.

"Where am I?" The light of the bedside lantern sent a blinding stab of pain through his eyes.

"Iskalt." Lochlan said from his seat beside the bed.

Griffin looked at his brother in his wrinkled clothes and a scattering of discarded books around him.

"How long was I out?" He leaned his head back against the pillows trying to make sense of his dreams.

"Since your arrival this morning. The night grows late."

Griffin flung the blankets aside and attempted to sit up. They had to leave. Now.

"I know you're anxious to be away with the moon, but you're in no condition to portal anywhere."

"We have to go, Loch." Griffin moved to the edge of the bed, letting his feet brush the floor.

"Just give yourself a moment to finish waking up." Lochlan handed him a goblet of watered wine.

"How long have you been here?" Griffin sipped from the cup, blinking bleary eyes at his brother. As Brea would say, he felt like something the dog threw up.

"Since I carried you in here this morning."

"You've sat with me all day and night?"

Lochlan must have seen something in his face. The king of Iskalt scooted to the edge of his seat and laid a hand on Griffin's knee.

"You are my brother, Griffin O'Shea. You're my blood. And you remind me of our father." He hung his head. "The absence of my memories plagues me, Griff." He rubbed a tired hand over his face. "How could I have left you alone like that?"

"Like what?" Griffin stared at him, not sure what he meant.

"You were just a babe when our parents died. And I just left you? Let you grow up with that awful woman?"

The haunted look in Lochlan's eyes tugged at him. "You were just a child yourself, Loch. Only four years old. What could you have done? By the time either of us were old enough to make sense of anything, too much time had passed. I was of Fargelsi, and you were of Eldur."

"I should have done better by you. I'm your older brother. It was my responsibility to care for you when our parents were gone."

"It's ancient history, Loch." Griffin stood up, feeling better than he had after Nihal played his song the first time. He vaguely wondered if that meant it wouldn't last as long this time.

"I haven't thanked you." Lochlan stood with him. "Not properly anyway."

"For what?" Griffin lifted his pack over his shoulder.

"For working so hard to bring my children home." Lochlan swallowed, casting his eyes down to his feet. "I have had a small rebellion to put down in a southern village, and my council tells me it could cost many lives if I left Iskalt now. I don't know what we'd do without you."

"I'll keep good on my promise, Loch. I'll bring them home."

Lochlan nodded. "Home." He smiled. "I hope you know this is your home too now. We're your family. All of us. You have a place here. A purpose."

Griffin nodded, not trusting himself to speak. How long had he wanted to hear such words from his brother? And how long would it last if Lochlan ever got his memories back?

"The others are waiting for you." Lochlan crossed to the door. "I'll open the portal to wherever you're going, and we'll set up a time and place to meet when you're ready to come home. I don't want you risking your health anymore. Not until we find out how to get your magic back."

Griffin nodded again, taking a moment after Lochlan had gone to collect himself. Was this what it was like to have a big brother looking out for him? Whatever it was, he didn't want to get used to it.

The woman's cries of agony still echoed in his mind. They had to move quickly. Griffin didn't know when it would happen or if it already had, but that woman was in trouble, and he was pretty sure Callum had something to do with it.

"Nihal." Griffin walked into the garden where everyone

waited for him. "You know who she is? The woman in the portal?"

Nihal nodded. "We have met."

"Do you know how to find her? She's in trouble, and we need to hurry. I know she's in a big city with tall buildings and thousands of cars and busses."

"You literally just described every major city across the human world," Myles muttered. "Can you narrow it down some?"

"She is in a place called New York City." Nihal dipped his head in Myles' direction. "I can take you to her."

"I've never visited New York," Griffin said, frowning, trying to think of the closest place he had portaled to before.

"I have." Lochlan stepped forward. "Brea likes to shop in the city from time to time."

"I like the Christmas shopping," Brea said, flushing pink. "For the kids."

"Right. For the kids." Lochlan shook his head. "There's a place in Central Park where I can take you," Lochlan said. "It's private enough no one should see you arrive."

"That should be near enough to our destination," Nihal said. "She lives in a place called the Upper West Side."

"Can you handle this, Myles?" Brea turned to her best friend with a bit of a grimace on her face.

"Who me?" He rubbed a tired hand over his eyes. "Guide one sick fae, two more stubborn ones, and a little boy with a penchant for trouble through one of the biggest cities in the human realm? Piece of cake. But I'm going to need a nice long vacation when this is over."

"Just try not to make a spectacle of yourselves, and you'll be fine," Brea said. "The Dark Fae will blend in with their natural glamours, but Griffin will need some help."

"Right." Lochlan approached Griffin, placing his hands on either side of his head to create a glamour that would last long enough for Griff to do what he needed to do in New York.

"We really need to get moving." Griffin couldn't explain it, but the woman needed help, and he didn't know how much time they had left.

Lochlan moved to the center of the garden and opened a portal into a land so green, Griffin could have sworn it was Fargelsi.

"This is a city?" Riona peered through the portal before she stepped through with Gulliver and Nihal right behind her. Myles and Griffin followed.

"Do not risk portalling back in your condition, Griff." Lochlan stepped through with them for a moment. "I will check back here every evening in case you have need of me," Lochlan said. "Leave a note pinned to the largest tree there with a time, and I will be here to bring you back."

"Thank you, brother." Griffin gripped his hand one last time before he backed away from the portal and into the quiet woods.

It was eerie, the way the forest cushioned the sounds of the city in the distance.

"Where to, Nihal?" Myles asked. "The Upper West Side is a big place."

"It is near something called West Fortieth and Fifth Avenue, between Grand Central Station and the New York Public Library."

"Okay. That was way more specific than I was expecting. Let's go. Chop, chop." Myles set off along a path through the woods. "We'll just hail a cab and be there in a few minutes."

"Minutes?" Riona glanced around them at the thick overgrown forest. They seemed miles away from anything resembling a city.

Griffin was as confused as the others, following Myles up a worn set of moss-covered steps to a wider trail. They encountered a few humans along the way. Such an odd thing to see them jogging along the trails with their dogs and their phones, going about their business in the middle of nowhere. As the trees began to thin and he could see the clear blue sky, anxiety gripped his chest. The woman had grown quiet. Whatever had happened to her, it was in the past now, and she needed help.

"We need to hurry, Myles." Griffin urged him to pick up the pace.

"Almost there." Myles glanced at his phone, following the directions the Google person gave him.

"Hey, Myles?" Griffin called.

"I know, keep walking." Myles ignored him.

"Are you sure Loch brought us to the right place?"

"Yep."

"But there's a castle. There, just up the hill. Like a fae castle."

"Do some humans live in castles?" Riona asked.

"Yep, we have castles here too sometimes, just ignore it." Myles led them up to a pair of iron gates at the head of the trail. Beyond lay a stone castle complete with a moat and a turret tower. A large plaque named the place as Belvedere Castle, but Myles had them turning off the trail before Griffin could see what the castle was all about.

For a moment, Griffin thought he'd stepped through another portal. Cars zoomed past them, blaring their horns, and pedestrians hurried around them.

"What just happened?" Riona took a step back, grabbing Gulliver's hand.

"Welcome to Manhattan." Myles raised his hand. "Some call it the best city in the world." A yellow car slowed to a stop in front of Myles.

"But we were just in the forest." Gulliver turned around in a circle. "Where'd this place come from?"

"We were in Central Park, smack dab in the middle of the city. Now get in and just go with it. We'll be there in a few minutes." Myles slid into the front seat with the driver, leaving Griffin and the others to pile into the back seat with Gulliver sitting on Riona's lap. "Bryant Park near the New York Public Library. And step on it. I've always wanted to say that." Myles slapped the dash, and the driver whipped into traffic, speeding along a wide road lined with trees.

Griffin's mind whirled with images as the streets past by in a blur.

"Anyone else sensing the irony here? We're looking for a lady with a book and we're going to a library?" Myles glanced back at them, but if the others were feeling anything like Griffin, they were a bit shell shocked by the sudden appearance of the largest city he'd ever seen. It seemed to go on in an endless grid of streets and people—so many people. With buildings rising higher than any he'd ever seen before.

"Not a chatty bunch today, are we?" Myles chuckled.

"Here we are," the driver said a moment later. Myles tossed some cash onto the seat as he stepped onto the curb, ushering the others out of the back seat. The little yellow car pulled away to join the thousands of others just like it.

"Nihal, are we close?" Griffin asked. "Where does she live?"

"Do you have the address? I can just ask Google," Myles said.

"She is close." Nihal started down the street, past the stone steps of the library with its enormous columns and arches that wouldn't look all that out-of-place in Fargelsi.

"Here. This building is where she lives." Nihal pointed to an unremarkable stone building that reached toward the sky.

Myles whistled, shaking his head. "Right on the corner of Fifth Avenue? This lady lives in style." Myles marched across the street. "I don't suppose you know this mysterious woman's name?"

"No idea." Griffin shook his head.

"Course not." Myles gave Nihal a questioning look.

"The lady goes by many names," Nihal said.

"Well, you're just a big help aren't you Nihally." Myles took the steps two at a time up to the front of the building. "Wouldn't want this to be too easy."

A man dressed in livery with an odd hat perched on his head stopped them at the door.

"Hello, there sir," Myles said, pausing to shake the man's hand. "We're here to visit my aunt on the fifth floor. We won't be long. The old dear needs some help moving some furniture."

The man nodded with a huge smile and tugged on the golden door handle to let them inside.

Myles stepped into the grand marbled lobby like he owned the place.

"Did you give that man something?" Gulliver followed Myles to the elevators—not one of Griffin's favorite human inventions.

"I bribed him with a fifty-dollar bill." Myles pressed the call button. "But we're going to need to find this lady's apartment. We can't just go knocking on doors along Fifth Avenue."

"Does the number seven hundred four mean anything to you?" Nihal asked, pinching the bridge of his nose. "B. Number 704-B. I think."

"Going on instinct, are we?" Myles sighed, muttering something that sounded like 'fracking fae' under his breath before he stepped into the elevator and slapped the button for the seventh floor.

Riona braced herself for the elevator, grabbing Griffin's hand and squeezing tight as the small closet moved up in an unsteady climb.

Griffin's anxiety for this unknown woman sent his pulse pounding the closer they came to finding her. *We might be too late.* He hoped he was wrong about that. This woman had to have the book. He could just feel it. They were so close.

Griffin was the first one off the elevator. He looked down the long marble corridor, but he didn't have a clue what they were looking for.

"Over here." Myles called to them, standing in front of a black door with a golden plaque carved with the numbers 704-B. The door stood open.

"Looks like we're not the first ones here today." Myles' voice sounded unsteady and a little less sure of himself.

Screams shot through Griffin's head, and he saw blood. So much blood. "She's hurt." Griffin shoved the door aside, stepping into a small room with a high ceiling. The zigzag wooden floors gleamed in the light coming from the windows in the next room. Views of Bryant Park stretched in a picturesque panorama from the large windows in the living room. White marbled columns flanked the wide-open doorways leading from one room to the next. The house was quiet. The only movement came from the open balcony doors where curtains fluttered in the breeze.

Griffin stepped onto the long, narrow balcony, and he was momentarily stunned by the sheer size of the city sprawling out before him. He almost missed it. The drop of blood on the slate tiled floor. There was another one and then another.

"Here!" Griffin called to the others as he raced to the end of the balcony, shoving chairs and tables aside. Lying on the ground in a puddle of her own blood under the drooping waxy leaves of a potted plant was the woman he'd seen in the portal. She was so pale, and there was blood everywhere, but her chest moved, rising and falling with her labored breath. The dainty string of pearls around her neck were smeared with blood and bruises marred her lovely face.

"Let's get her inside." Nihal moved to grab her shoulders. "Careful with her head. She's had a nasty blow."

Myles met them in the living room with towels and helped them get her settled on the sofa. He dabbed at her head wound with a white towel that came away soaked in blood. "Guys, she doesn't look so good. We might need to call an ambulance to take her to the hospital."

"We don't know what happened, Myles. We can't take her to a human doctor." Griffin checked her over for signs of further injury.

"Wha-what happened?" the lady murmured, her brow furrowed in pain and confusion as she began to stir.

"Shhh," Griffin whispered, smoothing the blond hair from her face. "We're here to help you."

Her eyes flew opened, and she let out a shriek.

CHAPTER THIRTEEN

Riona

Humans were strange creatures. Riona had never been in a human house before setting foot in Queen Brea's.

But that was not this.

This was a house in the sky overlooking a noisy city. In Myrkur, she'd always loved her quiet. When Egan let her have her space, she'd sit in the palace gardens under the oiche fruit trees. Before stepping into Fargelsi that first time, she hadn't known flowers could be any color other than black.

But she'd loved the black roses, loved the way their fragrant scent wafted through the gardens, and the softness of the petals in her hands.

But here, nothing was quiet. Riona examined the flowers on the balcony that grew from a pot instead of the ground. Was this more human magic?

If she were honest, she was tired of magic, tired of quests and information that didn't lead anywhere.

The music from Nihal's instrument drifted out through the open doors, wrapping her in a layer of warmth, of comfort that she didn't want. She didn't want to grow content among odd luxuries or happy with people she barely knew.

And yet the music had her stepping back inside, needing to hear more.

Nihal sat on the floor in front of the odd settee, playing a new song. It wasn't the song that gave Griffin strength, this one seemed … more. The melody floated out of him. Griffin perched on the arm of the couch, a contented smile on his face. Part of her knew that wasn't right, that Griffin shouldn't be lost in the music when the woman who'd brought them here was dying.

"I love using human washrooms." Gulliver walked into the room and stopped. "What are we … oh, that song is nice." He lowered himself to the floor beside Nihal.

Myles walked in from the kitchen carrying a glass of water. "I found some aspirin, but it won't really help with this kind of pain." He stopped. "What's wrong with you guys?"

None of them answered him, so he went on. "Riona, you're smiling. Stop. It's weird. Griffin, quit dancing or swaying or whatever you call that awkwardness. And Gullie…" His eyes zeroed in on Nihal, who appeared to be in a trance. "Hey." Myles put a hand on his shoulder. "Are you okay?"

As if Myles' words snapped Riona out of her stupor, she looked to Nihal, seeing for the first time the color draining from his already pale skin. His hair turned from blond to ashy gray. "What's happening?"

Griffin and Gulliver remained in their oblivious states, mesmerized by the song that no longer felt calming to Riona. "Nihal, what's happening?" She lowered herself at his side. "Stop playing. Please. This isn't right." Wrinkles appeared on his face and the darkness of his wings faded away, turning them to brittle white. "Nihal?" No, this couldn't be happening. "This magic is killing you."

And yet, he didn't stop.

Riona had been so wary of him after living her entire life thinking she was the only one of her kind remaining. "Please, don't do this." The fae was dying right before her eyes, and she wasn't ready. There were so many things she'd wanted to ask him, but hadn't. "No. I don't want to be the only one anymore." She blinked away tears.

Myles walked to the swaying Griffin and slapped him across the face. Griffin reeled back, the trance gone. "What was that for?"

"I've just always wanted to do it." Myles pointed to Nihal. "But you've been dancing to the song killing our new friend here."

Alarm flashed across Griffin's face, and he put himself between Nihal and the woman, crouching down to look into his eyes. "Nihal, stop."

They needed him. Yet, his body aged right before their eyes. Riona had to do something drastic to get him to stop. She reached around him for the tender spot she knew from experience was right below the joints of his wings. She reached up to hold his wing while finding the spot, but the wing tip broke off in her hand, crumbling to dust.

She backed away from him, her eyes glassing over. "He's … killing himself."

As the music continued, Nihal slumped forward. Myles tried to pry the instrument from his lips, but the grip he had on it was too strong, like it was aided by the magic he performed.

His eyelids drooped and slid closed. And still, Nihal played.

The notes grew quieter as they watched the man they barely knew slide into unconsciousness. He fell, his back slamming against the marble floor seconds before his head hit and the piccolo skittered across the tile, still playing its song despite having no player.

"He can't be dead." Riona knelt beside the prone Nihal.

Myles dropped to his other side. "We have to save him." Even the human knew how important this man was. He pressed his hands against Nihal's chest over and over.

But the fae didn't open his eyes.

Myles sat back on his heels, listening to the sound still coming from the instrument. "He's dead."

The music slowed before stopping altogether, sending them into silence.

Gulliver finally snapped out of the trance and scooted away from Nihal. "What was that?"

No one answered him because none of them were quite sure.

Nihal's body shrank in on itself before turning to ash and disappearing before their eyes.

Riona clutched the edges of her wings, needing the comfort only they could give her. She scrambled from the ground to find space to collect herself, to keep anyone from seeing the tears in her eyes.

A cough froze her in her tracks.

And then another.

She turned on one heel, her eyes going to the woman who'd been all but dead. Her chest rose and fell, breath entering her lungs. Blood still caked into her clothing and her hair, but...

"The wounds." Griffin examined the woman. "They're gone."

Riona focused on the spot on the floor where Nihal's ashes had even disappeared.

The woman coughed again, but this time, her eyes slid open.

"Gulliver." Griffin commanded. "Can you find the light switch? I need more than this lamp."

Gulliver's brow furrowed. "What's a light switch?"

"I've got it." Myles turned on the rest of the lights in the room, but his face looked exactly how Riona felt. Confused. Sad. A little scared.

"Are you okay, ma'am?" Griffin hovered over the woman.

She nodded. "Water. I need water."

"Gotcha covered." Myles handed Griffin the glass he'd had before. Griffin helped her take slow sips.

"Where am I?" Confusion had her body tensing.

In the light, Riona got a much better look at the woman. Long blond hair and sparkling blue eyes. Even now in her weakened state, her gaze held an intensity Riona had felt few times in her life.

They explained what happened to the woman, but Riona didn't want to stick around for that. She slipped through one of the doors at the far end of this sky house, entering a bedroom that looked more like what Riona was used to. Yes, the bed was probably more comfortable than any in Myrkur, but unlike the other human places they'd gone to, this woman seemed to live more like a fae with few possessions.

Riona ran a hand over the soft blanket on the bed. Humans lived in so much comfort, she wondered how they left their homes every day to work. In the prison realm, getting away from the busy palace to visit the villages was her favorite part of the day.

At least in Myrkur, their villages didn't have buildings reaching into the sky. It was unnatural for those who couldn't fly to live so high up. She walked to the large window looking out on the thriving city. Was there ever quiet here? Peace? Or did one have to find stillness in the middle of so much activity?

She couldn't stop thinking of Nihal and the song he played to his death. Had he known he was to die?

She replayed his words while he sat underneath that tree at the Robinson farm. He was a conduit, able to use certain spells without having magic of his own. But he'd also said it wasn't his only purpose. Riona glanced over her shoulder to the closed door.

With a deep sigh, she turned to the table near the bed. Whoever this woman was, the only thing it seemed she cared about were the paintings in frames along the room.

There was a man with auburn hair, violet eyes and a crooked smile. He looked like he was causing mischief.

He featured in a lot of the paintings, always wearing a hat, but he wasn't the only one. Two little boys ran along a beach by the sea. In the next painting, they sat on their parents' laps. On the table, two frames were connected, one boy in each. Riona lifted it, peering closer so she could see the tips of their ears poking through their hair.

Riona's eyes widened as she stared at the images.

Fae children.

She wiped the remnant of a tear from her face and burst through the bedroom door, letting it slam behind her.

"She's fae!" Riona sucked in a breath. "Everyone, back up." Riona didn't know if she was Light or Dark Fae. But if it was the former, she'd have magic, and could use it on them. "Move. She could be dangerous."

Myles pulled Gulliver away from the woman, but Griffin didn't move. He knew more than anyone how they needed to be sure of who to trust, yet he inched closer, never taking his eyes from the woman. Reaching out, he tucked her hair behind her ear—her very fae-like ear—and nodded like he'd expected it.

Griffin removed his hand. "You didn't think Nihal would lead us to a mere human, did you?"

The mention of Riona's distant kin sent pain searing through her. She didn't need the reminder she was once again alone in both words.

The woman sat up, ignoring the blood now staining her settee. "Nihal?" A tear trailed over the curve of her cheek. "Your final purpose is complete." She bowed her head in respect.

"Is anyone else not worried about this unknown fae woman who just killed Nihal?" Riona couldn't believe the rest of them were standing so close.

"Riona." Griffin's gaze filled with a weary softness. "She didn't kill Nihal. She ... well, I'm not sure what she did."

"It was the song. Nihal transferred his life force to me, healing me. He completed his purpose." The woman looked more sad than pleased about that.

"And why was his purpose protecting you?" Riona held the paintings close to her chest.

"Because I am descended from the line of Grainne O'Rourke, yet I do not believe in keeping the book of power hidden. I assume that's why he led you here?"

No one answered as they waited for her to say she had the book.

The woman sighed. "Would this make you more comfortable?" She mumbled something under her breath, and her features changed to that of a familiar old lady.

"Ashlin." Griffin scowled, taking a step back. "You led us to a dead end."

"I did. But much has changed since then. I only wanted to give myself time to get to the book. That has been my purpose here for twenty-six years. Those spells, they are meant to be used, to allow the fae to flourish and to learn from their past mistakes."

"What are you holding, Riona?" Myles looked over her shoulder.

"There are many paintings in that bedroom, but these ones … I think they have meaning."

"Those aren't paintings." Myles smiled. "They're photographs."

Riona couldn't fight the feeling that she needed to hide the paintings away, that letting everyone see them would change everything. Her heart hammered in her chest as she fought against the urge to destroy them. Sparing one look at the woman who'd returned to her normal features, Riona knew where the unfamiliar urge came from.

This woman was using magic to keep someone in this room from seeing the paintings she held.

Which made Riona fight harder. When Griffin's fingers took hold of the frame, the magic snapped, sending Riona flying backward.

Griffin landed on his butt with a grunt. His hands shook as he stared at the images. "It's me," he whispered. "Me and Lochlan." He lifted his eyes to the woman on the settee. "You're supposed to be dead, Mother."

CHAPTER FOURTEEN

Griffin

Griffin's life had never been easy. From forming a motherly bond with an evil queen, to having the entire fae realm forget him after his prison sentence, it all stemmed from a single circumstance.

His parents died.

There was never a question of either of them surviving, only who got them killed. Some said it was Regan, others claimed Callum had them murdered.

It was odd for the king and queen of Iskalt to leave the kingdom at the same time, but they'd traveled to the human world for a noble purpose, saving the daughter of their best friend, Faolan, the queen of Eldur, just like Finn now tried to do the same for Lochlan's children. That daughter? She was the weeks' old Brea Robinson. His parents exchanged her for a human baby, Alona—the same Alona who now ruled Eldur.

It was a profoundly important task because there were

those who wanted Brea dead for having both Eldurian blood and Fargelsian—meaning, the potential for both magics.

And boy, were they right. Brea was the most powerful magic wielder he'd ever seen. She pulled an entire palace down on top of Regan.

Griffin's parents never returned from that fateful trip to the human realm, and his life spiraled from there.

He couldn't stare at the woman he didn't know any longer, so he stood and crossed the room, yanking open the balcony doors. For once, he needed the noise, the activity of humans who were ignorant of the fae troubles unfurling right under their noses.

He stayed out there long after his supposed mother took a shower and retired for the night. Gulliver and Myles made themselves comfortable in a guest room.

Griffin closed his eyes, imagining how different his life might have been had he grown up in Iskalt with his mother and his brother after the death of their father. Would they have been happy? A family?

"Do you think she's the woman?" Riona joined him at the steel railing.

Griffin's grip on the rail tightened. He knew exactly the woman Riona meant. "She has to be." When he'd been trapped in his own portal, he'd seen a woman calling to him. It was his mother the entire time.

"She was exhausted. I'm sure she'll have more information for us tomorrow."

"I know." He did. He'd seen the injuries. Even if they'd healed completely, it would take a while for her to feel whole again.

Riona's wings curled into her back as she leaned over the rail. "I don't understand how they live so high in the air."

"You can fly. How are you afraid of heights?"

Riona stilled for a moment. "I'm not. But humans do not have wings. If they fell into the sky, they would crash down to the earth. Why don't they live near the ground where there's no risk of a building falling over?"

Griffin shook his head. "Most of the time, buildings don't just fall over. And there are too many people in this city for them all to live near the ground."

"That tells me they need to stop breeding."

A smile stretched Griffin's lips. He wasn't sure how Riona brought it out in him when he was still reeling on the inside.

"Are you angry with your mother?" Riona looked to him.

That was the question, wasn't it? All this time, his mother was alive, but without his father, she wouldn't have been able to open a portal home. But did that mean in all this time, she'd never found a way to get a message to them? Did she even try?

"I think I should be." He looked back over his shoulder at the dark room. "But I'm so tired of being angry." His met her gaze. "Aren't you?"

Riona hugged her arms across her chest. "I'm not angry."

"It's okay to admit it. To think of what your life could have been like if the people of your village hadn't been slaughtered. If Nihal..." His eyes turned sad as he paused. "If he was still here to answer your questions."

"Nihal's death doesn't make me mad, Griff. Only alone."

He got it then, the feeling he'd never understand. Riona grew up thinking she was the last of her kind. Nihal proved that to be a false assumption, but now, he too was gone. "Maybe we'll meet others like you."

She stared at him for a long moment, and he wondered what it was she searched for in his face. "No, Griff. I very much doubt we will. It's best not to craft hope out of nothing, because when it's gone, it takes a part of ourselves with it."

"Riona." Griffin edged closer to her and bumped their shoulders together. "You are *not* alone." It was the truth. They might have different end goals, different kings they wanted to be loyal to, but he couldn't imagine not at least trying to keep her on the right side of the fight.

The sides had become clear the longer they searched for the book. So many people wanted to keep it out of the wrong hands, and Griffin knew he had to be one of them. Once he freed Shauna and Nessa, he would defeat Egan.

He wasn't sure if this woman would be beside him or facing him across a battlefield, but right now, in the steady noise of a night in the human realm, maybe that didn't matter.

"Do you think she has the book?" Riona asked.

It was a question Griffin asked himself many times. "No. I don't." If she had it, he'd know, he'd feel it calling to him. He pictured the injuries on his mother. "Someone took it from her. Tonight."

Riona was silent for what felt like ages. "Egan won't wait forever."

"We can't return without the book." It was as simple as that. He couldn't give up until the book and the twins were in their possession.

Riona shivered. "I'm heading in for the night. I'll sleep on the floor of the room Myles and Gulliver took."

"You will not. Take the couch."

"The one with bloodstains on it?"

"Follow me. I'll show you a human trick." He re-entered the sitting room and went straight to the couch. "Humans need extra padding on their furniture because they don't like it when their bums hurt."

Riona gave him an incredulous look.

Griffin shrugged. "They haven't been bred riding horses or mules. All they know are their cars and sometimes these train things that go through tunnels. So, give them a break, okay? Humans aren't quite as ridiculous as you think."

"Says the fae pulling the bum pads off the settee."

"They call this a couch, actually." He held up one of said bum pads. "And this is a cushion." He flipped it and put it back on. "Now, the blood isn't a problem."

She marveled at the suddenly clean couch. "How did you learn that?"

"Myles. He got food on a cushion while we were at Brea's house. He flipped it over instead of cleaning it."

He walked to a door he'd seen his mother open for a towel. Searching through the linen closet, he found what he was looking for and returned to Riona. "A blanket."

She took it with a grateful smile. As Griffin turned away from her, she grabbed his wrist, forcing him to turn back to her. Her eyes studied him as if looking for something. "You're still not well."

"I'm okay." He swayed on his feet as if to prove her point.

"How will we help you without Nihal?"

He squeezed her hand but didn't let go.

Riona stepped closer to him. "Outside, you told me I wasn't alone." He waited for her signature snark or biting words, but they never came. "You aren't alone either, Griff. You don't have to figure everything out on your own. I believe in you, I believe in *us*. You, me, Gulliver, and even Myles. No one would think we could accomplish so much together, but we have. We've found your mother alive and come so close to the book. It's because of you. There's something I need to tell—"

Griffin didn't let her finish before pulling her toward him into a bruising kiss.

Riona tensed, her wings shooting out behind her in alarm. One hand came up, her fingers curling in Griffin's shirt. Instead of holding on like she'd meant to, she pushed him away so she could breathe. "Griff..."

His fingers traced over her dark skin. The tattoos swirled faster at his touch. "You can't say those things to me and not expect me to kiss you."

One of her fingers traced her lips. "We ... this isn't right, Griff."

"Why?" He leaned his forehead against hers. "You proved to me I didn't love Brea. You've trusted me during our journey even though I know you'd say there's no trust here. Do you know how much faith it takes to walk through someone else's portal?"

Her eyes met his, but she didn't speak.

"You earned my respect the day we fought in the pits. And again when you let both Gulliver and I go from Kvek's stronghold. Then you came to Fela and destroyed it, making me question everything about you."

A tear rolled down her cheek. "I didn't have a choice. I will never stop seeing the faces of your people in my mind. Destroying your village was a choice, my choice. But it's one that now haunts me. You should hate me, Griff."

He shook his head. "I know the worst of you. You know the worst of me. And yet, we're standing here together." His palm slid up one arm and over her shoulder to the hollow of her throat before pulling it back entirely. "There will be sides in the coming war if Egan destroys the prison magic, and I am pretty sure I know which side will have your loyalty. I've made that choice before. But until then, whatever this journey throws at us, we're in it together."

His fingers linked with hers before releasing her and stepping back. "Goodnight, Riona. Sleep well because I have a feeling tomorrow will change everything we know." He left her staring after him as he peered into his mother's room. She'd barely been able to speak after practically coming back from the dead. Shutting her door, he entered the room next to hers to find a pillow on the ground for him and Gulliver and Myles in the bed. Lowering himself to the soft rug, he closed his eyes, wishing he was the kind of man who deserved to give in to the feelings inside him.

Sleep never came for Griffin, and he was up long before the rest. His legs wobbled beneath him, but he gripped the kitchen counter to steady himself as he made his way to the fridge. He had to make sure Gulliver had something to eat when he woke. No one wanted to be around a hungry Gulliver.

Something tugged at Griffin and whispers echoed in his mind, not unlike what he'd experienced in his portal. He breathed deeply, trying to clear his thoughts.

Footsteps sounded behind him, and he turned, coming face to face with his mother. He stared at her, wondering how he hadn't seen the resemblance the moment they found her. She was the image of Lochlan.

Dark circles ringed her eyes, but she was otherwise unharmed. "Griffin." She spoke the name she'd given him, slowly, like she wasn't sure she was allowed to use it.

"Most people call me Griff." He cast his eyes toward the floor, unable to meet her penetrating gaze.

She nodded, a smile coming to her face. She took a tentative step forward, and Griffin backed up. "I just ... can I get to the coffee maker?"

Griffin slid out of the way. "Brea is obsessed with coffee." He guessed his mother's fondness for it came from living around humans for so long. "Brea is—"

"I know who she is. The fae communities in the human world are not ignorant of all that has happened in the kingdoms."

"Oh. Right." He drummed his fingers on the countertop. "So, the book."

His mother heaved a sigh as she filled the coffee maker and hit a button. "I barely had it long enough to make a dent."

"A dent?"

She waved the question away as she reached for a mug. "It is out of our reach now. That is why I didn't tell you about it last night. I did not want you chasing after it."

"I can feel it." He rubbed a spot over his chest. "It's getting farther away."

His mother nodded. "That's because it is probably back in the fae realm."

"You..."

"There are a great many things you need to know." She waited for her coffee to finish dripping into a pot before pouring a mug and leading him from the kitchen.

In the sitting room, Riona had already tidied the couch and stood in the middle of the room stretching out her wings.

"Nihal used to do that." His mother smiled at the

memory. "A Slyph's wings are like an extended muscle that must be treated well."

Riona caught sight of them and brought her wings in.

"Good morning." Griffin's emotions tipped from happy to see Riona to confused at being in the presence of his supposedly dead mother. He couldn't wrap his head around it.

"Both of you, sit." Griffin's mother lowered herself to the ground.

The wearier Griffin sat next to Riona on the settee.

The woman sipped her coffee before setting it on the table between them. "I guess I should just start at the beginning. My husband and I volunteered to bring Brea Robinson to the human realm. An Eldurian noble then took Alona, the human child back to Eldur through my husband's portal where we were to follow."

"But you never made it." Griffin rested his elbows on his knees and leaned forward.

"No. We never made it. My husband—your father—was killed by the one fae he trusted most on his council."

Griffin knew what she was going to say.

"Callum. His own brother. I'd always seen through Callum, but my husband had a soft spot for his little brother."

Griffin thought of Lochlan. Brothers betraying brothers. Would the cycle ever end in Iskalt?

"Callum didn't kill me. Instead, he trapped me in the human world. I met Nihal four years ago. I'd been living in Aghadoon to be close to the book."

"I thought that village only allowed descendants of Grainne to even see it?"

She gave them a grim smile. "I am Fargelsian on my mother's side. I don't know if anyone ever told you that, Griffin. I wasn't known to be royalty—we kept the small amount of royal blood a secret—but your father and I fell in love. My father was a lesser Iskalt nobleman, though, in those days it was still quite the scandal for a prince to marry so far beneath him. And then when Brandon disappeared and Regan came to power, I made the choice to hide my Fargelsian heritage—until I needed it to get into the village."

She took a long drink, and it seemed to fortify her. "The book ... I don't know how Callum tracked it to me, but this time he didn't plan to leave me alive."

Griffin jumped to his feet. "Callum was here? He did this to you?"

She nodded.

"Did he have children with him?"

"I'm sorry. He didn't." She looked to Riona. "Are these the twins we spoke of when I was Ashlin? The O'Rourke twins?"

Griffin pushed a hand through his hair and paced the length of the room. "Yes."

"My purpose in Ireland wasn't only to delay you and give me time, I wanted you to know that no royal Fargelsian twins could be normal kids. Their power…

"What?" Griffin stopped walking.

"Brea is a direct descendent of the O'Rourke Queens. Any children of hers would be as well. In the O'Rourke line, twins hold a significance, but there haven't been any since Sorcha and Grainne."

"You told us this before." Griffin was losing his patience. "What kind of significance?"

"There is much of the book only they will be able to read. And that kind of power is everything."

CHAPTER FIFTEEN

Griffin

"Loch will meet us in the park in a few hours." Myles slammed the apartment door closed behind him. "We'll just take a cab straight there and be out of here in no time."

"And why is it Griffin can't create a portal?" Enis asked. "He was born with the O'Shea magic." She settled her clear blue eyes on him, and Griffin shrank beneath their steady gaze.

His mother's name was Enis O'Shea, and she wasn't dead. Griffin couldn't seem to wrap his mind around that truth. Nor could he stop staring at her.

"He's sick," Gulliver explained. "He gets sicker when he opens portals, so Loch won't let him do it anymore."

"You and your brother have remained close?" Enis looked at him with a bright smile and a healthy color in her cheeks. "I feared you would become strangers when you were torn apart."

"We've only recently become ... friends."

"Of course, you've been in the prison realm for a long time." She patted his knee. "Without the full use of your magic, it's no wonder you're ill."

It was a little creepy how much she actually knew about them. Part of him wanted to rage at her for not working harder to come back for them. How different all their lives would have been if she'd returned to Iskalt to raise her sons together and hold the throne until Lochlan came of age. How many lives might not have been ruined? But another part of him wanted to hold on to her and not let her out of his sight.

"Did you ... prepare him?" Griffin asked, giving Myles an imploring look. He didn't want to shock his brother with the news of their mother's ... not dead situation.

"Warn him his mother has come back from the dead?" Myles shook his head. "That's not something you tell a guy in a note pinned to a tree. I told him to meet us just after moonrise, and we had someone who would be returning to Iskalt with us."

"What's our next move?" Myles sat on the chair opposite the couch Griffin shared with his mother and Riona.

"We have to catch Callum before he tries to enter the prison realm with the twins." Griffin didn't want to think about what would happen if Callum were to get away with the book and the children he needed to read it.

"How does this twin magic work?" Riona asked, leaning forward to hear Enis' answer.

"O'Rourke twins are powerful," Enis began. "And if my assumptions are correct about Brea and Lochlan's children, then they will be even more powerful for having the magic of all three kingdoms. Yet we will not know that for certain until they come of age.

"The twins usually have a unique skill set. One twin wields powerful magic while the other twin has only the ability to enhance or stifle the other's. In the past, these twins have rarely worked together for a common goal. The twin without magic doesn't often survive long if he or she opposes the one with the power. That is why Grainne escaped to the human realm with the book of power. She went where her sister could not follow."

"My niece and nephew are just children," Griffin said. "They are young, and they love each other. We have to get them back before Callum has a chance to destroy their bond.

"Tia already has use of her Fargelsian magic." Griffin smiled, thinking of his niece's penchant for getting into trouble with her magic.

Enis nodded. "She will likely come into her Iskaltian and Eldurian magic when she is eighteen. The book will be the key to increasing her Fargelsian power. It will show her brother how best to work with her to help her. In the wrong hands, the book is dangerous. Even more so with O'Rourke twins added into the mix."

"If it's so dangerous, why not destroy it?" Griffin asked.

"Because the book holds as much good as bad. It holds the key to all of our magic. Much of what we no longer understand. It cannot be destroyed."

"But what does Callum want with it?" Myles asked.

"I think he wants to destroy the tentative peace our kingdoms have created in the last years," Griffin said. "Right now the three kingdoms are all friends because our rulers have become like family to each other. But what happens in the future when that friendship is no longer what holds them together? When others are in charge? Maybe Callum doesn't want to wait for that kind of division to happen naturally over time. I believe he wants to bring the barrier down between Myrkur and the other kingdoms."

"But why?" Myles frowned. "What will that accomplish?"

"Chaos. Conflict and division." Griffin rubbed a weary hand over his face. "He thinks if he can flood the realms with convicted criminals it will throw the kingdoms into anarchy—likely war, which is when he will try to seize power and create even more division among us."

"And he needs the twins and the book to destroy the boundary," Riona whispered, sharing a look with Griffin. That was why they were here. What would happen if Callum did the thing Egan sent them here to do? And what would Riona do now that she knew exactly what her king needed?

"I think I'd like to not return to the human realm for a while," Gulliver said the moment he stepped through the portal into a fresh sunny day in Iskalt. "I mean, I like pizza and donuts, and Coke, but I'm quite sick of the time shift between worlds. It's like we're losing time." He crossed the moon garden to Brea's side, giving the Queen of Iskalt a fist bump.

"I feel the same way about the human world." Lochlan followed him through the portal, letting it close on the inky black night in Central Park. "It's the worst part about traveling frequently." He rested a hand on Gulliver's shoulder, his laughter a rumble in his throat. But Lochlan's laughter quickly turned into a strangled sound when Enis lowered her hood, her face pale in the sunlight.

"Mother?" Lochlan's voice trembled in uncertainty. He shook his head and blinked as if to clear his mind of whatever vision he was seeing.

"Lochlan." She nodded, folding her trembling hands in front of her.

"She's not dead," Myles announced, slapping Lochlan on the back.

"I can see that." Lochlan took an unsteady step forward.

"After your father died, I was stuck in the human realm and another mission took precedence." She fumbled with her cloak.

"She was protecting the book," Griffin said. "Turns out she's been the one helping us all along. She's worked with Nihal for years."

"Where is Nihal?" Brea asked.

"He died saving Enis after Callum attacked her and stole the book," Myles explained. "We have a lot to catch you up on." He steered them all inside out of the cold.

Brea busied herself with getting them settled around the table in the dining hall as an early dinner was served for their traveling guests. She beamed proudly when Enis complimented her on the changes she'd made from the formal dining with the full Iskalt court.

"It always seemed a bit much in my day to have all the nobles in attendance every single night. It's exhausting."

"Right?" Brea laughed, bouncing baby Ciara on her hip while princess Kayleigh had taken up residence on her long lost grandmother's lap.

"Now that we know Callum has the book, we can follow him." Griffin began the long process of catching them up to speed with everything that had happened. "We should leave as soon as we've rested for a little while."

"I'm sure it can wait until morning," Brea said. "You've not been well, Griffin."

"We don't have much time to catch up with Callum. I

don't have time to be unwell. Tia and Toby will be beyond our reach soon."

"Who?" Brea cocked her head in confusion.

"The twins." Griffin's blood ran cold at the blank look on her face.

"What twins?" Lochlan asked.

"Not this again," Myles groaned. "We're too late."

"Too late for what?" Brea frowned. "What's going on, guys? Why do you all look so devastated? Who are Tia and Toby?"

"They're your children, Brea," Griffin said, rising to take Ciara from her arms just as they went limp with shock.

"What?" Lochlan frowned. "That's absurd, we don't have twins."

"Yes you do. Callum has them and he's taken them into the prison realm. It must have been before we left the human realm. The boundary magic has made you forget they were ever born."

CHAPTER SIXTEEN

Riona

"How could we let this happen?"

Riona watched Griffin pace back and forth across the palace library. "Seven."

He stopped and turned to her. "What?"

"That was the seventh time you said that. The answer won't change, Griff. We failed to get the book."

Red crept past the collar of his shirt and into his face. "You think I care about the book right now?"

"You should. We know now Callum took the twins to Myrkur, to Egan. Everything is different now. Egan doesn't need us. He doesn't need to keep your people alive."

Griffin collapsed into a chair. "Shauna and Nessa. How could I have forgotten about them? Since the moment I realized Brea and Loch forgot the twins, it's like I have this all-consuming guilt. And fear."

Pain seared through Riona, and she clutched her head

with a quiet cry. The agony pulsed through her. She dropped to her knees. Egan. He must know she'd failed. "Callum," she panted. "He's reached Egan." That was the only explanation for the sheer anguish of his wrath.

Griffin scrambled from his chair and dropped to his knees in front of her. "Riona?"

The pain didn't go away like it had each time before. "It's him. The magic that ties me to him." Her wings shook as they folded around her.

And then another set of hands were on her, a comforting touch. Griffin pulled her to him, holding her as Egan's magic sought to remind her she didn't belong to herself or to Griffin.

Her body quaked in his arms as she burrowed closer, hiding her face in his chest. Her wings stretched to their full size and wrapped around them both like a cocoon. Riona hated relying on anyone else, she hated that Griffin had to hold her together.

But she didn't hate *him*. Maybe she never had. From the moment they met, Griffin had an honor about him.

"We've made a habit of saving each other, haven't we?" He rested his chin on top of her head. "How is the pain?"

Being in Griffin's arms, she'd barely noticed the pain ebbing away. "It's almost gone."

They stayed there beneath the shield of her wings as her heartbeat returned to normal and Egan's magic left her. For now.

Griffin's warmth soothed her, and she wasn't ready for the moment to end.

"We have to go back to Myrkur." Griffin's voice was no more than a whisper.

She leaned her head back to meet his gaze, wanting to

contradict him, but he was right. "You need access to your full magic, or…"

"Or I'm going to die." He heaved a weary sigh.

It was a realization Riona had come to over the last week or so. Every time Griffin fell ill, it was a deeper sickness, more serious, and it lasted longer each time. Eventually, he wouldn't wake up.

He gripped her chin, his thumb moving over her lips. "There was a time you'd have welcomed my death."

She nodded because it was true. And since then, she'd followed a fae who was brave and selfless. One who didn't look at her tattoos and wings in disgust. "Egan once told me there was a reason the Dark Fae were trapped in the prison realm along with the criminals." Her wings retreated from around them and Riona sat back on her heels. "The three kingdoms weren't prepared for the likes of us. He claimed there'd never have been any kind of peace if Sorcha hadn't erected the magic generations ago. He claimed the Light Fae … aren't supposed to mix with Dark Fae."

Griffin rubbed his chin. "That might be so. The Light Fae are not ready to find out there are ogres in this world and fae with wings or tails or horns. They may not understand how your magic comes from a different place than theirs. But…" He dipped his head. "Riona, look at me."

She lifted her chin to meet his gaze.

"Just because a fae is not ready for something doesn't mean it shouldn't happen. Egan wants the magic down so he can march his army through Iskalt and beyond, an army of Dark Fae who think the outside world has forsaken them. He thinks the only way to exist together is for one kind of fae to dominate the other."

"Isn't that the only way?" Riona frowned, unable to fathom a world where there was true peace among all fae.

"No. You do not know the lands of the Light Fae as I do. They do not yearn for conflict. Eldur's ruler is a human and Fargelsi's is a former servant. I think, given time, we could continue to be a world at peace, one who accepts all kinds of fae no matter how different they are."

Riona closed her eyes and released a long breath. "How do you do it, Griff?"

"Do what?"

"You lived in Myrkur for ten years, and yet, you have this faith, this hope."

"You wouldn't want to know the man I was before. I never questioned Regan even when she did things I knew weren't right. Not until a girl made me rethink everything I knew. I did my worst to her, even trapping her in a marriage bond. And yet … she had faith in me. She was my anchor, the first fae who ever believed I could be more, good."

"You were lucky to have Queen Brea."

"I was. I can be that fae for you. Riona, you are not Egan's puppet. You don't have to continue to dance to his tune. Let me believe in you. Let my faith help you believe in yourself. I think you need me."

Tears welled in Riona's eyes, and for once, she didn't wipe them away. No one had ever told her she could be good, that she had more to offer than the pawn she was. She rose up on her knees and closed the distance between her and Griffin. One corner of her mouth curved up. "You're right about one thing, Griff." She steadied her breathing. If she was going to admit to this feeling, she had to be calm, confident. "I do need you." She leaned in, her last words only a whisper on his lips. "I don't know if I deserve your faith, but I want to."

Griffin pressed his lips to hers. Her body relaxed under his touch. This kiss, this connection was what they needed. Riona wrapped her arms around his neck, drawing him down on the library floor.

Both of them knew the dangers coming for them, that they had to return to the prison realm and there was a chance they wouldn't make it out again. Once they crossed the border, they would be forgotten once more, and this time, there would be no portals out unless Griffin got his magic back.

They didn't hear the door open, but Gulliver's snicker was undeniable. Riona pulled back to find Gulliver with Enis, looking down on them.

"So, is this what people do in the library once they know how to read?" Gulliver's smile spread across his lips. "I figured there had to be a good reason why anyone would sit in a dusty old library reading instead of exploring outside."

"Gullie." Griffin shook his head. "I'm going to make sure you learn how to read."

"Why would you do that to me?" Gulliver pouted. "Come on, we can make a deal. I distract your mother so you can, uh, continue, and you don't try to cram useless information into my head."

Griffin pushed to his feet. "Reading isn't useless."

Riona stood and met Enis' strange gaze. "Listen to the kid, Griffin. He's smarter than you."

Gulliver reached his fist out, and Riona bumped hers against it in the odd way Myles taught them.

"I'll let you guys talk." She tried to step around Enis.

"I actually wanted to talk to you, Riona." Enis smiled. Riona found she did that a lot, but something didn't feel right about it.

"Oh." Griffin's face fell. Riona knew how much Griffin wanted to spend time with his mother before leaving for the prison realm, but she'd been busy studying the few pages from the book of power found in the Iskaltian archives, presumably put there by Nihal years ago.

Enis led Riona out into the hall. "Would you like some tea? I'll have it brought to my rooms."

"How do you fall back into life as a royal so quickly?" Riona looked to her. "I'll never be comfortable in a palace."

Enis smiled. "Because I'm home. This palace hasn't changed. It still feels like my husband will walk around the corner or there'll be two little boys running through the halls."

Riona hadn't talked to Enis since they arrived from the human realm a few days ago. Enis assured them all it would take a while for Egan and Callum to understand the magic they wanted to use … to understand the twins. Which gave Griffin time to rest.

Enis pushed into her rooms—rooms Riona had learned were hers all those years ago. A fire burned in the hearth. Enis stopped the servant on the way out. "Might we have a tea cart brought in?"

He nodded. "Yes, my lady. I'll fetch it myself."

Enis gestured to the white velvet settee, and Riona took a seat. She didn't know what the woman could possibly want to talk to her about. Without Griffin as a buffer, Riona had little to say.

Enis sat in a chair near the fireplace. "I don't know if I'll ever get used to the cold of Iskalt again. Especially after living in the human realm with a heating system where I only had to turn up the temperature on a little box to make it warmer."

Riona had stopped being amazed by human things. She'd accepted their lives were just different. "Couldn't you heat this room with your magic?"

"Ah, my magic. I do not have Iskaltian magic like my boys. A long time ago, I was able to use Fargelsian power. But I'm out of practice and wouldn't be able to recall the right words without some time to study."

"You didn't memorize spells from the book?"

She shook her head. "It was in my possession for only a short time. I only intended to keep the book safe."

"Why? Wasn't Aghadoon protecting it?"

"That depends on what you mean by protecting. They had it hidden away unused, not accessing the enormous amount of information and spells it can reveal. Over the years, some of the pages have become part of the archives in the three kingdoms, like those found here, but we know so little of its true contents. We cannot have such a powerful book out there if we do not understand it."

"That ... actually makes sense."

Enis smiled. "Dear, I have spent so many years away from the fae realm, letting other kingdoms raise my children. Four years ago, I met Nihal, a Dark Fae who'd become a conduit of the book. He offered to bring me home, to let me give up on my mission. But I couldn't do that."

In a way, Riona understood her. Riona had spent most of her life on some mission or another for Egan. There'd been a time she thought the raids and the fights in the pit were part of loyalty to the king, and there was a nobility in that.

Enis stood and walked into the adjacent bedroom, returning a moment later with a small stack of parchment.

A knock sounded on the door, and Enis hid the parchment behind her back as she answered it and let the servant in. He pushed a silver teacart in front of him. Two sterling pots sat on top with china cups. A plate of pastries accompanied them.

"Thank you." Enis smiled. "We can pour our own tea." The servant bowed and left them in peace.

Forgetting the teacart, Enis sat beside Riona. "I learned a lot about your kind from Nihal, but he never told me where he'd come from. I now know it must have been Myrkur, but what I don't know is how he escaped the prison magic." She paused. "That is not why I asked you here." Enis stood and poured two cups of tea, not asking Riona how many sugar cubes she preferred. "There is a line almost hidden on this page." She handed a worn parchment to Riona. "Look at the bottom."

Riona leaned closer, trying to make out some of the smaller text. "A being from the land and the sea, born in darkness will bring out the music in the magic." She lifted her head to look at Enis. "What does it mean, 'music in the magic'?"

Enis set her teacup on the tray and walked to where her human sack she called a backpack sat. She pulled out a familiar looking instrument. "This music was not the purpose spelled out in Nihal's tattoos, but he was the only being I ever found who could bring about a sound from this specific instrument." She handed the piccolo to Riona.

Riona wrapped her fingers around the instrument. "And you think I can do the same?"

"To be honest, I don't know. I tried playing it myself, but no sound came. There was a page of the book that I believe now is displayed in Fargelsi. It isn't a spell, only an explanation. It says 'with music all spells are possible.'"

"With music, all spells are possible," Riona repeated as she looked down at it. "But I don't know how to play."

"Try. Please just try."

Riona recalled watching Nihal play the instrument. She mimicked the image in her mind. But when she blew across the opening, nothing happened. No sounds, not even a squeak. "I can try again."

Enis slumped. "No, it will be no use. Nihal could play it instinctively. Like it was impossible for him to hit the wrong notes. It was the magic of the book."

Riona held out the instrument for her to take, but Enis shook her head. "You may yet find someone to play it in the prison realm. Guard it with your life, Riona." She looked to the door as if making sure it was still closed. "I have one more request of you."

"What is it?"

"Those books you have that allow you to communicate with the Dark Fae king..."

Riona sucked in a breath. How did she know? "What do you want with them?"

"I want to speak with Egan."

CHAPTER SEVENTEEN

Griffin

Failure came in many forms, but Griffin often wondered if he'd ever know what success felt like.

He sat on the snow-covered bank of the pond where he'd first seen Tia and Toby skating. Nessa would have loved that. She'd have loved the sun beating down on her, and the other children to run and play with. Even now when two of them were missing, the Iskalt palace teemed with the children of servants Brea allowed to play where they liked.

"You're going to catch a chill, brother." Lochlan lowered himself to the ground beside him. "In your condition, you need rest. Why don't we push off your journey a few days?"

Griffin snorted. "You wouldn't be saying that if you remembered your kids."

Lochlan's brow scrunched. "I've tried. Every night, I try to conjure images of them in my dreams. During the day is the worst though. Brea is mourning them, despite not remembering the kids we've lost. It's … torture, Griff." Lochlan hunched forward, a tear rolling down his cheek.

Griffin couldn't remember ever seeing his brother cry.

"I'm sorry I failed you." Griffin stared into the distant snowfields across the pond. "You can't imagine how sorry I am." He'd made a promise to Brea to bring them home, a promise only he remembered now.

Lochlan shook his head. "I may not remember them, but I feel like I know you now. You would have tried your hardest."

For the first time in Griffin's life, that was the truth. There'd been no ulterior motives in his mission. He hadn't chosen to back the wrong king over his family.

And still, it made no difference.

"What is it like, Griff? The prison realm."

Griffin rested his arms on his knees. "I don't think you want to know."

"I do. I have to."

A sigh hissed past Griffin's lips. "It's always dark, but you get used to that part. Its inhabitants are stripped of magic. I think that was the worst part for me. We live in villages with the Dark Fae." He smiled as he thought of his people. "I lived in a place called Fela. We took care of each other, sharing what little we had, working for the good of the community. For more than ten years, we evaded the king's notice."

His shoulders slumped. "Before I left on the king's mission, we were attacked, our village destroyed."

Neither of them said anything for a long moment. Lochlan put his hand on Griffin's shoulder. "I'm sorry for the people you've lost."

That should have been the other way around, Lochlan needing consolation for his loss.

"My best friend was Shauna, our village healer." Griffin smiled at the memory, but it dropped quickly. "The king is holding Shauna and her young sister, Nessa, at the palace to make sure I return."

"I should have been there." Lochlan dug his hands into the snow. "If you were trying to rescue my children in the human realm, why wasn't I there with you?"

"You're a king, Loch. You couldn't just leave."

"But they were my kids. I don't remember them, but I feel their loss right here." He put a hand over his heart.

"You had a purpose here too."

"It shouldn't have mattered."

"But it did." Griffin turned toward him. "We have gathered important pages from the book because you and Finn traveled each kingdom, searching through the libraries and archives while I was busy in the human realm. We have much of our knowledge of the book because of you two."

Griffin never could have imagined the prison boundary to be as complex as they'd learned it was. This wasn't like Regan's boundary spell around Fargelsi. The greatest magic wielders from all three kingdoms came together to pick apart that boundary piece by piece. The prison boundary wasn't so simple.

"But is it enough to be any help?"

The scroll Lochlan and Finn found in the palace in Eldur contained their biggest clue yet. The wall itself was responsible for holding all the memories and magic. The page from the book of power claimed the exterior wall absorbed the memories, becoming stronger as more people crossed the boundary, while the interior wall absorbed the magic from those who entered.

"Griff!" Gulliver called.

Griffin turned to see him stumbling across the fresh layer of snow, his boots getting stuck in its depths. He waved a leather book over his head. "Griff." He panted as he reached them. "Riona, she…" He bent over, unable to breathe and handed Griffin the book.

Griffin gave him an odd look before flipping the cover open. "It's empty. Gulliver, what's going on?"

"Last. Page." Gulliver finally caught his breath. "Flip to the end. She didn't have time to erase it."

Griffin did as he asked, his eyes widening as he reached the page that had a line of black text scrawled across it. "My king, we have the knowledge you need. We're coming home."

Griffin growled. "Whose is this?"

"Riona's."

Something shattered inside him as the betrayal sank in.

"Griff." Gulliver's eyes flicked between Griff and Lochlan. "She's gone. And…"

"And what, boy?" Lochlan's icy gaze latched onto him.

"Enis went with her."

The brothers shared a look. Their mother?

"Follow me." Lochlan stood and together they trudged back to the palace. Griffin interrogated Gulliver as they stomped through the snow.

"Why did she leave this behind?" Griffin gripped the book in his fist, the evidence of her betrayal.

"Because I'd already found it." He huffed out a breath. "I hid it in my room this morning, and I watched her search every inch of her own room before Enis arrived and said they had to go."

"How long ago was this?"

Gulliver shrugged. "Enis did some Fargelsian spell to lock me in the room, but it wore off after a few hours."

"I thought Enis said she didn't have magic anymore." Lochlan's jaw clenched.

"Does it really surprise you she lied?" Gulliver's tail flicked with annoyance.

A guard opened the door for Lochlan, Gulliver, and Griffin. They made their way through the palace halls before stopping at the royal bedchamber.

Lochlan led them inside to find Brea rolling on the ground with her remaining children. A sad smile graced her lips, but it dropped when she saw her husband's stormy expression. She sat up. "What's wrong?"

Lochlan looked to Griffin. "Give her the book. If it's spelled to erase messages, it can be spelled to remember them."

"What's going on?" Brea stood and scooped the baby into her arms.

"We need your Eldurian magic. It's still daylight, and this has to be done now."

"Of course." She took the book. "What is this?"

"Riona's communications with the king of Myrkur."

Brea's face darkened. "The man Callum took my kids to?"

Griffin wondered if it was harder to deal with the kidnapping if they remembered the kids or not. It was a special kind of pain for a parent to know they didn't hold the one thing that connected them with their kids. Memories. The kind of memories that deepens love.

With Ciara in her arms and Kayleigh pulling at her leg, Brea concentrated on the book. A yellow ring of magic trapped it in Brea's power. The cover flipped open, and the blank pages flew past of their own accord until Brea reached the last page with the visible message. With a satisfied smile, she closed the book and handed it back to Griffin. The leather was warm in his hands.

It used to be moments like this when he fell more and more in love with Brea Robinson, but he knew now it had never been right. Without the marriage magic creating deeper feelings, he was left with respect. Respect and loyalty. He looked from Brea to Lochlan to Gulliver.

Riona betrayed him, and that crushed something inside him. But these people ... no matter what side Riona chose, he would never again go against his brother, his ex-wife, or the boy he'd raised as his own.

Griffin perched on the wooden arm of the settee and opened the book to find Riona's handwriting.

Brea leaned back. "I wasn't able to recreate the responses, but every message she sent is there."

Lochlan stepped closer, and together with Griffin, they read through Riona's growing betrayal. She'd kept Egan abreast of their movement, every progress they'd made. She'd told Egan about Griffin's illness, about the twins. Anger brewed in his gut. It was only days ago he'd told Riona he was so tired of being angry, yet he couldn't keep it from rising to the surface now.

Was everything fake? Designed to help her get close to him and learn all his secrets? The book fell from his fingers and tumbled to the ground, spine up.

Riona Nieland was now an enemy of the three fae kingdoms. She chose her side repeatedly, every time she wrote to Egan.

But Griffin ... was she an enemy of his as well?

The sun was still in the sky when Griffin returned to his room to prepare for the journey to the prison realm. He didn't have much to pack, so his mind was left to think about Riona, about their time in the library.

When he'd kissed her, he felt her respond. And her words … Throughout his life, Griffin learned how to decipher lies from truths, but in those moments, he'd truly believed her, believed in her.

Just like she'd wanted him to. He slammed his fist against the wall, ignoring the pain in his knuckles in favor of the pain in his heart.

Was this how Brea felt when Griffin had chosen Regan over her again and again?

What about his mom? He barely had the capacity to think of her as being alive, let alone alive and a traitor.

Yet, she'd gone with Riona. Back to the man who wanted to bring the magic down to move his army across the fae lands. Griffin wondered if the Light Fae would ever be ready for the Dark Fae.

Griffin grabbed his bag as he stepped into the sitting room he'd shared with Gulliver and Riona to find Gulliver sitting on the settee, his back hunched.

Griffin dropped his bag on the floor and approached the boy. "Gullie."

Gulliver turned hurt eyes on his surrogate father. "You're leaving tonight." It was an accusation more than a question.

Griffin nodded, letting his anger at Riona fade away. Gulliver didn't deserve to stand in the path of his rage. But once it was gone, his energy slipped away as if it had been fired only by the strong emotions. "I am."

"And you're not taking me with you."

Griffin slumped onto the settee next to him. "I don't ever

want you to enter that realm again. It's my job to protect you."

"But my friends are there. Shauna and Nessa are still trapped."

Neither of them said their real fears. The girls were trapped—if they were still alive.

"What about the twins?" Gulliver pleaded. "I want to help."

Griffin slid an arm around him. "I need to know you're safe. Going back there … it scares me, Gullie. I might end up trapped forever if the magic remains in place. I might…" He sighed.

"Die," Gulliver finished for him. "You can say it, Griff. You might die." A tear leaked from his cat-like eyes. "Why do you get to risk your life and I don't? I can help you. I *need* to help you. I'm the last ally you have who remembers everyone. Riona has gone back to the king's side. Myles returned to Fargelsi to prepare his kingdom should the magic come down." He turned to meet his gaze. "It's always been you and me, Griff. That doesn't change just because it's dangerous. We're all we have left."

Griffin pulled the boy into a hug, not wanting to let go. "When did you get to be smarter than me?"

"I've always been smarter than you."

They both laughed as they released each other. If felt good to laugh.

Griffin studied him, the boy who'd had to grow up too fast. "Okay." He hoped he wouldn't regret it, but Gulliver was right. He needed to make his own choices. "We don't have much time. Pack your things. We're traveling the old fashioned way, no portals."

"Not a boat again?" Gulliver shrank back.

"No. There's only one place we can enter the prison realm. Be prepared for some long days in the saddle, Gullie."

Gulliver groaned. "I'm guessing I'll soon understand why humans need bum pads on their settees."

Griffin chuckled and bumped Gulliver's shoulder before pushing to his feet. "I need to see the king and queen before we go. I'll meet you at the stables at dusk."

"I won't let you down, Griff."

"You never have, Gullie."

He left Gulliver to prepare for the journey and found Lochlan and Brea in the moon garden.

Griffin approached cautiously.

Lochlan took one look at his eyes. "You're leaving, aren't you?"

"I must. We have to get to Myrkur before they figure out how to use the twin magic. I've promised this before, but this time, I won't fail. I *will* bring your kids home to you." Part of Griffin wanted to tell Lochlan to go to the human realm and stay there until Griffin passed the prison magic. It was the only way to remember him. But he didn't know how long it would take him to reach the border, and he'd never ask his brother to leave his family and his kingdom for that long, not for a brother he barely knew.

Brea gave him a sad smile. "Are we going to forget you again?"

Griffin nodded. It was the hardest part about leaving. "As soon as I cross the threshold, you won't know I was ever here."

He wondered how close Riona and Enis were to the magic barrier. They hadn't crossed yet if he still remembered them. But they were a future problem.

"Loch, if the magic comes down, the king will bring his

force to travel across the realms unimpeded. I've seen his army, it's the stuff of nightmares. You must send word to Queen Neeve and Queen Alona. Your combined armies must be there at the border, ready to face whatever comes."

Lochlan nodded. "We'll be prepared."

This was the hard part. "I wrote this for you last night." Griffin handed him an envelope with the words 'You have twins and a brother in the prison realm you've forgotten. Read this now!' written in a hasty scrawl on the front. Inside, Griffin had left instructions for Loch and Brea. "You probably won't trust my instructions so as soon as I leave, write a letter to yourself about what must be done and who I am. Put it someplace you will find it."

Lochlan's brow furrowed as if he didn't like it, but he nodded.

Griffin gripped his arm. "Promise you'll do this. We will fail without your armies."

"You have my word."

Griffin stepped back. "I'm glad I got to see you both again. I don't think we'll meet in the future." Sadness exacerbated the weakness inside him.

Brea pulled him into a hug. "We may not remember you, Griff, but you will always be in our hearts. We will not fail you."

Griffin stepped back, his eyes glassing over. "We will not fail each other."

He tried to smile as he looked from his brother to the girl he once loved. "It was always meant to be you two. I'm sorry I ever tried to take that away." They didn't remember his actions of the past, but he'd never forget them.

"Right here." Brea placed a hand over her heart. "Always."

He ripped his eyes away, knowing if he stared at them too long, he wouldn't want to leave.

Going to the prison realm the first time had been for penance, maybe even redemption.

But now … he was going for love. Shauna. Nessa. Tia. Toby. Even for Brea and Lochlan.

And that gave him a strength he'd never had before.

CHAPTER EIGHTEEN

Riona

"The king's soldiers will be waiting for us on the other side." Riona stood, staring at the crumbling boulders flanking the path before her. Only a few more steps and she would be home, and everyone she'd met on this side of the border would forget she ever existed. Including Griffin O'Shea. "You can wait here and enter after they've taken me to Egan."

"No." Enis shook her head. "I go wherever the book goes."

"You realize he won't give it to you no matter what you do?" She glanced at the former Queen of Iskalt, still wondering why she'd come with her and not with Griffin.

"You let me worry about that." Enis took her final steps into the prison realm.

With a deep breath and a reluctant heart, Riona followed. Passing through the barrier magic was like walking through a cold shower. It left her shivering. She'd grown soft in the human realm with all its comforts.

Riona blinked in the dim light of the sun on this side of the barrier. Anytime she'd visited the border in the past, she'd thought the sunlight here was blinding. But in reality, it was like the softest of sunsets in this no-man's-land that wasn't Myrkur or the Northern Vatlands they'd just left.

"I thought it was always dark here." Enis glanced around the barren landscape.

"It will be when we get there." Riona waited at the center of the path. Egan's men would be along any moment on their patrol of the border. "The light fades the closer you get to Myr until it's completely dark, and only the light of the moon and stars will guide you. The palace is an hour's ride from here on horseback."

"Riona, ye returned." A garbled voice grated at her. "We didn't expect ta see yer lovely mug here ever again."

"Oh, my." Enis moved behind Riona, putting her between herself and the ogres heading their way. "What on earth is that?"

"Lady Enis, meet your first ogre, Uthar." Riona turned toward the loyal soldier. He was actually kind of a nice guy—as far as ogres went. "Uthar, can you take us to the palace? I have news for the king."

"Right 'way miss. Th' cart's just o're the hill." Uthar ran ahead to prepare for their ride to the palace.

"Good Heavens!" Enis gaped at the cloud of dust Uthar left in his tracks.

"Right." Riona turned toward Enis. "Ogres are faster than they look." Uthar and his brother looked like a pair of identical eight-foot-tall boulders come to life with their cracked gray skin and mossy green hair that grew down their broad bare backs.

"Told yer." Uthar grumbled at his brother Gunthar. "Her brought a lady queen wi' her."

"Hey Gunthar, how's it hanging?" Riona climbed up into the ramshackle cart the ogres used for transporting newly arrived indentured. Egan liked to scare the bejesus out of the Light Fae prisoners by having the ogres greet them.

"Er, wha'?" Gunthar stared down at her, scratching his armpit with long, knobby fingers.

"A human expression I picked up." Riona shoved him playfully. She liked the ogres. Most of them were fun, though some were just downright mean.

"You been 'round humans?" Uthar helped a shocked Enis into the cart, lifting her by the collar of her fancy riding dress. "Whas it like out there?"

"Big and scary," Riona said.

"Truly?" Gunthar snorted like a horse as he took up the harness to the cart.

"Bigger and scarier than Kaltrick on his grumpiest day." The Ogres' father was widely known as the meanest ogre in all of Myrkur.

"The little Slyph's having' a go at us, 'rother." Uthar's laughter sounded like rocks tumbling together.

"Hold tight." Gunthar called over his shoulder.

"He means it." Riona shoved a rope in Enis' hands. "Don't let go unless you want to fall out." The ogres took off, running up the winding road to the mountains that led into Myrkur.

Enis let out a loud yelp and clutched the rope, cowering down into the cart as the bland landscape passed them by in a blur. Riona stood at the helm of the cart, holding onto the reins behind their ogre mounts. "We'll be there in half the time this way," Riona called to her fae companion. Which didn't give her much time to decide her next steps, because Riona still wasn't sure which side she was on.

The ogre brothers dropped them off at the outer palace gates, which left them to make their way through the slums just inside the walls.

Riona had always turned a blind eye to those who lived among the tents, most of whom were the untouchables, cast offs from the palace. To her, they'd always been lazy fools who never worked hard enough to prove their usefulness to their king. But something had changed since she was here last. The filth and grime were worse. The smell of unwashed bodies permeated the air along with the night fires that kept them warm in the darkness of Myrkur. They'd truly fallen on hard times in her absence.

Enis walked beside her with a cloth over her nose, and a tear in her eye at the sight of young women and children starving and begging for the scraps the palace threw out. "I don't know what I expected, but this is heartbreaking."

"They bring it on themselves." The words were out of Riona's mouth before she could even contemplate them. It was something she'd said a million times before, but now she wondered how true that was. Was she just repeating what she'd heard others say about the slum rats?

"The palace is much better." Riona marched toward the inner gates, refusing to look anywhere but at her destination. How many times had she walked the main road and not seen what was happening right under her nose?

No one blocked her way as they passed through the palace gates. It wasn't as grand as the palaces she'd visited on her journey, but Riona had everything she needed and more in the barracks as one of the king's favored.

"Come with me." Riona led Enis up the grand staircase to the guest rooms. She scowled at the clutter in the halls. The staff had fallen down on their cleaning duties of late. "Let's get you settled. The king will meet with you in the dining hall this evening." That was protocol for guests—who were normally Myrkur chieftains.

"No, no, you're not leaving me in this hellhole." Enis hissed at her when she opened the door to their finest suite. Well, it was their finest, though it was rather bare in terms of what Enis was used to.

"I have something I need to do before the king knows I'm back. Just … don't leave this room. You'll be fine."

"Riona, don't you dare leave me here." Riona shut the door behind her, twisting the key in the lock and pocketing it before she thought better of it.

Servants and guards had seen her return, so she didn't have much time to make her decision. If she knew Egan at all, Shauna and Nessa had started off serving him in his quarters, but for as long as Griffin and Riona had been gone, and as many excuses as she'd given him, they were likely working in the kitchens or the laundry by now. Both were terrible jobs, but still better than what awaited them should Egan decide Griffin and Riona had failed—and he would decide they'd failed when he discovered they had allowed Callum to beat them to the book and to the twins he needed to read it.

She also knew Egan well enough to know he'd forgotten the girls the moment they were out of his sight. Riona made her way to the kitchens at the rear of the castle, crossing the courtyard where punishments were carried out. She flinched at the familiar crack of the whip as two young boys were beaten for some slight against the king.

How had she let herself become blind to such things? Beatings were an everyday occurrence here. Riona used to sneak into the kitchens whenever she was hungry, and it had never bothered her before.

That was before she'd known another way. Another life where people didn't go hungry at the whim of a cruel king. Where children weren't orphaned and then beaten for stealing a loaf of bread when they had no other means of feeding themselves. Where indentured servitude wasn't even a thing. No one in Fargelsi or Iskalt had to spend their lives working in the king's opal mines until they were too old to be useful or died from lack of nutrition.

She found Shauna and Nessa in the washroom behind the kitchen, scrubbing filthy pots and pans, their hands cracked and dry from the harsh lye soap. Both wore the backless dresses of the female indentured. It was easier to punish them with the whips if they weren't protected with layers of clothing.

Shauna's back was covered in stripes from the whip master's attentions. Some had scabbed over, and some bled. Little Nessa wasn't much more than skin and bones, her back blistered from a recent beating.

There was no decision to make. It was already made the instant she laid eyes on the two most important people in Griffin's life. "Shauna?" Riona whispered, creeping into the washroom. Shauna looked up from the pot she was scrubbing. Sweat poured down her face from the heat of the water and the kitchen fires from the next room. Shauna backed away from her work, grabbing Nessa from the enormous cauldron she was busy cleaning. She shoved Nessa behind her.

"Don't you want to get out of here?" Riona bent so they could hear her whisper. "Griffin is coming back, and you need to be far away from the king before Griff gets here and does something stupid and heroic." She believed Griffin would do the right thing, and she wanted to give him that chance. And that meant getting his family to safety.

Shauna scrambled to her feet, taking Nessa's hand in hers. "You mean like trade himself for us?"

"Exactly."

"We have to get Hector too," Nessa said, her sweet face still managed to hold on to the innocence of youth. Something rarely seen in Myr.

"Hector? Who's Hector?" Riona growled.

"He's working out in the slums," Shauna said. "We can't leave without him."

"He's not in the castle?" Riona urged them to follow her into the darkness behind the kitchens.

"He's helping people escape the slums." Shauna limped behind her. "But he's also one of the king's indentured, patrolling the streets."

"Then he can help himself." Riona tugged Nessa's hand.

"He's here because of us," Shauna hissed. "We have to tell him we're leaving with you. That Griffin is returning."

"Fine." Riona rolled her eyes. "Where do we find him?"

"Follow me." Shauna led them around the outbuildings where the castle provisions were stored to a narrow dirt path that lead behind the castle to the rear gates.

"Get behind me." Riona moved to put herself in front of the indentured girls. "Put your heads down and act like you're scared."

"Won't need to act much," Shauna muttered, gripping her sister's hand.

"Where you heading with these?" An ogre soldier stopped them at the gates.

"These two are being put out for stealing food from the king's table." Riona gave Shauna a shove.

Shauna let out a pitiful wail, stumbling past the guards with a loud moan.

"Get her out of here." The soldier shoved her with a boot to her back. "And keep her quiet, I don't want to hear her wailing anymore tonight."

"She'll get what's coming to her." Riona sneered at Shauna's back, hauling her up by the tatters of her dress and marching her through the gates. Nessa rushed along right behind her.

Once through the rear gates, Shauna guided them into the slums far away from the night fires. From the back side of the slums, Riona noticed a huge difference from her prior visits.

"The tents here are empty. Why have the people moved so close to the main road?" Back here it was vacant and almost … clean. Fresh grass now grew where mud trails once cut deep ruts into the ground.

"Hector has been moving people out of the slums, but we don't want the king to know yet. Every few days we move the remaining people closer to the road so it looks like it always does to those who pass by, giving little attention to the conditions here. A few disappear each day, but there are always more to replace them."

"And where are you taking them?" Riona glanced around. Curious how they'd managed to move so many people out without the king's notice. Not that many paid much attention to the cast offs.

"The villages where they'll be safe." Shauna cast a wary glance at Riona. She couldn't blame her for not trusting her.

"Kiaren, where is Hector?" Shauna stopped to ask an older woman Riona vaguely remembered seeing in Fela before it burned.

"Shauna, what are you doing out here?" The old woman grabbed her hand. "The king will have your head if he catches you gone from your duties."

"We're leaving, Kiaren."

"Finally come to your senses then?" The woman led her along the back row of tents. "He's just about to leave."

"Kiaren." Shauna pulled the woman to a stop. "Griffin is returning."

"Then you need to be anywhere else but here when he arrives. What is *she* doing here?" Kiaren glared at Riona.

"She is helping us."

"Why?"

"Well, she's been with Griffin all this time, so my best guess is his annoying goodness has rubbed off on her."

Riona snorted at that. Griffin would never have considered himself good, but these people obviously did. Before she could say anything, the women pulled her into a tent.

"Shauna?" A man with a ring through his nose pulled her into a hug. He was Dark Fae, with horns like a bull. He turned menacing eyes on Riona, an irritable snort escaped his nose.

"Time to get us out of here, Hector," Shauna said.

"That must mean Griffin is back?"

"He won't be too far behind me," Riona said. "As long as he believes Shauna and Nessa are under Egan's thumb, he won't think clearly. And as far as Egan is concerned, we've failed in our mission."

"And when Griffin shows up, Egan can't have anything to use against him." Hector nodded in understanding. "I'll get them out of here tonight."

"See that you do." Riona turned to leave.

"Wait, what will you do, Riona?" Shauna grabbed her arm. "You should come with us."

"I can't." Riona pulled away. "It's time I return to my king." She hung her head as she left them to their escape. Egan would kill her if he found out, but she owed this much to Griffin.

Back in the palace, Riona wrinkled her nose at the layer of ash and filth covering everything. Her accommodations within the barracks might have been more comfortable than those residing in the slums, but she was just as trapped as they were. Even more so, having the undivided attention of the king.

The king who would soon know she had returned. If he didn't already. Riona climbed the back stairs up to the guest quarters. Fishing the key from her pocket, she let herself into Enis' room.

"It's about time." Enis stood up from her seat on the bed. "What do you mean locking me in here?"

"I had something I needed to do first." Riona paced to the aged wooden chest in the corner and splashed her face with water from the basin. Checking her reflection in the cracked mirror, she thought she looked like the Riona Egan would remember. Though there was little of herself she recognized anymore. The black shadows creeping across her wings now covered half of the white membrane. Riona didn't know what would happen if they turned full dark.

"Don't think you can swoop in and steal the book out from under me. I've sacrificed too many years to let that happen."

"I don't want your book, Enis." Riona dabbed her face dry with what she'd once thought was the finest cloth. That was before she'd slept under the silken sheets in her room at the palace in Iskalt. "I just needed a moment to see to Griffin's family here before Egan knows I have returned." She crossed the room to face Enis.

To Riona's surprise, Enis didn't ask about this family of her son's. It was becoming harder to believe she would come to care for her children at all.

Riona pushed the thoughts away. They were for another time. "We're about to walk into the dining hall to meet with Egan and likely Callum too. They need to think I've come straight to them with you as my guest."

"Very well. You will introduce me to your king, and I will take it from there. It is important we find out where he is keeping the book."

"Don't forget your grandchildren are here too." Riona frowned at the former queen. She was as cold as ice.

"Of course. Their safety is obviously of great importance as well."

"Of course."

Griffin

"You ready for this?" Gulliver wrapped his arm around Griffin's waist, hoisting the bulk of his weight on his young shoulders. If it weren't for him, Griffin wouldn't have made it this far.

"Ready as I'll ever be." A coughing fit wracked his lungs.

"Hold on a little longer, Griff. We'll find Shauna, and she'll make you all better."

"Thanks buddy," Griffin wheezed. "Time to go home." Together they hobbled forward, through the barrier that would make all those he loved forget about him all over again.

He could feel the magic wash over him. Cold, icy tendrils trickled through his veins, searching for magic he didn't have, drawing out the last of his energy.

They were already waiting for him. Three muscular,

bearded soldiers paced the barren land at the entrance of the prison realm, their ivory tusks jutting from their angular jaws.

Black spots danced in front of Griffin's eyes as they approached. "Gullie, don't let them catch you. Go find Hector." Griffin took a step toward the soldiers and collapsed face first onto the dry dusty ground.

Someone splashed water on Griffin's face.

His lids slid open, and he blinked the water from his eyes. Torchlight greeted him, along with the sounds of raucous laughter. Shaking his head, he realized that was the only part of his body he could move. His arms and legs were bound to a whipping post.

It all came back to him then. He was home. Back in Myrkur where he couldn't help but think he belonged.

Gulliver? He looked around, not seeing the boy anywhere. He could only hope the soldiers hadn't caught him after Griffin passed out. With any luck, he was a long way away from here where Hector and their friends from Fela were taking good care of him. Not that he'd ever known Gulliver to follow instructions.

"Ah, he's awake." A familiar voice sent a wave of revulsion through him. "Welcome home, young Griffin."

"Egan." Griffin managed to answer with a firm voice, though he felt as if the only thing keeping him upright were the ropes binding him to the whipping post.

"You forget your manners, Griff." The king's bushy brows arched at him. "I'll let it slide this time. I hear you've been through quite an ordeal."

That was when Griffin saw her. Riona stood behind the king seated at the high table. She wore an icy expression. Nothing of the woman he'd come to know was reflected in her countenance. She stood like a rock, not meeting his gaze.

He wasn't surprised to find his Uncle Callum seated at the king's table, eating his finest food and drinking the sour wine Egan boasted was the best in the land. It probably was, but that wasn't saying much.

Griffin was shocked to see his mother seated opposite Callum. He gave her a wary look but didn't speak. He couldn't fathom what she was up to, but her presence here felt like a betrayal.

"You've failed, Griffin." Egan sliced into a ham, serving himself and his guests from the same knife he used to eat his own food. The man was even more vile than he remembered. "I sent you through the barrier to collect what information I needed to destroy the magic keeping Myrkur in the dark, and you did not deliver."

"I never wavered, my king." The words were like ash in his mouth. "I nearly had it."

"Nearly." Egan stuffed a slice of ham into his mouth. "Nearly is not good enough, my boy. Your uncle has brought me all that I need, so what use do you serve me now?"

"Callum will never give you what you want. You would be wise not to trust him."

"Now is that any way to talk to your uncle?" Callum shared a scathing look with the king.

"You've betrayed everyone who ever had the misfortune to call you family." Griffin erupted into a coughing fit. Sweat trickled down his brow. He was dying and Egan knew it. "What do you want, Egan?" He was so tired, he just wanted an end to this torture.

"My healers tell me you have the sickness," Egan said. "Your magic is unbalanced. Supposedly, all you need is the full use of your magic, and all will be well again. Yet, I cannot return your magic to you until I know I can trust you. You see what a conundrum that is, don't you?"

"Uncle Griff!" A child's voice commanded his attention away from the high table. "Don't listen to him. He's a bad man!"

"Tia, Toby. Are you okay?" Griffin tried to get a good look at them, but they were just out of his line of sight. He could tell they were in some kind of cage on display for the whole court watching the proceedings with glee.

"We're okay, Uncle Griff," Toby called in a weary voice.

"Take good care of each other, kids. No matter what happens, that's your greatest strength." He hoped they were wise enough to understand what he was saying. No matter what, they needed to work together and not let the unique-ness of their magic tear them apart like it had for the twins who'd come before them.

"Uncle Griff." Egan chuckled and Callum joined him in a good laugh at Griffin's expense. "How adorable." Egan returned to his wine, draining his cup of the dark red, bitter wine he thought was the sweetest vintage.

"More wine, Callum?" Egan offered.

"Please." Callum barely concealed his grimace. He was clearly disgusted by the Dark Fae king with his scraggly beard, beady black eyes and ivory tusks. Not to mention his poor hygiene and even worse table manners. He was a king unlike any his uncle might have seen. Even Enis sat with a rough linen napkin over her nose to block out the malodorous scents wafting through the dining hall.

Griffin managed a wry smile. Egan thought he was an

impressive king, trotting out his best food and wine to two Light Fae who'd spent their lives with luxuries Egan couldn't even imagine. They were appalled, and he had no idea.

"Where are Shauna and Nessa?" Griffin asked, fearing the worst. If Egan considered him a failure, they likely would pay the price.

"It seems they are unwell. Suffering from the plague sweeping through the villages. I can't imagine they will survive it, as weak as they are from the work they've been doing."

Griffin fought against his restraints. If he'd failed them so miserably, the only thing he wanted now was to take Egan with him when he died.

"Your Majesty, we've found the boy," a voice as familiar as his own stirred hope in Griffin's chest.

"Excellent work, Hector. Griffin, I believe you know my loyal servant of Fela." Egan's smile spread wide across his face.

Hector was once Griffin's closest friend other than Shauna. He was as close as a brother. But Hector was an indentured now, and he held a squirming Gulliver in his arms.

Many of the fae who'd ever meant anything to him were caught up in Egan's clutches now. Griffin had thought he could save them all. What an arrogant fool he'd been. He'd allowed himself to reach for power, only to fall flat on his face … again.

No, this time it wasn't a throne he'd reached for. It was worse. This time he'd tried to become the savior of all those innocent souls trapped in Myrkur. And he'd failed every single one of them. Doomed himself and everyone he loved to a terrible fate.

CHAPTER TWENTY

Riona

Griffin hated her.

That much was apparent every time Riona looked into his eyes, trying to say words she couldn't voice with Egan watching her every move.

"Sire, perhaps we should remove Griffin from the post."

Egan's hard eyes landed on her. They'd finished their meal, and Callum left to take the twins to their room while Hector carried Gulliver off to the cells. She'd never forget that image. Hector was supposed to be Griffin's friend. But then again, wasn't she supposed to be his friend too?

Egan, Riona, and Enis now stared at the auburn-haired Iskaltian prince who could only lift his head to skewer Riona with the betrayal in his eyes.

"Perhaps you've gotten too close to this man on your mission." His eyes narrowed. "A mission you didn't complete.

Tell me, Riona, why shouldn't I tie you up next to our prince here?"

"No, Majesty." She dipped her head in response. "I am sorry. I only meant that he is weak, and you don't wish to kill him."

Enis stepped forward. "She is right. It isn't time to kill him yet."

The *yet* was the problem.

Egan stared at Griffin, and Riona could only imagine what he wanted to do to him. "Okay. I'll play by your rules for now, ladies. Enis, you may untie your son and take him down to the cells. But he will pay for his failures. Publicly. And soon." He turned toward the door. "When you are finished, Enis, come to my chambers. Riona, come with me."

She cast one final look at Griffin. As his mother untied him, he collapsed to the floor.

"Riona!" Egan stomped a foot against the ground.

She had no choice but to follow him through the palace Riona grew up in, the one she'd called home in the years after her village was massacred.

Egan sighed once they were alone in the safety of his private sitting room. He collapsed onto the black settee in front of the fireplace and rubbed his eyes.

Riona used to love times like these when it was just the two of them, when he brought her in to his confidence. She took her usual place by the fire that was never allowed to go out. Without even considering her actions, she reached for the wooden box on the mantel and began to pack his pipe.

"Griffin is really sick, isn't he?" Egan's king act faded away, leaving only the man who'd been like a father in so many ways.

Riona nodded, stretching her feet toward the hearth.

"He's been ill for a while now. I wrote to you about it. Have the others with the sickness recovered?"

"One has."

Only one? Those weren't good odds.

He rubbed his chin. "A young man from Griffin's village. We had word he'd come down with the sickness after a portion of his magic was returned, but last week, he was part of a force that tried to burn their way in to Kvek's stronghold.

"Kvek?" There was only one way into the fortress. The river. Burning their way in wouldn't have worked.

Egan nodded. "We don't think they meant to take it. There have been raids all over Myrkur while you've been gone. I've had to send my soldiers to protect the chieftains."

That was a mistake. If Riona had been here, she'd have told him sending the king's forces would only sow more unrest in the villages. The people weren't happy as they starved and suffered under constant taxes and raids.

She pictured Fela and the destruction there. "Egan." She dropped the formalities as she'd always done when speaking with him alone. "Tell me, how close are you to bringing down the magic?" She handed him his pipe.

He let out a harsh laugh before he took a puff of his pipe. "The book is useless. Callum and I have tried to read parts of it. I thought it would help as much as the pages I had—"

"You had pages from the book?" He'd never shown her, but it was confirmation of what she'd suspected.

"I am Dark Fae, Riona. Just like you, I have no magic. But the pages I have … they taught me how to direct magic from the wall back to the fae it belonged to originally."

So, that was how he'd returned Griffin's portal magic to him. They were right.

Egan stood and rounded the settee to reach a secret compartment in the wall. Riona was the only fae who knew it was there. He yanked it open and pulled out a thick leather tome. Walking back toward Riona, he dropped it to the floor at her feet. "Useless. May as well throw it in the flames."

Only useless as long as he couldn't read it. "Callum brought no answers?"

He shook his head. "He's been here for weeks, but all he brought was this book and two brats who say they know nothing of it."

A knock sounded at the door, and Egan answered it, letting Enis and Callum in.

Riona reached forward and lifted the heavy book into her lap. How could a book hold so much power? Did Egan even know what it contained?

Enis walked toward her as if drawn to the book. "May I?"

Riona shrugged and let Enis take it from her. This book had changed everything in Riona's life. She now knew how wonderful life could be outside Myrkur, how the sun felt warming her skin. The taste of really good food. A full belly. Sweet wine and silk sheets. Her eyes were opened to the endless possibilities that lay beyond the borders of the only home she'd ever known. Could she give that up and go back to her former life? Leave it all behind?

Leave Griffin behind?

Gulliver?

If she had a choice, she'd free Gulliver from the cells and take him and Griffin far from this place, all the way to the sea where her ancestors once ruled. They didn't need magic if it only caused conflict.

Enis sat on the floor, running a hand across the broken leather. "I barely had the chance to examine it before Callum arrived." She shot Callum a scathing look before returning to the book.

Egan grunted. "Don't waste your time. It's written in some language that probably doesn't exist anymore. The magic in that book is useless."

Enis shook her head. "No, not useless. Just incredibly ... specific."

"What do you mean?" Riona barely knew this woman. On their ride from Iskalt, she hadn't revealed her motivations for betraying her children. But then, Riona hadn't either.

"The pages will open only to those they are meant for. Otherwise the language will appear as unreadable symbols."

A growl sounded in Egan's throat. "Speak plainly, woman."

Enis opened the book and flipped through the pages, landing on one with a hand drawn image of the instrument Riona had all but forgotten was in her bag.

Below that were a series of symbols. Riona leaned forward to stare down at the book as the symbols changed and morphed into lines of musical notes.

"What do you see here, your Majesty?" Enis lifted the book to show him.

Egan's brow furrowed. "Nonsense. How are we to know what those scribbles mean?"

"*We* aren't. Only Riona is. Because this page relates to her. Riona, what do you see?"

"Musical notes." She could practically hear the song in her mind.

Enis smiled, her eyes alight with ambition. "You see? You must find the parts that pertain to you. The information you seek is in this book, your Highness. You just need to find the people who can decipher it. The twins will be vital to the interpretation of much of this book since they have the magic of all three realms. Though it may be some time before they will be able to learn all this book has to teach them." She thumbed through the pages, her eyes scanning for those that might pertain to her.

Callum remained quiet, but his dark eyes never left the book. "Lord Egan, we need to see what the twins can read of this book."

Enis crossed her arms. "You mean to say you've had my grandchildren and the book all this time, but you haven't yet asked them to interpret it?"

He grimaced, his expression darkening.

Oh. Riona got it now. "They couldn't? You already tried."

"We went through every page." Callum sighed. "Nothing."

"Everyone out." Egan's words were so quiet they almost didn't hear him.

"What?" Enis shared a confused look with Callum, but Riona knew Egan's tempers more than most. She recognized a king ready to explode.

Red crept up Egan's neck. "You are all useless to me. I asked for a way to bring down the barrier magic, and you bring me a book I can't even read? Get. Out. Before I have you all whipped for wasting my time."

The three of them scrambled toward the door.

"Riona?" Egan called her back. "Take the damn book. But do not let it out of your sight."

Riona lifted the heavy book, feeling like she carried all the hopes of magic wielders everywhere.

Callum was gone by the time she stepped into the hall, but Enis leaned against the wall. She kicked away when she saw Riona with the book.

Enis held her arms out for it, but Riona shook her head. It

was like the book called to her, not wanting her to let go now that she had it.

There were so many things Riona needed to do. Help Griffin. Find Hector and figure out why he'd brought Gulliver to the king. Free Gulliver and the twins.

Instead, she listened to the book, hearing its whispers grow louder and louder until it was all she could hear.

Not wanting to take the book into the barracks, she headed for Enis' room. She couldn't trust the woman when it came to Griffin, or the kids, but the book ... she'd never harm the book. Riona could see it in her eyes. These spells were the only thing that mattered to the woman.

Riona pushed open the door to Enis' room. It was much smaller than Egan's, with the sitting area and bedroom all one open space. Enis shut the door as Riona threw the book on the bed and backed away.

"How could you do it?" Riona hugged her arms across her chest. "Betray your family for a book."

Enis sighed. "If I remember correctly, you also betrayed them."

"No. I returned to Myrkur to save them. To make sure Griffin's people didn't suffer upon his return."

"And yet, you stood at Egan's side today. I know you wish for loyalties to remain clear, but life is more complicated than that."

"Why can I read the music?"

"Oh, I suspect there's a great deal you can read." She pointed to the book. "Every answer you've ever wanted is in this book. The purpose of your tattoos. The reason your wings grow darker each day. The truth to the prison magic. All you have to do is look."

Riona backed away until she hit the settee. "I … no." It was all in front of her, this path she'd never asked for.

Enis' eyes changed from blue to black the longer she stared at the book she'd spent so long trying to steal.

The whispers entered Riona's mind again, and she clutched the sides of her head. "I can't … make it stop." Her tattoos heated, sending bolts of electricity through her as they moved along her skin. Pain speared through her head. She couldn't do it, couldn't open the book.

Enis' eyes cleared as she looked to Riona. "I can save Griffin."

"What?" Her heart thundered against her ribs.

Enis moved to sit beside her and flipped through the pages before finding the one that spoke to her. "Many of the spells in this book are Sorcha's. But a few are from my ancestor, Grainne O'Rourke, her twin. I can see her spells. They call to me like the book calls to you. And this one … has the power to restore magic."

"Egan has a page that has taught him to do that," Riona said.

"He is simply funneling pieces of magic from the barrier to the one who owns it. The spell he is using is very limited. The only real useful aspect of it is that it allows him to control those he's forged a magical connection with—even if they didn't have magic before. That is why people are getting sick. Abilities like Griffin's portal magic need something to hold on to—his root magic—Iskalt magic. Without it, he will die. And very soon. Others—like you—I suspect, he can't give magic to you, but he can form a magical connection that causes pain. He uses that to control those under him."

Riona thought to the times she'd felt Egan tugging on her, the pain in her head. Had he been using these spells?

Enis scanned the page in front of her. "The amazing thing about much of this book is one doesn't need Fargelsian magic to wield its power, only the words. This spell here is different. This is restorative magic. But ... I need Tia to do it. I don't know why the twins lied to Callum, but they have to be able to read most of this book. The barrier takes magic from Light Fae, but if I'm right, we can use this spell to fully restore it."

"You're forgetting one thing, Enis." Riona moved to sit beside her on the bed. "No one has magic here in Myrkur. Not even Tia, and I doubt Egan will return her magic in full. I don't even know if he can if his spell is as limited as you say it is. But if you can help Griffin..."

Seeing Griffin tied up, barely able to move of his own accord was an image Riona would never forget. "We have to convince the twins to help." Not only that, but they had to do it without Egan or Callum's knowledge.

Enis smiled. "Leave the details to me. I have a plan, but first, I must speak with Callum. Don't leave this room. There are people who would kill you for this book." With those words, she rushed into the hall.

Once the door shut behind her, Riona climbed up onto the bed. "Okay, whispering book. You have me here. What is it you want to show me?" A page flipped of its own accord and then another. Riona watched with wide eyes as the book came to life, stopping at a page at the back. "What's this?"

She leaned closer. The O'Rourke family tree. Riona read the text under the title explaining how the pages updated every time a new descendent was born—only the most direct descendants were recorded here. "That's kind of creepy." Yet, she couldn't take her eyes from the tree. Enis and her family were descended from Sorcha's twin, Grainne, but they weren't of the royal lineage, so they weren't recorded. Riona traced her fingers down ancestors dating back a thousand years before reaching Brea O'Rourke-Cahill-O'Shea, daughter of Brandon O'Rourke and Faolan Cahill, queen of Eldur. Each of Brea's children were represented with vines connecting them to Lochlan.

Riona's breath caught in her lungs as they begged for more air. Her finger shook as she traced the vine from Tierney and Tobias O'Shea. "This isn't possible."

But she couldn't doubt the accuracy of the book.

The twins controlling the fate of everyone in Myrkur were the children of Griffin' O'Shea.

CHAPTER TWENTY-ONE

Griffin

The magical noose tugged at Griffin's neck as he followed Egan through the ranks of his soldiers preparing for battle. Experiencing the king's powerful hold for himself, he could almost understand Riona's betrayal. Almost.

Ogres and horned, hoofed Dark Fae fell in line as the king passed, while scaled Asrai fae took on their land forms to collaborate with the king's generals. A battalion of bat-winged Slyph flew overhead like a swarm of locusts.

"Even if the three kingdoms gather their armies once we've brought the borders down, they'll never match the might of the Dark Fae. Their magic tricks will be nothing against our brawn." Egan's barrel chest puffed up. "They won't know what hit them."

"It is true, the sight of such an army will shake them to their core, your Majesty." Griffin stood, defeated. He was too weak to act. Too weak to think. Egan gave him just enough magic to keep him alive, so he would get a front-row seat to the destruction of the Light Fae. Only, Egan truly had no idea what he was up against. He thought he understood magic when he'd never really seen it at work. He expected three separate armies. The weaker Fargelsians who had use of their magic at all times. The stronger Eldurians who had use of their magic during the day, and the Iskaltians with their night magic.

Egan's army was a fierce horde of brute strength, and they wouldn't go down without a fight. But the Light Fae were united in a way they never had been before, and at the helm of their collective massive army, were the strongest rulers the lands had ever known. They would defeat Egan with their magic. But at what cost?

And it was all Griffin's fault. He'd failed to find a way to free the innocents of Myrkur and remove the tools Egan now had in his possession—Griffin's own niece and nephew.

Egan tugged his leash, spurring Griffin to follow him as he regaled him with the feats of his army and his own prowess as a mighty ruler.

"What of their magic?" Griffin said in a disinterested voice.

"What magic?" Egan stared proudly at the thousands of Asrai soldiers—creatures of the sea come to do battle on land —with their vicious claws and teeth and scales that gleamed like armor in the torchlight.

"Make no mistake, the three kingdoms will come at you with the full force of their magic."

"What is magic against might?" Egan clapped him on the shoulder with a laugh. "We will come at them with the stuff of their worst nightmares. They will run at the very sight of the Asrai, and then my Slyph will pick them off like carrion."

"And what about the sun?" Griffin asked. The sunlight would blind them, just as it had with Riona.

"My soldiers are used to patrolling the border. They know of sunlight."

Griffin nodded. He had no doubt Egan would fail in his arrogance and willful ignorance. "Clearly, you have thought of everything, my Lord," Griffin murmured with disdain Egan was too distracted to notice. "So what need do you have of me?"

Egan shrugged. "Leverage. You and those kids." His laughter sent him into a coughing fit.

"Which you wouldn't have without Callum. Who wouldn't be here if I hadn't gone into Iskalt and led him to the information he needed to gather the book and the twins." Creative truths.

"So you're saying you didn't fail me?" Egan's voice took on a harder edge.

"My mission might not have been a success, but it wasn't a failure either." Griffin turned toward the king of Myrkur. "The fact that my uncle walked into the prison realm with everything you needed doesn't mean I failed. It means you shouldn't trust him."

"And I should trust you instead?" Egan frowned. "Callum is in my pocket. We're two of a kind. He wants power. I shall give him Iskalt once I defeat your brother."

Griffin couldn't hold back his own laughter, which turned into a bout of coughing. Spitting blood on the brown grass at his feet, Griffin took a deep breath. "Callum won't be satisfied with that."

"You let me handle your uncle. I've plied him with my finest rooms and my best wine. He's dined on the riches of Myrkur. He's even developed a liking for Dark Fae women."

Egan laughed. "He is my creature now. One I won't turn my back on."

"You truly have thought of everything, your Highness." Griffin shook his head, eager to see Egan hang himself with a noose of his own making.

"Indeed, I have." Egan turned his attention back to his soldiers. "Once Enis and those kids finish reading the book, we'll bring that barrier down. And then we march."

"With your bravest, most loyal servant at your side." The words burned like acid in his mouth.

"Riona's faith isn't what it once was." Egan sighed with something that sounded like deep regret. "I've gifted her to Callum. She will come back to me in time, but she needs to be reminded who and what she is. When Callum proves no longer useful, she will kill him."

"You did what?" Griffin choked on the tightening of the noose that seemed to grip his heart and lungs like a vise.

Egan laughed at the look of horror on Griffin's face. "She is my servant, to do with as I choose. She always has been and always will be. Now leave me, O'Shea. I have things to do."

The knot around Griffin's throat loosened, and he retreated into the castle. The king's men knew not to let him stray outside Egan's walls, but otherwise left him alone.

Griffin made his way to Riona's rooms, but she wasn't there. He hadn't spoken to her since he arrived back in Myrkur. Not since the sting of her betrayal hit him so hard. That she'd left him in Iskalt still hurt. But she didn't deserve to be traded like she meant nothing.

Griffin was almost running by the time he reached Callum's rooms. Though they may have been the finest Egan had to offer, they paled in comparison to what the former king would call luxurious.

The door stood ajar, but it was silent inside the room.

"Riona?" He pushed the door open, just waiting for Egan's magical tug that would send him back to his own pitiful rooms near the dungeons where Gulliver remained a prisoner beyond his reach.

A muffled sound of outrage greeted him in the dim light of the large, sparse room.

The furnishings were quite fine—for Myrkur. Clean and simple, but well made. The heavy four-poster bedframe lay in shambles on the floor, and the white linen bed curtains meant to billow in the breeze from the open windows, were wrapped around Callum O'Shea, binding him to the bed. A vibrant bruise marred his eye, and he was bleeding from various injuries, though a ball of fabric acting as a gag kept him quiet.

Riona sat in the lone chair by the window. Fury shone in her eyes.

"I saved him for you if you'd like to do the honors." She finally acknowledged Griffin. "I figured the least he deserved was a few more hours to fear his death."

"Did he touch you?" Griffin's voice came out rough.

"He thought to try, but he didn't get very far."

"Good for you." Griffin's mouth lifted in a hesitant smile.

"Griffin, I…" Riona trailed off like she was uncertain how to begin.

Griffin shook his head. A thousand thoughts passed through his mind, but the right words failed him.

Riona held a jeweled dagger clutched in her hands. Nothing so fine had ever belonged to Egan. She must have taken it from his uncle. He pried the knife from her blood-stained hands, letting his palm trace the furious lines of her face for a moment. He may have imagined it, but for a second she seemed to relax at his touch.

Turning to his uncle, Griffin gripped the knife and took a step toward the remains of the bed. From the bruises across his body, Riona must have thrown him against the heavy wooden bedposts as thick as young tree trunks.

Callum fought against his restraints, crying out in alarm as Griffin approached. He managed to shift the rag in his mouth, spitting it out as he took a deep breath.

"You're going to kill me, just like that, Nephew? Have your woman do the fighting and gut me like a coward?"

"She doesn't belong to me, or anyone else." Griffin scowled at the man he hardly knew. The man who was responsible for the path his life had taken when he was just a child.

"Get on with it, then." Callum sighed. "I can't take another moment in this hellhole with that absurd man who dares to call himself a king."

Griffin gripped the dagger and bent toward his uncle, sawing through the linens that bound him. "Leave." Griffin pointed toward the door. "I don't care where you go, but I never want to see your face again." Griffin's shoulders fell.

Callum scrambled from the shambles of the bed, adjusting his clothes until he found his dignity once again.

"You are as much as fool as your father," Callum spat.

Griffin smiled. "That is the highest compliment anyone's ever paid me."

"I take that back. There is much of me in you, Griffin." Callum's eyes darkened with menace. "Both second sons who would have made better kings than our brothers. Both with the thirst for power. Perhaps I should have kept you and raised you as my own."

"We are nothing alike," Griffin spat. "I love my brother and his family. I would never take what belongs to him."

Callum laughed in his face. "You really don't know, do you?"

"Callum, don't." Riona rushed forward.

Callum's laughter erupted, his eyes shining with tears of mirth. "The mighty Queen Brea's magical twins." Callum laid a hand on Griffin's shoulder. "They're O'Shea brats for certain, but they're not your brother's gets." His triumphant grin split his face. "They're yours." Callum's eyes widened, startled as he looked down to see the dagger protruding from his belly.

Griffin pulled back before plunging the dagger into his uncle a second time. "The first one was for me. That one is for my brother and father, and all of Iskalt, you worthless swine." He shoved Callum back on the bed.

Dropping the knife, Griffin left Riona staring at his retreat.

CHAPTER TWENTY-TWO

Griffin

"Where is Gulliver?" Griffin sat stiffly beside Egan at his table in the dining hall. He had little appetite with his waning health. If he had a choice, he would still be in his bed, but Egan's magic pulled him from the relative warmth and comfort he found there and forced him to join the king's court.

"The boy has taken up residence in my dungeons. Considering Shauna and the girl conveniently disappeared from the kitchens upon your return, your boy will take their place."

"I thought you said they were working in the mines." Griffin stared at the king.

"Mines, kitchens, what does it matter? They are gone."

"What do you intend to do with Gulliver?"

"If you please me in the coming battles, I may send him to work in the mines instead of the brothels. I'm told he has a talent for finding valuable things. Perhaps he will earn his keep."

"I haven't the strength to stand." Griffin sighed. "What makes you think I will be of any use to you?"

"You found the strength to kill your uncle." Egan raised a bushy brow at him. "My men discovered his stinking corpse this morning."

"It was I, my Lord." Riona's voice rang out across the din of the feasting soldiers seated below the king's dais. Riona captured Egan's gaze, making her way slowly, almost seductively, through the throng of staring men and women. "I found him rather useless, your Majesty." She took the steps up to the dais to his side.

Egan looked to her with pride in his eyes.

Dressed in fresh leathers, and her colorful tattoos drifting lazily across her skin, she looked every inch the warrior Griffin knew she was. With her increasingly shadowed wings fanned out behind her—the remaining white shining like a beacon, she was glorious.

"Your wings?" Egan reached out to touch the dark shadows along the edges of her diaphanous wings.

Griffin thought he saw her wince at his touch, but she recovered quickly, smiling for the king she seemed to adore. He couldn't stomach the look in her eyes.

"It is nothing, your Majesty." Riona folded her wings in, coming to stand beside Egan, completely ignoring Griffin. "I know I must accept my punishment for killing your man." She cast her eyes down.

Egan took her hand, chuckling. "You did me a favor, my dear. Callum O'Shea was baggage I no longer need. We have the twins, the book, and Enis is hard at work interpreting it. What need have we of a fool like Callum who couldn't seem to handle the prize I gave him." Egan's smile turned Griffin's stomach. "Besides, we have our own O'Shea here to open portals when we've need of them." Egan slapped Griffin's shoulder.

"I'm afraid he won't be opening any portals any time soon." Riona gave a hearty laugh. "Not without the use of his magic in full. He too, is useless. Though, as you say, I suppose we'll need him, eventually. As I told you, there are marvelous things to be had in the human world. Things you will no doubt want access to when the time comes." Riona bumped her hip against Egan's throne-like chair.

"One thing at a time, dear one." Egan joined her laughter. "One thing at a time."

"The humans have the best wine." Riona flashed her dark eyes toward Griffin, a perfect sneer on her face. "Rich and sweet. Perhaps you can keep this O'Shea strong enough to travel when you've need of him."

Without asking for the king's leave, Griffin stumbled to his feet and fled the dining hall to the raucous laughter of those Egan favored.

Griffin's mind reeled with thoughts of Riona. Of his uncle's warm blood on his hands, and the last word's he'd spoken.

Lies. It had to be lies. A final cruel joke. The twins couldn't be his. It wasn't possible.

But it was. They were ten years old. Not eight like he'd originally thought. Griffin had been gone for a bit over ten years. The math worked. Brea woke up one day and forgot she'd had another husband once. One she'd loved because the marriage bond made it so. He'd fooled himself into thinking that was enough, that one day she'd love him truly. But then she discovered she was pregnant. Naturally she would believe Lochlan to be the father. She would have no reason to think otherwise.

His gut churned in horror. It was bad enough that he'd let their sham of a marriage happen in the first place. Even worse, that he'd pretended for a short while that they were happy. But that there were now children involved? The possibility that he could be Tia and Toby's father ... it was heartbreaking to even consider it. That he'd missed their whole lives.

And the thought of telling Brea ... Lochlan. Griffin shook his head. They could never know. He wouldn't be responsible for hurting their family like that.

"Stop." Two of the king's guards blocked his path.

"I need to see them." Griffin gathered all the strength he had, desperate to see the twins. To search their faces for a trace of his own.

"They are resting. They spent the morning working with Lady Enis."

Griffin snorted in disgust. He could only imagine how hard his mother had driven the children—her own grandchildren—to find the magic she sought to learn from the book. That was all she cared about. Power. He supposed that was where he got his own thirst for power from.

Griffin searched his pockets, pulling a coin purse from his pocket. "Will this buy me a moment with them?" He handed the gold to the men who likely hadn't seen such riches in all their lives.

Together, they nodded, stepping aside and pocketing the gold without further thought.

Griffin charged into the room Tia and Toby shared. He heard sniffles coming from the bed where they lay hugging each other for comfort.

"Uncle Griff?" Tia sat up, wiping her eyes. "Is that you?"

Griffin crossed the room to sit between them, pulling them into his arms. "Yes, it's me." He ruffled the soft silky hair on their heads, one strawberry blond and the other a dark brown like Brea's.

"We're going to get you home." He tried to give them all the comfort he could. "I promised your mother and father I'd bring you back to them."

"I miss Papa." Tia sniffed. "And Mama."

"Of course, you do." Griffin held them tight, surprised by the severity of how much he wanted it to be true. That something so beautiful and good could have come from the travesty of his marriage to Brea.

He would never and could never take the place of Lochlan in their hearts. To the twins, he would always be Uncle Griff.

But he had to know. Somehow, he had to make it through all of this and make good on his promises to deliver Tia and Toby safely into the arms of their parents. And then he would find a way to discover if his uncle's parting words were more than just a cruel joke.

"I knew you'd come," Tia whispered, looking up at him with such trust. "Just like my dreams. You came for me."

He cupped her delicate cheek. "You knew I'd choose the right side in this before even I did." The words were mostly to himself, but Tia offered him a soft smile.

"Griffin, you can't be here." Riona's familiar voice brought him out of his blissful, too short moment with his brother's children. No matter what happened or what he discovered, he had to think of them that way.

Tia and Toby had been almost asleep when he found

them, exhausted from their efforts to read the book that held the key to their escape from the prison realm.

Without a word to Riona, he tucked them into the large bed and kissed their foreheads. "I'll be back soon." He just had to lay eyes on them, just once, to know they were okay. Reluctantly, he turned to follow Riona from the room.

Once they were outside, crossing the empty courtyard, Riona slowed her pace to match his. "We have to talk."

She was more herself without the eyes and ears of the castle on her. This was the Riona he knew. The one he wanted to pull into his arms and erase the wide gulf standing between them. But she'd betrayed him right when he'd needed her the most.

Griffin's steps faltered as a realization struck him. He knew how Brea must have felt when he was the one who'd done the betraying. How much it must have hurt her to have someone she cared for turn against her when she'd had no one else to depend on.

For once, he was truly grateful Brea couldn't remember him.

CHAPTER TWENTY-THREE

Riona

Riona glanced back over her shoulder to the guards standing along the outer walls of the palace. They kept their eyes on those entering the palace, not leaving it, but she knew the Slyph patrolled the skies.

She'd never noticed how many guards Egan employed. Even a few Light Fae walked the grounds from the palace to the slums beyond.

"Are they indentured?" Griffin asked.

Riona had expected another question first, but she understood if he wasn't ready. "No, Griff. The guards come here of their own volition, choosing to work for the king. Indentured fae become servants, or take up roles as the king sees fit, others are sent to the mines, or worst, cast out as useless."

"We didn't know." He rubbed the back of his neck. "In Fela, we stayed out of the king's way, assuming the troops Egan sent to terrorize the villages and collect taxes were the worst of it. We knew about the mines … but we just lived our lives, trying to keep each other going in our small corner of Myrkur." His shoulders stiffened as if he just remembered who he was talking to.

Riona sighed. She was so tired of playing this game, of trying to please a king who was never satisfied, one who'd unleash his army to destroy all the beauty Riona witnessed in the three kingdoms.

Which was why she was still here, why she'd betrayed Griffin. Egan needed to be stopped, and she wanted to be the one to do it.

Griffin's steps slowed as they reached the barracks. "Riona, whatever you need to say to me better be good because I can barely stand."

"We're almost there." She opened the door to the barracks and led Griffin to a room at the back. Dark Fae watched in curiosity. They'd probably tell Egan of this rendezvous, but Egan wouldn't care as long as he still believed she was loyal to him.

What were his words when he'd found out she killed Callum? Oh right, "Now you have to seduce the other O'Shea." He wanted information on the three kingdoms and their armies. Information he believed only Griffin could give.

Riona shut the door to her small room, so different from the suites she'd stayed in on her trip through the human and fae realms. A single bed sat along one wall with a short set of drawers for her few belongings.

"This is where you live?" Griffin eyed the cramped space.

"I don't need much." She pushed past him. "For now, we can speak in private here."

The door opened again, and Hector slipped into the room before closing it behind him.

Griffin looked from Riona to Hector. "What's going on?"

Riona took his arm and led him to the bed. "You look like death. Sit down."

Griffin took care lowering himself. "Hector..."

Hector grinned. "Bet you didn't expect to see me here?"

Griffin's eyes hardened. "You ... both of you betrayed me? Why am I here?"

They shared a look before Hector gave a short nod. "It was Gulliver's idea."

Griffin's hands clenched. "What was his idea?"

"For me to bring him here as a prisoner. While you've been gone, I became one of the king's men. The king wanted Gulliver, but I didn't want to let anyone else find him. I tried to hide him, to send him with Shauna and Nessa, but he wouldn't go. Not without you. Seems to think you need him to stay close. I have loyal soldiers watching over Gullie. He is safe."

"You mentioned Shauna and Nessa." He sucked in a breath. "They're safe?"

"They are." Hector put a hand on Griffin's shoulder. "You have your friend here to thank for that."

Griffin lifted his gaze to Riona's, a tear escaping the corner of his eye. All these months Griffin worried about the two girls, and now they were free. But Gulliver was in more danger than ever.

"You helped them?" Griffin's voice was small.

Riona hugged her arms across her chest. "I only got them out of the palace. Hector did the rest."

Hector sat on the bed next to him. "You've been gone a while, Griff, and to be honest, none of us knew if you were coming back. So, all this time, I've been thinking about what you would do to save our people. We have a network now." Excitement shone in his eyes. "We're focused on freeing indentured and Dark Fae who wanted to escape the army. It's the first time the villages and the king's own have worked together."

Exhaustion weighed on Griffin, but it wasn't natural, he knew that. The bits of magic keeping him alive weren't enough.

"Why am I here?" Griffin hung his head. "So you two can tell me you were only playing at betrayal?"

Hector gave him a long look as if comparing the Griffin who left with the one who'd returned.

Riona saw both. She saw a defeated man who couldn't save anyone with the lack of his magic draining him.

"How is Sinead?" Griffin asked.

Riona recognized that name, but it took her a moment to recall why. Sinead was one of Egan's test subjects. He'd returned bits of her magic and watched as she weakened.

Hector sighed. "She's dead, Griff."

Riona snapped her eyes to Griffin's. If Sinead died of the illness, they needed to find a way to recover Griffin's full magic as soon as possible. She couldn't trust that Egan truly understood the magic he was using to keep Griffin alive.

Hector looked to the door. "I have to go. I'm on patrol tonight."

Griffin grunted a goodbye, and Hector stood. "Take care of him."

Riona only nodded as he walked out the door, leaving her alone with Griffin. She paced the small room in front of him, not knowing exactly how to start. Every hate-filled look he sent her cut deep into her core.

"You really saved them?" He lifted his head to look at her, vulnerability in his voice.

"I…" She stopped moving. "Yes. It was the first thing I did when I came back."

He nodded as if he was unable to muster a smile. "I'm so tired of this, Riona. Tired of feeling the life drain from me every moment. Tired of not knowing who to trust or who has betrayed me."

She sat on the bed beside him, her shoulder brushing his. "Me. You can trust me."

"Can I?" He rubbed his eyes. "You left me, Riona."

"I needed Egan to think I was on his side. You, Griff, are important to him. I no longer am. If I wanted to survive this homecoming, I had to make it look like I betrayed you. That is what he expected me to do."

"And that makes sense logically. But Riona, I don't know what's happening in this palace. Shauna and Nessa escaped, but now Gulliver is trapped. The king doesn't trust me, yet he showed me the might of his army. Hector is somehow involved in everything. And you … I don't know what your goal is."

"My goal?"

"Why are you doing this? We'll probably fail. A lot. I don't know if we can bring the magic back."

"We don't need to." She slid to the floor, reaching under the bed. "I found out how Egan, a Dark Fae with no magic, is giving magic to Light Fae trapped here." She pulled a thick book from under the bed.

"Is that…?"

Riona nodded. "The book of power. It's the key. It will show you anything within its pages that pertain to you and your needs." She dropped the book on the bed.

Griffin ran a hand along the worn leather cover. They'd spent so long searching for it, and now here it was, hidden beneath a bed in the prison realm. "How did you get this?"

"Egan gave it to me to guard. In his ignorance, he sees the book as useless because he can't read it, but he doesn't trust Enis with it."

"Yeah," Griffin sighed. "Neither do I." His mother was not the same fae who'd left her kids behind. She spent too long chasing this book. Now, it was all she cared about. He pictured Tia pouring over the book as Enis watched with a steely gaze. "Is Tia okay?"

"She's scared. So is her brother. They know they're special, but right now, they think it's because they can read most of the book."

He didn't think he'd ever understand the Fargelsian twin magic, but the thought of Tia and Toby in the prison realm was a nightmare.

Riona could see a question in his eyes. He wanted to ask her about what Callum said of the kids' parentage, but something held him back.

"Griffin." Riona turned to him. "I need you to make a decision right now. I know I betrayed your trust and broke the friendship we had, but that's in the past. And our future is bleak. It consists of keeping people alive long enough to thwart the king. So, right now in the present, you need to decide if you trust me, if you can work with me." Her eyes pleaded with him. "I can't do this alone."

Griffin stared at her for a long moment as if trying to see past the issues separating them. A sigh rattled from his lips. "I do. I trust you. At least I want to. Just don't make me regret it again."

Riona suppressed a smile and nodded as he pulled the heavy book into her lap. "Enis thinks there is a page missing."

"Lots of the pages must be missing. Spells from this book are spread across the three kingdoms."

"Yes, but this page is important. It infuses magic into someone who has none. Enis says Nihal believed the book could give out magic. But then she saw Egan, and she believed it too. The twins have scoured the book looking for this particular spell, but it isn't there. We think he's using it to siphon magic from the barrier. It's how he returned your portal magic and how he's giving you bits of it now to keep you alive."

"If he's funneling magic from the barrier, does that mean he can bring it down on his own?"

"I don't think so. I believe whatever spell he's learned is extremely limited in its use."

Griffin ran a hand through his hair and looked away. "What Callum said to me before ... is that in the book?"

It had been a few nights since Riona discovered the family tree, but she'd looked at it again and again. It never changed.

She flipped open the book, going straight to the last pages where the O'Rourke Queen's lineage was depicted.

"I don't understand. This is Sorcha's family?"

"The Iskalt queen was descended from Sorcha, so are her children..."

Griffin traced the lines before finding Brea's name. Below her were each of her children. Two of them had lines leading to Lochlan. The other two ... "The twins really are mine." He couldn't take his eyes off the names. "How is this possible?"

"I think you'll find a great many things are possible with this magic. The only thing stronger than the wall around

Myrkur is this book." She closed the book and slid it toward Griffin. "We've discovered that each fae can only read the parts that relate to them. I wonder what the book will show you?" She lifted a brow in challenge.

Griffin stared at the worn cover.

"Go on. Open it."

Long fingers slid under the cover, flipping it open. And nothing happened. "Are you sure it's supposed to show me something?"

"Do you hear it? The whispers?"

His brow creased. "Whispers?" He closed the cover. "When I was trapped in my own portal, I heard them. And in Aghadoon outside the library. What did it show you before?"

Riona had been prepared for the question. Over the last few days, she'd gone through every bit of the book it let her read, but there was one part the book hadn't revealed to her, and she'd been too scared to ask the twins. She lifted a hand, watching the swirling marks dance across her skin. Nihal claimed the tattoos told of her destiny and that the book would help her discover what that was.

"Many things," she whispered, answering his question. "But not enough."

CHAPTER TWENTY-FOUR

Griffin

Egan wanted Riona to seduce Griffin, to learn the secrets he had lurking inside him. Secrets about the queens and kings of the three realms, about their readiness and willingness to fight.

What he didn't understand was the kingdoms were used to battles, ten years of peace didn't erase their history of war with Queen Regan. Only now, all three kingdoms would have a common enemy. In all the histories of the fae realms, Griffin couldn't recall a time when Fargelsi, Eldur, and Iskalt bonded together as a unified army. If Lochlan heeded the letter Griffin left for him, they'd be ready.

Griffin just had to make sure those he loved on this side of the barrier were ready as well. He rolled onto his side, his body aching from spending the night on Riona's floor. When he left in the morning, the entire palace would assume he'd slept in Riona's bed, that she'd obeyed Egan's command.

Noise sounded in the dark, and Griffin sat up, trying to make out the figure.

Riona.

She stood with her bare back to him, her wings folded in. Griffin averted his eyes as she finished getting dressed.

"You can look now." Her words weren't hard, only resigned. "Today is going to be awful." She slipped a tiny dagger into her boot before letting her trousers cover it. Another knife hung at her waist next to her fire opal encrusted broad sword.

"That sword was a gift from the king." It wasn't a question, only a statement. The opals gave it away. Opals the indentured were forced to mine.

Riona swept her dark hair up out of her face, tying it with a black ribbon that matched the tight vest she wore over a dark shirt.

Griffin's eyes went to the single window. It was always dark in Myrkur, but the position of the moon told him it was still very early. "Where are you headed?"

"I must join the king. We have some duties to attend too."

"Is part of me trusting you not asking questions?" He looked up at her from his bed on the floor.

A pained expression flashed across her face. "Not today, Griff. You don't want to ask what I'm doing today." She wouldn't look at him.

Griffin considered what evils she might do in the name of her king. "It's a village, isn't it? You're being sent to get the fae in the villages to fall back in line."

"No, Griff. Today's mission is about one fae, no other."

One fae. He pushed himself off the floor with all the strength he could muster. "What are you going to do to him?"

Gulliver.

Riona stopped with her hand on the door. "I'm going to try to save him, Griff. But Egan wants to control you, and he knows the way to do that is through that boy."

And the twins. Had Callum told Egan they were Griffin's children? Gulliver was capable of taking care of himself.

"Help him. Please." He had to choose. Gulliver or the twins. But it was never a real choice. He didn't have a way to help Gulliver. Griffin's heart cracked in two as he pictured Gulliver tied to the whipping post.

Riona nodded once, scooped the book into her arms and left.

Griffin's legs cried out with weakness, and he fell onto Riona's bed. How was he good to anyone in this state? He'd fail them all. Riona. Gulliver. Brea. The twins.

But he wouldn't stop trying, not while he lived. He pushed himself up again and yanked open the door. Rows of soldiers slept on cots in the main hall of the barracks.

He crept through the sleeping soldiers, reaching for the main door right as it opened. Griffin reeled back as Toby's frantic gaze found his. His ... son? Griffin couldn't unpack those emotions right now, not when they were all in so much danger.

"What are you doing here?"

Toby cast a nervous glance behind Griffin at the sleeping soldiers. "I ... well, you see..." He couldn't get the words out as his voice trembled.

Griffin grabbed him by the shirt and pulled him into the barracks. He held a finger to his lips as he led Toby back to Riona's quarters.

Once they closed the door, Toby released a long breath.

"You shouldn't be here, Toby."

The kid kept his eyes trained on his shoes. "Tia told me I had to come."

What was that girl thinking? "Weren't guards watching you?"

Toby shrugged. "During the day they sit outside our rooms laughing and rolling dice. But our night guards usually fall asleep, and it's so early I managed to get out before they woke."

Griffin lowered himself to the bed. "Toby—"

"You can barely walk," he blurted, crossing his arms.

"I won't begin to guess how you found me here, but—"

"Oh, the entire palace knows you stayed in Riona's room last night. Why do they care where you sleep?"

"It's not about sleeping," Griffin muttered. "I'll ask again, why have you come?"

"We waited for you to find us. In the human world. Tia kept promising me you'd come. That you were one of the good fae who'd rescue us."

"I tried, Toby." Griffin scrubbed a hand over his face. "We couldn't reach you. It wasn't until you crossed into the prison realm that I knew where you were."

"Is it true? That Mama and Papa have forgotten us?" His bottom lip quivered at the mention of his parents.

Griffin wanted to say no, to tell this kid his parents could never possibly forget him, but the lie stuck in his throat. Tears slid down Toby's reddened cheeks.

Griffin couldn't handle it anymore, he stood and pulled Toby into a hug, the kind of hug a parent gave. Toby trembled in his arms. "Are we ever going to see Iskalt again?"

Griffin pulled back and looked down at him. "I will do everything in my power to get you home."

Toby nodded, clinging to Griffin once more. Heat seared

from his touch, but Griffin couldn't pull away as if the magic held him in place as it flowed from Toby, the twin born without magic.

"Toby, what's happening?" Strength wound through him, wiping away months of weakness, of feeling ill. Griffin had almost forgotten what strength felt like.

Toby pulled away. "We found a way. In the spell book, we found an entire chapter on Sorcha's prison boundary and copied it before they took the book from us. We don't understand most of it yet, but Tia used those pages to figure out how to isolate one fae's magic from the barrier that took it. She hadn't tried yet to direct it in to a real fae. Enis called it restorative magic."

Griffin stepped back, magic tingling along his skin, a familiar power. His own. "You could have killed me."

"The sickness would have killed you."

"But how? You don't have magic."

Toby stepped back, dropping his gaze.

"Kid." Griffin leaned down toward him. "Answer my question."

A small smile appeared on his lips. "You sound just like Papa when he's irritated."

Griffin didn't know if the twins would ever learn the truth, but now wasn't the time for family reconciliations. "Toby..."

"No one knows we can do it. Not even Mama."

"Do what, exactly?"

Toby rubbed his hands up and down his arms. A nervous tic. "Mama taught us a long time ago how I could boost Tia's magic, but that we needed to be careful. She said we should always agree on how to use our magic together as a team. She said my magic is just as important as Tia's even though I can't do much with it on my own and most people would think I don't have magic at all. But that's not all we can do. Tia ... she can funnel her magic *through* me when I'm not at her side. The spell that returned your magic ... Tia performed it just now, but I was her conduit."

All the implications of this rolled through Griffin's mind. The two of them could do great things together or they could be used for great evil.

"Toby." Griffin put a hand on each shoulder and looked into his son's eyes. "You can't tell anyone what you've done here today, that I have my magic inside the prison realm."

Toby nodded. "We know how to keep secrets."

"Good, then let's get to the palace before the morning guards take their shifts."

Ten years without magic, and Griffin hadn't lost a beat. He reveled in the feeling of the Iskalt power swirling within him. But he couldn't let it free. Not yet. Even during the day in Myrkur, the moon provided him with the power. If this realm wasn't so terrible, it could be an Iskaltian's dream.

He hunched his shoulders, trying to seem like he was as close to death as they all assumed.

Toby stopped in front of a door and knocked. A crashing sound came from inside before Toby knocked again, looking sideways down the hall. "Tia, it's me."

A grating sound echoed in the hall as Tia unlocked the door and ushered them in. Griffin tried to find something of him in there, but both kids were so like Brea.

A teacart lay on its side with a rusted metal kettle leaking tea out on to the woven carpet that surrounded the bed. Griffin righted the cart.

The book sat atop the bed, open.

"Uncle Griff." Tia wrapped long arms around him.

He rested his chin on the top of her head. "Thank you."

She smiled as she looked up at him. "It was Toby's idea that we test what we found on you."

Even now while performing no magic, the power swirled in Tia's eyes, stronger than he'd ever seen before.

"Egan returned my magic to me a few days ago so I could translate the passages he wants from the book." She shrugged. "He underestimates me. I learned his spell the moment he murmured the words, and that told me what to look for in the book so I could help you."

Griffin released her. The girl was young, but she had a good head on her shoulders.

A grunt came from under the bed. "Blasted wood." Gulliver slid out, clutching the top of his head. "Griff." He grinned up at him.

Griffin crossed his arms. "What are you doing under there?"

"We thought it was the morning guards knocking on the door."

Reaching a hand down, Griffin pulled Gulliver up and yanked him into a crushing hug.

"You're kind of cutting off my air, Griff." Gulliver's tail poked at Griffin.

"Sorry." He backed away. "How did you escape?"

Another grin slid across his lips. "Well, that was the easy part. Hector threw me in a cell just like we'd planned, but after I'd already stolen the keys from one of the guards. I stayed there for a couple days so I didn't cast any suspicion on Hector, but last night I saw my chance. My guard was part of the network Hector has created. He pretended he didn't see me escaping the dungeon. Tia has been hiding me all night."

"Good. We can get word to Hector to extract you."

Gulliver's cat eyes narrowed. "If you think I'm leaving my friends to fight this battle, you don't know me at all. I won't go, and you can't make me."

Tia intertwined her finger's with Gulliver's. "It's okay, Gullie. You don't have to go." She glared at Griffin as if challenging him.

"Fine." Griffin pointed at Gulliver. "But—and this goes for all three of you—you are not to try anything dangerous. If you need help, you will come to me, no one else. Not Riona, not Enis, not Egan."

Tia's scowl deepened. "But Riona has been helping us. Want to see?"

He let her lead him to the book on the bed. "Riona already told me how the book shows you what you need, but I've tried. I'm not important in this story." The book showed him the family tree he couldn't stop thinking of, but nothing else.

"No, you don't get it. The book doesn't show *you* what you need to see. It shows your magic what it needs. So, when you had such a small amount of magic..."

"But Riona doesn't have magic."

Tia shook her head. "You're wrong. The book says all fae have magic. Every single one, even those like Toby. Most people say he doesn't have a lick of magic, but he does. It's just different. The Dark Fae can't perform spells or open portals, but their magic is in their nature. Their wings and horns and even tusks. You could say they're more magical than even the Light Fae."

Gulliver looked to Griffin. "Try it. Now that your magic has been returned."

Fear ripped through Griffin, but he inched closer to the four-poster bed. He ran a finger along the spine before opening the cover. The pages started flipping of their own accord, and he jumped back in surprise. When they stilled, he forced himself to look.

On the page were familiar symbols. They flickered and shifted across the page before text appeared beneath them. He'd seen these before. "Why am I seeing this?" It was a symbol translation, the kind that could tell Riona the destiny her tattoos spelled out.

Toby climbed up beside Tia, stopping short of taking her hand.

"You're important." Tia shrugged. "Not in the same way as us, but no less. This book ... the people here, everything and everyone is preparing. You talked to Callum back in Iskalt, leading to our kidnapping and finding the book. Then you saved your mother, and she ended up here. Gulliver says Riona used to be an enemy, but now she too is ready to choose the right side. The book speaks of a single fae who sets it all in motion and is key to getting everything into place. A fae who knows everything that needs to happen, even if he doesn't know he knows."

Griffin shook his head. "I've done nothing. I didn't retrieve the book or save you."

Tia shrugged. "That's because you weren't supposed to save us yet, but it doesn't mean you haven't done exactly what you were meant to. And now the book is showing you the key to Riona's markings. There is meaning in that."

Griffin looked down at his niece—or his daughter. That term scared him more than the other. "Be careful, Tia. I think this book is more dangerous than we know. Be cautious trusting in something so powerful." He looked down at the book that was still open to the page of symbols. "Can I take this page?" He didn't want it to fall into Egan's hands or anyone else.

Tia nodded, carefully ripping it from the book.

Griffin turned to Gulliver. He didn't like that he was here, but if there was one fae who could move around unseen, it was him. "Do you think you can get a message to someone close to the king?"

"Of course." He nodded eagerly.

Griffin didn't want to do this. He'd rather Gulliver hid under the bed all day. And yet, here he was.

"I need you to find Riona. Tell her to come to my rooms tonight."

Gulliver's brow creased. "So, I'm a booty call messenger?"

One day, Griffin would get back at Myles for teaching Gulliver about human TV shows. "Just do it, Gullie." He turned toward the door. "And pick up this mess." He didn't want Egan to send an indentured to their rooms. "You're royals, not pigs raised in a barn."

"I'm not." Gulliver grinned. "I'm a dirty rotten thief."

"Well, Mr. Dirty Rotten Thief, help the prince and princess clean up the tea I'm sure you spilled."

Griffin left them to their mess. His magic buzzed along his skin, making him feel alive for the first time in so long. He clutched the page about Riona's tattoos in his fist as he pushed into his rooms.

It didn't escape his notice how he stayed in the palace—crumbling or not—and Riona lived in the army barracks.

With his new strength he wanted to run, to sit atop a horse, or simply walk down to the slums to find out more about Hector's network.

But he couldn't. Instead, he studied the page from the book of power and waited for Riona.

CHAPTER TWENTY-FIVE

Griffin

Griffin couldn't sit still as he paced the length of his room. At least here there was no noise except the magic getting used to him once more. It filled his every sense, every part of him.

It was home.

He wasn't meant to live without magic, but it was a consequence of his prison sentence that he'd learned to accept. .

He walked to the window and clutched the frame, looking out onto the sleeping palace grounds. It didn't take long to grow used to the changing of night to day and day to night. When the sky remained dark, you had to use other markers.

Like the moon, perpetually full, hanging overhead. The stars scattered across the sky.

A knock sounded on his door. He steeled himself, letting

his shoulders hunch and his steps falter before pulling the heavy door open.

Riona stood on the other side wearing the same clothes as before, but it wasn't her clothing that drew attention. Red lines stretched down her cheek and shoulders with blood crusting the edges. "Come in." He didn't take his eyes off her as he shut the door.

Riona held her chin up, not cowered by anything Egan did to her. "He thinks I have come here to extract information, to lure you into your bed. So, we'll have most of the night."

"Riona," he whispered, reaching a hand to grip her chin and turn her head for a better look. "What did he do to you?"

She didn't push his hand away like he'd expect her to do. Instead, she stilled her quivering lip. "I'm okay, Griff." She sighed. "You'll be happy to know Gulliver has escaped. He's probably far from the city by now."

Griffin's brow creased. "He didn't get a message to you to come here?"

She shook her head. "I..." She released a breath. "He struck me ... Egan ... " She clutched her cheek. "When we didn't find Gulliver in his cell. He turned his whip on me, not stopping until Hector stepped in and calmed him down. But then ... what if Egan no longer favors me? That is when the real damage will happen."

His hands skimmed her shoulders and cheeks, up into her hair. "I won't let anything happen to you." He removed his hands and stepped back. "You asked me this morning to trust you. And I do, Riona. I trust you." He turned to the table where he'd set the page from the book. "Right now, I'm asking for the same. You and I will get out of here, we will save our families, our friends. That is our destiny. It doesn't matter what this page tells us. We choose our own paths."

Riona's wings gave an agitated shake, but her expression hardened. "Griff, what did you find?"

"If what Tia says is true, I found nothing. The page found my magic."

"Your magic," she breathed. "It makes perfect sense. The book didn't react to you because..." She stumbled back. "You have your magic now. All of it?"

He nodded, lifting a hand to show the power sparking across his fingertips. Riona approached him cautiously, rising on her toes to look into his eyes. "They're violet. Griffin, your magic ... it's beautiful."

He shook his head and held up the page. "Wait until I show you this."

Riona took it from him, her eyes scanning the symbols. "I don't know what it means."

"You can't read the symbols?"

She shook her head. The images on her skin moved with more speed than they had before. "My tattoos ... how?"

He stepped toward her. "I don't know why the book showed this to me. Tia has her theories. But it feels right. I think I'm supposed to have found it. I'm supposed to shape your destiny with the writing on that page."

Gathering every ounce of courage she possessed, she handed the page back to him. "Okay." She nodded. "I think I'm ready."

Griffin knew she'd been waiting for this her entire life. To finally understand what her tattoos meant.

Riona pulled every knife she had free, setting them on the table. She unbuckled her sword belt and let it fall to the ground with a clang.

The page said the symbols must be read in a specific order to spell out what Riona needed to know.

Griffin's magic directed him to leave the page on the table. He'd only read the symbols once, but the power inside him remembered. It wouldn't all make sense until he matched the symbols he'd read about with the ones sketched across her body.

"Give me your hands."

She held them out. On the left was a horseshoe. He rubbed his thumb over it before reading the second, a symbol that looked like praying hands. A human symbol.

"Faith will mean more to you than luck." The words poured out of him. "Faith in yourself and in the people around you." The two symbols kept swirling, unable to be still. Griffin leaned forward, pressing his lips against each. "I have faith in you."

Riona shivered. "Please, just keep going."

He ran his hands up her bare arms, finding the next marking and its equally vague meaning about loyalty. He bent forward to repeat the kiss on the tattoo on her arm. "You have my loyalty." Egan raised her, but she'd betrayed him so many times for Griffin. She chose to be good, and Griffin wouldn't forget that.

He moved up to her neck. "This row of white flowers means there is a purity about your task." She remained still as he pressed a kiss to the blossoms pulsing around her throat.

"Griff," she whispered, lifting her chin for him to move the kisses up. He pressed his lips to the mark of a whip across her face, and she closed her eyes, bringing her fingers to the laces of her vest. "Don't forget what we're doing."

He grinned against her skin. "Detours are allowed."

Her fingers shook on the laces, and Griffin put a hand over them. "Let me."

She nodded and dropped her hands. Griffin fought with the laces, and she helped him slid the vest and shirt over her head. He didn't stare at her nakedness, instead keeping his eyes on hers. His fingers skimmed her sides before settling on the next tattoo—a pattern of colorful lines weaving together. "You're going to change the course of fae history forever."

Riona held an arm across her breasts as Griffin's heated gaze left her eyes, trailing down to the single mark on her stomach. It reminded him of a compass rose with lines and arrows pointing in every direction. His fingers flitted over it, and his eyes flashed violet. "This one, right here, says a handsome fae will come into your life and make you question everything you thought you knew."

She smiled. "Well, it'll be nice when that happens."

Griffin laughed and pressed a kiss to the symbol. "It points to more than one path."

"That's impossible. You can't have more than one destiny."

Griffin rounded her to find the symbols on her back and stopped. His fingers skimmed across the raised welts, and she gasped at the pain.

"He did this to you?"

She nodded. "Egan loves his whip."

He stood, rounding her once more. "I will kill him one day. That I promise you. He will never touch you again."

She swallowed, her eyes glassing over. In true Riona fashion, she didn't let a tear escape.

Griffin moved back around her, letting his lips skim over the bruises between her shoulder blades. Rage raced through him, but the magic was stronger and it wanted him to continue.

He closed his eyes, touching the intricate knots swirling and curving over her sides. "You will be integral to much magic you were not born with. The instrument—"

Riona gasped. "Nihal's piccolo."

That part scared him. They'd seen first-hand how unpredictable and dangerous the music from the book was.

Griffin continued to read the clusters of symbols across her hips and back that held bits of information that wouldn't make sense until their true meanings were fulfilled. When he reached the last moving tattoo at the center of her back, he placed a palm over the colorful circle full of swirling blue and orange fae symbols, seeing flashes in his mind. "There's a crown." It came to him so suddenly he wasn't prepared for the onslaught of images racing through his mind. He fell back onto his butt. "Riona..." His eyes widened. "This tattoo speaks of your destiny." He stood, turning her to face him. "You are the keeper of Myrkur. That was once the role of your people in ancient times. Each generation a keeper rises. It is her responsibility to name the true heir of Myrkur and to guide them in their rule. When the time is right, you will know our rightful king or queen ... and you will place them on the throne. The keeper is ... a kingmaker." The tattoo revealed endless possibilities, but one thing was clear. They would defeat Egan.

Riona's face turned ashen as she trembled and dropped to her knees. She gasped, searching for her breath. "I feel ... empty somehow. This purpose, it no longer belongs only to me." She looked up at him, her eyes glassy and dazed. "You've set it in motion."

Griffin rose up on his knees, his hands shaking as he

reached for her. "Naming a king or queen ... it's like having the power to end a war."

"Or start one."

He reached forward and tucked a braid behind her ear. "We don't know what the future holds, Riona. But now we know your role in it. And—"

"And what?"

"There have been so many misunderstandings between us, so many betrayals. And we're still here, still standing."

Griffin watched the war going on in her eyes. Without warning, she grabbed Griffin's shirt, pulling him into a bruising kiss. He kissed her back with everything he had, every bit of magic and power went into the kiss, sparking between the Dark and Light Fae.

Griffin ran his hands down her spine just beneath her wings, and she shivered under his touch. "Riona," he whispered against her lips.

"Hmm?" Her eyes found his.

"I think—"

"No." She cut him off. "We won't do the declaration thing. Because a war is coming for us, and we don't know what will happen."

Griffin pushed to his feet and extended a hand down. She took it and got to her feet. Griffin slid his shirt off over his head before pulling Riona to him once more. They collapsed onto the bed in a tangle of limbs and wings.

"Sometimes, Griff, moments are just that. Moments. A space in time that can never exist again."

Griffin pressed a kiss to her lips. "And sometimes moments are part of a lifetime, bigger than themselves."

He gave himself to her in every way, because she was

right about one thing. They didn't know how much time they had.

That night, after Riona had curled against him under a fur blanket, the truth of her tattoos ran through his mind. She was a kingmaker, the only fae alive with the ability to recognize the true heir of Myr. If anyone else found out, they'd kill her.

He tightened his arms around her, wondering how a man who was sent to the prison realm after a lifetime of betrayals now had so many fae to protect.

Griffin

Griffin forced his hand to tremble as he lifted a spoon of porridge to his lips, nearly letting it fall back into his bowl before he managed to get the food in his mouth. Pretending to be a weakling when he had the full use of his magic was nearly as exhausting as actually being that weak.

They were finally learning the way the magic of the book worked, and how it revealed certain spells to certain people based on their need of the magic and their destiny. And the limitations of such magic in this realm. Egan had used the pages he and his forefathers had gathered to gain control of Myrkur. For the longest time, he was the only fae with any magic at all—with the ability to give and take magic, seemingly at will. It made him seem all-powerful to those without magic of any kind. But that wasn't the case. Now that Griffin understood Egan's limitations—it weakened the Dark Fae king in his eyes. He wasn't all-powerful, and now that Griffin had his magic back, he wouldn't rest until Egan was defeated.

He still maintained his hold on Griffin, but the king had no idea how strong Griffin was now—and Griffin meant to keep it that way.

"The troops are ready to move at a moment's notice, my king." Riona stood beside Egan's table in the dining hall. She never dined with them, but she was always there beside her king, ever the loyal servant. Except she was no longer loyal. Griffin could see that now. All her flirtations and menacing attitudes were a facade. Probably always had been. He doubted if Riona had ever shown Egan her true self.

"Very good, my dear. If we can ever decipher that cursed book, we'll be ready to march."

"I am told the child is nearly ready, my lord." Riona tilted her head toward her king, catching Griffin's eye, she gave a sly wink.

He ducked his head to hide a smile.

"I need you to understand something before we march for the border," Griffin said in a weary voice.

"For a man at death's door, you are quick to voice your *needs*, considering I am the one keeping you alive." Egan sneered as he stuffed his face with runny eggs, the yolks dripping into his beard.

"Tia is a child," Griffin reminded him. "The Light Fae are born with magic, but most will not have use of it until they are of age. Which Tia will not be for eight more years."

"I know all of this." Egan waved away his concerns. "The child is special—"

"Special though she may be, she is still a child," Griffin interrupted. "She, like all Fargelsian children, has use of her Gelsi magic she inherited from her mother and grandfather."

"Her magic will be more than enough to destroy the barrier once we have translated the instructions." Egan went back to his eggs, ignoring Griffin's concerns.

Griffin slammed his fist down on the table, making the king's plate rattle at the opposite end. Egan glared at Griffin, a hint of worry crossing his face, and Griffin could have kicked himself for displaying such strength.

"No," Griffin whispered, letting his shoulders slump forward and his voice grate in his throat. "It will likely not be enough. Fargelsi children Tia's age grow up learning the language of power, using it for simple tasks like lighting a fire or making flowers grow. It takes them a lifetime of study before they can master their power. What you are asking of Tia far exceeds reasonable expectations of a child her age. She is special, and she will try, and it might prove to be enough, but I need you to understand that magic is not a simple matter of wishing for results and willing them into existence. This could kill her if she is pushed too far. And if you care nothing else about her, remember this—she is a valuable tool now, think of what she will become if given the opportunity to live long enough to master the magic of the three kingdoms running through her veins. Do not waste her power, your Majesty. Think of how she may serve you in the future."

It was all he could do for his daughter right now. If he could sweep her and his sons far away from Myrkur and beyond Egan's grasp, he would without a moment's hesitation. They were trapped, and Tia would have to do this. But he would not see it kill her if he could help it.

"Very well." Egan sipped from his goblet, sloshing watered wine down his chin. "You make a valid point. But I will not be easily swayed—"

They all turned as Enis barged into the dining hall and marched up to the king's table, shoving her way past guards and soldiers. "It is done." She slammed the book onto the table. "We have deciphered the last of the spell work needed to bring the barrier down."

"And can the child actually do it?" Egan glared at Griffin.

"Of course, she can." Enis stood proudly. "My granddaughter translated most of the spells herself. She is more than capable."

"Then we march." Egan wiped his hands on a stained linen napkin and stood. "We leave for the border in an hour." He strode from the dining hall, yanking on the magical chain that held Griffin prisoner. He had no choice but to follow the king.

Torchlight flanked the king's entourage as they made their way along the main road to the border. Egan sat tall in his saddle. His feeble mount struggled under his weight, but the poor animal was the finest horse in the king's stables. Griffin rode on a mule behind him with Riona at his side. Enis rode in the king's carriage with the twins.

The horde of the Dark Fae army followed in their wake.

A sick sense of déjà vu swept through him as they neared the invisible barrier holding them captive. He'd been here before. Though last time a barrier like this was broken, he'd been on the wrong side of the battle. This time, he meant to be on the right side. He could only hope Lochlan had followed his instructions. If Tia managed to get the wall down, he prayed all the realms where there with their armies, waiting to flatten Egan's army with their magic. Magic Egan and his loyal soldiers couldn't fathom.

The king's party came to a halt at the entrance to the prison realm, marked by two large boulders on either side of the narrow path.

The dim sunlight shone here at the border, the no-man's-land between Myrkur and the Northern Vatlands. The king's army shielded their eyes, squinting into the light they weren't used to. If they only knew what awaited them on the other side, how many would turn back now?

Griffin watched as Enis led Tia and Toby from the carriage, clutching the book under her arm.

Riona and Griffin moved to dismount, but Egan stopped them. "We will wait at the ready."

Griffin took a deep breath, trying to find the patience to deal with the king's idiocy. "Your Majesty, we need to make camp."

"We will make camp on the other side. I will not spend another night in captivity now that I have the means to see it end."

"Your Majesty, this will take days, not minutes or even hours. This is the most complex magic most of us will ever see. It took the best magic wielders of all three realms to create this boundary magic hundreds of years ago. It has only strengthened over time. And we are counting on a child to break through it. It is not a simple matter of blowing up a wall made of brick and mortar."

"Griffin is right," Riona interjected. "I have seen the Light Fae use their magic. It is impressive, but it does take effort, your Majesty. Perhaps you should send your army home and summon them when this is done?"

"No." Egan slid from his horse. "We will make camp here.

I want my soldiers at the ready the moment that wall of magic crumbles. We don't know what awaits us on the other side."

"Very well, sir. I will see to the soldiers." Riona made it seem like making camp now was all the king's idea to begin with. She handled him well.

Enis approached the barrier with Tia and Toby at her side. She set up a podium to hold the book, lowering it to Tia's height. He could tell even from this distance that Tia was scared to death. She looked over her shoulder back at him, her eyes glinting in the fading light. "Uncle Griff?" She clutched her grandmother's hand.

"Your Majesty, may I?" Griffin gestured at the twins.

"You get two minutes, so make it count." Egan waved him toward the children as he sauntered off into the swarm of his army.

Griffin rushed to their side, pulling Tia and Toby close.

Tia threw her arms around him and buried her face in his shoulder. "I don't want to do this," she whispered. "It's wrong."

"It'll be okay, Tia." Toby patted her back.

"Toby's right." Griffin pulled back so he could see her face. "It's not ... wrong." He searched for the right words. "There are thousands of people stuck here that don't deserve it."

"Really?" She sniffed.

"So many." Griffin smoothed the reddish blond hair from her face. In the golden light here, her hair was redder. Like his. "Do the best you can, Tia. Trust your gut, and if you can't do it, we will find another way. I won't let anything happen to you."

"Don't fill the child's head with lies." Enis shook her head.

Griffin stood, holding the twin's hands. "You should try to remember that they're your grandchildren, and you're supposed to love them. Not sacrifice them to get your hands on the book you gave up your own children for." Griffin looked down at the twins. "I will be right behind you."

He backed away, a little piece of himself broke, leaving them to take on such an enormous task. Tia looked so tiny as she approached the podium, flipping through the book to find where she'd decided she should start.

While the others made camp, Griffin sat at the center of the dusty path that had led him here nearly ten years ago. A wave of dizziness washed over him, but he assumed it was exhaustion. He had slept little since returning to Myrkur.

"You know, you should go find your tent and get some rest." Riona came to sit beside him. "You said yourself this would take some time."

"I can't just leave them." Griffin shivered as Tia reached out with her magic, testing the boundary.

"I've ordered several tents to be set up right here, so you don't have to leave them, and you can make sure they're getting the rest they need."

"Thank you." Griffin reached for her hand but stopped. He wanted to wrap his arms around her, to let her give him comfort, but Egan had eyes everywhere, and he couldn't know about what truly happened between them. He thought he'd sent Riona to seduce him, that it would mean nothing. Griffin wasn't exactly sure what it meant, but he knew it wasn't nothing.

For hours, that first night, Griffin and Riona sat on the dusty road, watching Tia, grasping Toby's hand as she worked her way through the complicated magic. Griffin and Enis were the only ones who could see she was making progress, albeit slow progress. Every time she touched the barrier with her magic, it lit up the night sky for a moment, displaying the intricate and complex weave of spells that held them trapped inside Myrkur.

"This is utter nonsense." Egan paced furiously. "Nothing is happening, we should be well on our way to Iskalt by now. This child will not make a fool of me!" He kicked a pebble in the road, snorting and pacing like a big cat irritated by the confines of its cage.

"Will you be quiet, you fool of a king?" Enis turned, staring at him with her hands on her hips. "I've had quite enough bluster out of you for one night. This is highly stressful, complicated work you clearly don't understand, so why don't you go drink some more wine with your soldiers and leave the magic to us?"

Egan blustered some more, taking a menacing step toward the former Queen of Iskalt.

"My King," Riona interjected, putting herself between Egan and Enis. "Perhaps the children would feel less … intimidated if you left them to it?"

Egan started to argue but thought better of it. "You are right, my dear." He patted her hand. He sought his tent after that, giving Enis one final glare that could cut glass.

Griffin wondered if his mother would make it out of Myrkur alive after that outburst.

Eventually, Griffin insisted they stop for the night, carrying Tia to her bed inside the tent she shared with her grandmother. Riona carried Toby, equally weary from his long day of amplifying his sister's magic—something Egan still didn't realize the boy could do. To him, Toby was useless, and Griffin wanted to keep it that way.

"Eat something." Riona shoved a plate of eggs and bacon into Griffin's hands. The sun was hardly up yet, and Tia was already hard at work again. The barrier flickered and darkened with every murmured part of the spell she spoke, sending wave after wave of magic against the wall.

"I'm glad Brea's not here to see this. It would kill her." Griffin ate mechanically, the food tasting like sawdust in his mouth.

"What do you mean, Tierney O'Shea?" Enis raised her voice, her face screwed up in anger.

Griffin set his plate aside, rushing to find out what was amiss.

Tia shrank under her grandmother's furious glare.

"What do you mean Tobias is your *conduit?*" Enis had gone red with rage.

"Take a step back." Griffin took his mother by the shoulders, moving her away from the twins. "You're tired and frustrated." He turned to find Tia crying. Her head braced on Toby's shoulder.

Griffin bent toward Toby, placing a gentle hand on his small shoulder. "Why don't you tell me what's going on?"

"Tia's scared." Toby lifted his head. "She's better when I'm with her."

"Of course, she is. You're the most important fae she has."

Tia nodded, sniffing back her tears.

"But if she doesn't physically *need* the boy here to funnel magic through him, then we could use him elsewhere," Enis insisted.

"I think we *need* to do whatever makes the twins comfortable. And we *need* to remember they are young children."

Griffin glared at his mother, wondering how she'd become so cold.

"It's true, I am Tia's conduit," Toby said, squaring his shoulders. "She can do magic through me or take my energy to strengthen her magic."

"Right, we know that." Griffin nodded. "What seems to be the problem about that?" He played ignorant, hoping Enis wouldn't figure out he already knew how Toby's magic worked.

"The child said she doesn't need to *touch* him to conduct magic *through* him," Enis said, her shrill voice catching more attention from the bored soldiers than Griffin thought was necessary.

"Go take a walk, Mother. Get something to drink."

"I'm fine." She folded her arms across her chest.

"It wasn't a suggestion." Griffin's voice took on a razor-sharp edge.

Enis walked away, leaving Griffin alone with the twins.

"Why does this make Grandma so angry?" Griffin asked, kneeling down beside Toby.

Toby took a deep breath. "It means, she can send me to another part of the barrier, and Tia can whisper the spells through me. We can work to weaken the barrier in two places at once."

"I was told the boy doesn't have magic." Egan's gravelly voice nearly made Griffin jump out of his skin. "You know how I feel about lies, O'Shea." The noose tightened, squeezing around Griffin's heart as a reminder of who was in charge.

Griffin stood in front of the twins. "He doesn't have magic of his own," Griffin explained. "He is simply a conduit for his sister's magic."

"We will send him to another axis point of the barrier." Enis came up behind the king. "This is a good thing, your Majesty. It means we will get through this wall faster."

Tia started to cry when the king ordered a contingent of his soldiers to take Toby away. "Toby! No. The magic scares him when I'm not with him."

"It's okay, Tia. I will go with him." Griffin moved to follow his son, but the tears of his daughter cut right through him. How did Brea and Lochlan do this?

"Uncle Griff, stay with Tia. I'll be okay." Toby lifted his chin.

"I'll keep an eye on Toby," Riona whispered. "I'll fly to wherever he is and make sure he's okay. For now, I'll send someone I trust with him."

Griffin nodded and watched her walk away with his brave little boy, so like the loyal father who'd raised him.

He was proud of Toby. Proud of Tia. And wherever Gulliver was, he was proud of him too.

CHAPTER TWENTY-SEVEN

Griffin

Griffin felt so helpless, watching Tia work tirelessly, following the complex spell work from the book. She spoke the words of power until her voice was hardly more than a rasp in her throat. But Enis plied her with special teas and honey to give her the strength to keep going.

And now, somewhere at another part of Myrkur, Toby did the same while Riona watched over him.

"What is happening with the lights?" Egan came to sit beside him. "I can see it now, she's burrowing right through it, taking it apart piece by piece."

Griffin looked up at the night sky. It was late, far past the time when a ten-year-old should be awake still. Colorful lights flew through the sky. Reds and yellows, purples and oranges. Every color of magic he'd ever seen danced like the snúa aftur lights that danced along the over Eldur border.

And in the distance, over the rocky mountains separating them, Griffin could just make out the lights glimmering over Myrkur where Toby worked.

"It's just as you said," Griffin lied. "As she burrows through the weaves of magic, she's discarding the substance the wall is made of. It will dissipate to nothing without the other pieces holding it together."

"It's quite beautiful," Egan murmured. With nothing else to do but watch and drink, the king was more than a little drunk.

"It's the most beautiful thing I've ever seen." Griffin smiled into his own goblet of wine. And it really was. Each of those fragments of light belonged to a fae inside Myrkur. Some living. Some long dead. But as the light made its way to its owner, it carried their magic back to them. All across Myr, Light Fae who were either sent here or born here were getting their magic back, right under the king's nose.

Griffin had watched for hours before he realized the barrier was made up of the magic it took from those who entered the realm, using it to strengthen the spell work Sorcha and her contemporaries had set in motion three generations ago.

And now, Tia was giving it back.

The king left him after midnight, searching for his own bed.

Just as Griffin carried Tia into her tent, he heard the unmistakable flutter of Riona's wings. She was back from checking on Toby.

"He's safely asleep for the night, and I've arranged to have a local woman watch over him." She smiled, clearly proud of herself.

"And who is this local woman?" Griffin asked.

"Shauna." Riona nudged him with her elbow. "She and Nessa are caring for him, so you can relax."

Griffin heaved a grateful sigh of relief, but he wouldn't relax until this was over and the twins were safely home with their parents where they belonged.

"I just don't understand it." Enis snapped the book closed with an irritable sigh. "Something isn't working."

Griffin and Riona joined her around the fire, taking a seat on the dry dusty ground. "It seems to be working just fine," Griffin said. "If not a little slow."

"It shouldn't be this slow. At this rate we'll be here for months." Enis wiped a weary hand over her eyes. "I've gone through every part of this book I can access and so has Tia and Toby. There is something important I'm missing. Something the book hasn't shown to those involved."

"Maybe there's another role?" Riona suggested. "Some aspect of the magic you haven't covered yet?"

Enis nodded. "It seems that way, but the twins should cover all the aspects of magic. They have Fargelsian, Iskaltian, and Eldurian magic. And if the book seeks more mature magic, I have Gelsi magic, and Griffin has Iskalt magic."

"What about the magic of the Dark Fae?" Griffin asked.

"They don't have magic, Griffin." Enis leaned back against the log behind her and stifled a wide yawn.

"Not of the traditional sort, but they are magical beings. Nihal certainly had his own kind of magic." He glanced at Riona.

"We've tried that. Riona couldn't read the pages."

"Well, Griffin read the pages concerning my tattoos," Riona admitted softly. "I understand what they mean now. Most of them."

It was as if Enis didn't hear her. "Nihal. That's it." Enis

grabbed the book, flipping through the pages. "Can you read this?" She handed the book to Riona.

Riona's brow creased as she studied the page. "It's a song. There are bars of music here I recognize."

"Do you still have Nihal's piccolo?" Enis asked eagerly.

"Yes, I've kept it with me." Riona rummaged through her bag, retrieving the instrument.

Griffin looked over her shoulder, scanning the odd symbols on the page. "You can read this?" He frowned. It looked like gibberish to him.

"Try to play the song," Enis urged, ignoring Griffin.

"We've tried that. The piccolo wouldn't play for me."

"That was before you translated your tattoos. I take it you have discovered your purpose among your markings?" Enis asked.

"I have." Riona ducked her head.

"Your people draw great strength from the discovery of their life's purpose. It changes you. Griffin is right, *that* is your magic, Riona. I think the piccolo will respond to you now."

Riona held the instrument in unsteady hands. "How will I know what this song will do? How will I know if it will … drain my life the way it did for Nihal?"

"Read the song before you play it. I believe its purpose will come to you."

Griffin watched as Riona studied the strange symbols on the page. As she lifted the instrument to her lips, Griffin stopped her.

"Are you sure?" he asked. "Don't do it if you're uncertain." He would not sit here and watch her fade to ash in front of his eyes.

"It is a song of … destruction." She frowned at the words. "More like a song of undoing. It won't hurt me."

Griffin nodded, afraid to let go of her hand.

She gave him a reassuring smile, and she began to play.

Griffin clapped his hands over his ears. The sound was horrendous. Like a hundred cats fighting.

"I'm sorry." Riona pulled away. "That was awful."

"No, keep trying." Enis beamed at her. "It's working!"

"Oh." Riona stared at the flute again. "It didn't make a single sound last time."

"Try it again. Take your time."

It took her several nauseating tries—literally nauseating —but she finally made it through the song without making anyone sick.

"Play it again." Enis instructed as Riona finished her second nearly perfect play through.

Enis stood, gesturing for Griffin to join her. "Look." She pointed toward the barrier.

As Riona played the now sweet melodic notes, the barrier lit up in a soft white glow the color of Riona's wings. The intricate weaves of magic binding the wall began to loosen the more she played.

"Yes, yes, keep going." Enis fairly vibrated with renewed energy. "Let's get Tia." She turned toward the tent.

"No. Let's not." Griffin stepped in front of her. "It's late and everyone is exhausted and if you disturb my ten-year-old niece while she rests, we will have a serious problem, Mother."

"Oh, Griffin." She reached to touch his cheek, sadness filling her eyes for a moment. "You are right. I'm a terrible grandmother. Of course, she needs to rest. We all do."

"We will start again at dawn." Riona slipped the piccolo back into her bag.

Things moved faster with Riona's song. Much faster.

Griffin was relieved to find that Riona's playing not only helped Tia pick apart the magic holding the wall together, but it also calmed Tia, giving her a strength he hoped trickled down through the twin bond to her brother.

Griffin stood beside Tia, feeling useless as she murmured the spells, flipping back and forth through the pages of the book. Somehow, she knew exactly which pages she needed and when. To him, none of the words on the page made sense, but her eyes flew across the lines of spells that should be far beyond her years. This kind of magic was far beyond most adult magic wielders, and she charged through it like it was nothing. His girl was an impressive sight to behold.

Tia's voice suddenly rose into a crescendo, shouting out words of power he'd never heard in all his time living in Fargelsi. Wind swept through the camp and a rolling thunder boomed across the sky. Griffin stumbled as the ground began to shake, but Tia's voice remained as strong as Riona's music.

The soft white light that reminded him of Riona's silky wings, burst into a brilliant blaze to rival the sun.

Griffin covered his eyes until the wind died down and the ground settled beneath his feet. When he opened them, the white light of the barrier was gone. She'd brought the inner wall down. The layer made up of the magic of those held within its borders.

The outer wall shifted and swayed. The iridescent glow

of the magical weaves seemed to flicker and gutter like a candle flame about to burn out.

"Toby," Tia whispered, her voice raw from shouting. At the sound of her voice, the remaining weaves of magic seemed to turn toward Griffin's daughter, like a sentient creature recognizing its master. The bright light gathered into a serpentine streak, winding and twisting like a snake.

The last threads of the barrier erupted like a blast of white-hot fire and shot toward Tia, striking her through the chest.

"Tia!" Griffin's hands fell at his sides as he stared helplessly at the still form of his daughter lying in a heap at his feet.

CHAPTER TWENTY-EIGHT

Griffin

"Tia." Griffin dropped to his knees, turning Tia's body so he could see her face. He pushed the fine strawberry blond hair away with a finger, almost burning himself as he did.

His hand drew back in surprise. Her skin blazed with the heat of whatever swirled inside her. White ropes of power moved under her almost translucent skin as if something lived inside her.

"Griffin!" Riona yelled.

He jerked his head up to see what she'd seen. The white wall that had remained after the magic barrier was gone, and this was his only chance to save Tia. He had to get her out.

"Get to Toby!" He didn't know who he yelled that to, either Riona or his mother, but he could only save one of the kids. It was up to his allies to save the other. This was the moment Tia knew would come.

She'd never lost faith he'd save her.

Sliding his hands underneath her small frame, he lifted her and cradled her against his chest. Magic tugged at him, Egan's leash. Griffin could have broken the magic when he first recovered his power, but Egan would have known.

Now, with nothing left to lose, he sliced through Egan's hold on him. Griffin O'Shea was finally his own man again.

A man who had to save a little girl.

"It's okay, Tia. I've got you." He avoided touching her heated skin as her head fell against his shoulder.

He looked back at the army who could now sweep through the three kingdoms of Light Fae.

Not on his watch.

"Where are you going?" His mother cried.

Griffin didn't know. He had to get Tia out of Myrkur.

Tia murmured words that made no sense to Griffin as he took off, running toward the place where the barrier stood only moments before. He ignored the fae yelling to him as he picked up speed. It had been months since Griffin had his full strength, and now, nothing could stop him getting Tia to safety.

She bumped against his chest as he ran, and a million thoughts flooded his mind. He had to get her to Brea—or maybe to Brandon, her grandfather. He understood Fargelsian power more than anyone.

Dust kicked up underneath his feet as he clambered through the mountain pass, moss-covered boulders narrowing his escape route. The sounds of armored footsteps followed him through the pass, and he looked up to find three Slyph flying above his position.

He was out of time.

"I'm sorry, Tia." He wasn't her true father, the one who'd

raised her. Griffin knew that. But he still felt the crushing knowledge that he couldn't keep her safe. Griff set her down, glancing over his shoulder to find two of the Light Fae criminals who led a contingent of Egan's army.

And they too had their magic back.

Blood red streams of power narrowly missed Griffin as he gathered his O'Shea magic in the tips of his fingers and drew a line in the air, a portal into the human realm.

Picking Tia up again, he prepared to step through the opening when an arrow flew past him, lodging in the throat of one of the Light Fae. The magic faded from his eyes as he crumpled to the ground.

Yellow ropes of magic shot up to the Slyph, narrowly missing one of them, but they weren't so lucky when a second arrow sliced through her shoulder, making her tumble from the sky and slam against a boulder.

Griffin looked from the portal to the path where his two allies must have been hiding. He'd recognize that yellow magic anywhere.

They'd come.

Brea and Lochlan barely knew him. They didn't remember their twins. And yet, they were here.

Another arrow hit the remaining Light Fae in the chest, while the Slyph above tried to avoid Brea's Eldurian magic, made powerful by the blinding sun overhead. Seeing his comrades fall, he took off back toward Myrkur.

The remaining Dark Fae lifted higher in the sky before following the other back toward Egan's camp.

Griffin's heart hammered in his chest as he tried to control his breathing.

"Wow." Lochlan stepped into view. "I guess that letter to myself was right. There was an O'Shea brother here that needed my help." He looked to the portal, one eyebrow raised. "You must be Griffin. You going to go through? I wouldn't recommend it. That kid in your arms can't be helped in the human realm."

Brea followed Lochlan onto the road. "I don't get to use my magic enough. That was fun." She looked to her husband. "And you wanted to wait to approach the barrier at night so you were the one with power. This man and his daughter would have died if you had your way."

Lochlan's armor had a crown etched on the helmet marking him as king. He creaked with each step. Brea, on the other hand, wore fighting leathers that suited her.

"We should get off the road." Lochlan looked back the way they'd come and turned to march down the road to the tree line.

Brea kept a sympathetic eye on Tia, but Lochlan didn't look at them again. "The barrier is down, isn't it?"

"It is." Griffin shifted Tia, looking down into her face. It had never struck him so hard before, the forgetting. That her parents could look into her face and show no recognition. No emotion. "The Light Fae inside the prison realm have had their magic returned."

"You mean the criminals?" Lochlan asked.

"Some. Not all." Griffin didn't have the energy to explain everything he'd already taught Lochlan, everything his brother forgot once Griffin returned to the prison realm. "I'd worry more about the Dark Fae army."

Brea looked back at him then down at Tia. "Those fae had wings."

Griffin nodded. "As do many others. Are you prepared for an onslaught of things you've never seen before?"

They stepped into a clearing, sloping down the side of the

mountain, and Griffin stopped. Every inch of space was occupied by a tent or a soldier. They didn't wear Iskaltian blue, there were no Iskalt flags.

Instead ... "This is the Fargelsian army."

As if that called him forth, Myles sprinted through camp. "What happened?" He looked from Brea to Griffin. "Who is this guy?"

Before, having Myles remember him had been helpful. But now that Myles too was a part of the world that forgot Griffin, he had no time for get-to-know-yous. "Is there a healer here?"

Brea was the first to answer. "Myles, go find Neeve's personal healer."

Myles ran toward another part of camp. "Where are the Iskalt forces?" The Fargelsian army was impressive, but also the weakest of the three.

Lochlan looked sideways at him. "We have them meeting with the Eldurian army at the border in case this king of yours manages to get past us. They will be here soon."

"Uncle Griff?" Tia moaned as her eyes fluttered open.

"Hey, sweetheart." He smiled down at her. "You're going to be okay."

A tear trickled down her cheek. "I was strong."

"You were." He held her close. "You were so strong, Tia."

"I feel hot, Uncle Griff. There's magic inside me that isn't mine. I feel it moving under my skin. Get it out. Please, I don't want it anymore. I just want Toby."

"Riona went to get Toby. She'll bring him to us soon."

Neeve walked through the camp, looking every bit the warrior. There was once a time when kings and queens didn't stand with their soldiers.

That time was over.

Neeve reached them and looked down at the girl with a smile. "You brought down the magic. I can see the Fargelsian power lighting through you."

Tia hiccupped a sob. "I don't want this power."

"You're a hero." Neeve smiled down at her.

Tia shook her head. "I'm not. I want to go home. Mama." Her eyes found Brea's. "Take me back to Iskalt. I don't want to be here any longer."

Griffin could see the struggle in Brea's eyes as she tried to remember her daughter.

"Papa," Tia cried.

Tears shone in Lochlan's eyes. "I'm trying."

It was then Griffin finally realized the prison magic wasn't any easier for those who forgot. They had to live with that burden.

"Hey." Griffin hugged her closer as the heat from her skin permeated her clothes. "We're going to get Toby, and we will all find our way home. I've got you, Tia."

Griffin wasn't the true father of these kids. He didn't delude himself. But Lochlan currently looked at Tia like a puzzle piece he was trying to place, and Griffin didn't like it.

"Uncle Griff, can you put me down?" Tia asked, wiping away her tears.

Griffin set her on her feet, getting a good look at the pure white power thriving inside her.

Neeve looked to Tia. "Dear, I can try to draw the magic out if you'd like."

Tia nodded. "Just make it go away, Auntie Neeve, please."

Neeve looked startled at the endearment.

Brea walked off, yelling orders to her sister's army. They had to be ready to face creatures they'd never imagined.

And still, Griffin hated the sight of Brea leaving her daughter.

Neeve and Tia sat across from each other on the forest floor. "Repeat what I say."

Tia nodded and copied every odd word that fell from Neeve's lips. The power pulsed, a bright light shining out of Tia. She screamed as the light poured out of her, blinding those nearby.

Griffin covered his eyes until the light dimmed. As they continued the spell, tendrils of white magic floated from her, not altogether different from when Tia and Riona took down the wall.

Only this time, Tia didn't need help from a magical instrument.

Something tightened in Griffin's chest as a slithery bit of magic struck him, warming him from the inside out.

His heart pounded as beads of sweat dotted his brow. He searched frantically for the one fae who'd lessen the turmoil inside him.

Because it was back.

As magic wound through the camp, Griffin realized Tia returned to him the one bit of magic he did not want.

Marriage magic.

Broken by the prison realm barrier and healed by that same magic.

Brea stood across the clearing, but he could feel her eyes on him. He turned, meeting her gaze.

And he knew.

Tia had changed the course of their lives forever.

Tia slumped forward, her skin returning to its pallor, with nothing beneath the surface. She looked as if it took everything in her just to lift her head.

Griffin stepped toward her.

"Tia!" Brea shrieked, sprinting across the camp sobbing her daughter's name. Lochlan ran from another direction, scooping Tia into his strong arms.

"I'm sorry. I'm sorry. I'm sorry." He held her tight, repeating the words as if that could make them truer.

Brea reached them, wrapping her arms around both her daughter and her husband. Griffin watched their family, a pit opening in his stomach.

Neeve pushed herself off the ground with a weary sigh. "I didn't know." Something haunted her gaze. "When the wall came down, she internalized every forgotten memory."

"The outer wall was made of the memories it took from the world each time someone stepped through." Millions of memories spanning generations and they'd filled Tia, but they hadn't defeated her.

Myles walked toward them, rubbing his temples. "I'm guessing we don't need a healer anymore?"

Around them, Fargelsian soldiers prepared for war, but a different war raged inside Griffin.

Neeve slipped her arm through Myles'.

"I didn't remember you this last time." Myles gave him a curious look.

Griffin rubbed his eyes. "Because you were in the fae realm when I crossed the barrier."

Neeve couldn't take her eyes from Tia. "That girl ... I'm not sure there's another fae alive who could hold that much power and survive it."

Griffin nodded. It was on the tip of his tongue to call her his daughter, but as he watched Lochlan torment himself over not remembering her, he realized blood didn't make her his daughter. Lochlan raised her, he protected her, he loved her.

Tears stained Brea's cheeks. "Where's your brother? Where's my Toby?"

Griffin was the one who answered. "I sent someone to rescue him."

As if the words alerted them to Griffin's presence, all eyes turned to him.

Lochlan's jaw clenched.

"Hello, brother." Griffin didn't know what else to say. Ten years had passed, ten years of Lochlan and Brea not knowing Griffin existed, not remembering enough to even question the twins' births.

Brea looked to him with softer eyes. Even after everything he'd done, she was the one fae who'd always believed he could be better, do better. It was why he'd fallen in love with her in the first place.

Riona's words came back to him, questioning if his feelings for Brea were real. At the thought of Riona, the marriage magic wrapped around his heart, squeezing it painfully.

What he didn't know was whether they remembered his time in Iskalt recently, when he'd been a brother to Lochlan and a friend to Brea.

Myles stepped forward, despite Neeve trying to hold him back. "I feel like I need to step in here and remind everyone Griffin is not the same fae. Try to look for those recent memories, guys. He was kind of a mopey dude on our trip, definitely didn't get my jokes, but he still tried to save the world, and he risked his life to bring Tia home. So, you know, maybe we shouldn't kill him."

"Myles." Lochlan growled. "Shut up."

"Yes, douchey Loch, king sir." He gave an elaborate bow. "It's just…"

"Myles." Neeve yanked him back. "Maybe we should go prepare to meet the Myrkur army should they march."

"Prepare? Is this like that training you thought was so necessary? As if anyone in Fargelsi doesn't know how to march. One foot. Two feet. I mean … it's not like anyone has three feet so they should know to go back to one."

"Myles." Lochlan sent him a dark look.

"Yeesh. Harsh crowd. Smile. It's not like we're about to march into a kingdom with no sun, an evil king, and an army of people who could just fly above us. Oh wait, this is totally like that. Come on, wifey. Let's go make sure our warriors know which end of their sword to use."

Silence descended as they walked away.

This was not how Griffin ever imagined a reconciliation. If it could be called that. "Look, Loch, I know you hate me, that you never expected to see me again. But I'm here now, courtesy of your daughter." He almost choked on the word *your.*

Brea reached up on her toes to whisper in Lochlan's ear.

"You saved my daughter." It looked like it pained Lochlan to say. "I won't kill you. Yet. But you, Griffin O'Shea, are not part of my family."

The words stung more than Griffin expected them to. He hadn't imagined any of this would be easy, but he'd hoped they'd give him a chance at least.

"Papa." Tia's eyes glassed over again. She pushed away

from him, forcing him to set her down. "Uncle Griff isn't bad."

"You don't know what you're speaking of, Tia."

She shook her head and wrapped her arms around Griffin's waist, her face tilted up at him. "I love you, Uncle Griff. Even if my papa can't see it, you don't have to be bad anymore. You saved me just like the dream."

He crouched down in front of her. "You, Tia O'Shea, are the one who saved us all."

"And Toby."

He nodded, fear lancing through him at the idea of Toby still in Myrkur. "The path forward won't be easy, but I have faith in you." In his daughter who could do amazing things. "Never forget that, okay? Wherever I am, I will always believe in you."

She sucked her bottom lip into her mouth and nodded.

Griffin straightened and turned, preparing himself for the hike back to the boundary where Egan's forces were no doubt preparing for battle.

"Stay," a quiet voice said.

Griffin didn't realize how long he'd stood there looking into the mountains or that only one fae remained looking at him.

Turning to Brea opened a gulf between them. Pain flashed across her face, and she rushed forward at the same time he walked toward her.

They collided in a crushing hug, the marriage magic inside Griffin releasing, letting the pain ebb away.

"I've missed you, Griff." Her words were muffled by his shirt.

He rested his chin on top of her head. "You haven't remembered me, so I don't think that's true."

"There's been this hole in my memories, and I was never able to figure it out. For ten years, I lived my life knowing something was different. And whatever Lochlan admits, so has he. I remember everything now. All the bad you did, but also the good."

She looked up at him, tears glistening on her cheeks. "You belong with us, Griff."

He didn't know where he belonged, only that it was with his people. Brea and Lochlan were only part of what he needed. Gulliver … Shauna … Nessa. Riona. They were part of him now.

"It's back, isn't it?" Brea sighed against him, probably realizing what he already had. The only reason she didn't hate him as much as Lochlan was because of the magic tying them together.

"Yes."

"It hurts. The magic tying me to Lochlan is at war with the magic tying me to you. I don't think we're supposed to have both."

Griffin looked over her shoulder to watch Lochlan glare at them. He pulled away. "I love you Brea, I always have. But I'm not in love with you. Not anymore. Whatever the magic tries to tell me, I know the difference now."

She wiped her face and smiled. "Then maybe there's hope for all of us." She threaded her fingers through his. "Fight beside me. Beside your brother."

"He won't want me at his side." He slipped his hand from hers and crossed his arms, taking a step away from Brea.

"He's in shock, Griff. We all are. Just please … don't give up on us."

He pulled her into another hug. "It's never been me giving up on you."

"We're here because of you. Our people have been called from their homes to protect the three kingdoms. Lochlan didn't remember you, but he trusted you in a way I've never seen him trust before. That couldn't have been fake. You're brothers."

That word ... brothers ... it stoked something deep inside Griffin. He wanted it. He wanted a chance to prove he deserved that trust.

Lochlan and Brea were family, and family never quit on each other.

He glanced toward the mountain path Egan and his army would traverse soon enough. "Okay, Brea. I'll stay. I'll fight at your side." For his people still stuck in Myrkur, for the twins he could never claim, and for the woman he needed to find.

If they all stood together, Egan didn't have a chance.

CHAPTER TWENTY-NINE

Riona

Riona had little experience carrying a fae as she flew. Her wings flapped harder, trying to get as much energy into each movement.

The kid—Toby—slipped in her arms, and she hiked him higher, needing a way to get him down the mountain to wherever Griffin went.

But Egan's soldiers were everywhere.

An arrow whizzed past her, and she veered to the left to avoid a contingent of ogres who were surprisingly good with the bow.

Egan's vast force spanned the length of the border, not letting a soul cross. She didn't know if Griffin was safe, but she had to believe he was to keep going.

If she couldn't get across the border, she had to find safety farther back in Myrkur.

The farther she flew, the heavier Toby became, until she had to find a place to rest.

Drifting toward the ground, she landed in a village that looked like it had been abandoned in a hurry. Smoke rose into the dark from nearby chimneys.

Choosing a small hut, she kicked the door open and set Toby on the simple bed. Stale air permeated the inside, and Riona stepped out, sucking in gulps of fresh air.

Toby had only woken once as she flew with him, but his skin was hot to the touch. She needed to find water.

Going from thatched-roof hut to hut, she kicked open doors, searching the belongings. Finally, she found two ceramic jugs. One was water, the other wine. She slipped two cups under her arm.

Hurrying back to where she'd left the kid, she poured him a cup of water and held it to his lips. "Toby, drink this."

The magic that had flowed through him wasn't his, so when it drained him, it found no magic to take, using his life force instead.

Sitting on the floor, she leaned back against the mud-brick wall with a sigh and uncorked the jug of wine, not bothering with a cup as she took a swig, letting it calm her.

"Tia." Toby groaned.

Riona scooted toward him. "We'll find her, kid."

She didn't know if the words were true or fantasy. A lantern sat near the bed, and she brought it to life, holding it up so the glow illuminated Toby's ashy skin. Sweat made his face shimmer.

She leaned her head back. "I tried, Griff. I promise I tried." Using the lantern, she pulled her wings around her so she could check the edges.

The black that had crept from the edges of her wings,

now covered almost half of each wing. Was it the destiny? Did reading her tattoos change the color of her wings?

"I'm supposed to recognize the king when the time comes." She whispered to herself. What time? And how would she know?

And what happened if she died before fulfilling her destiny?

She closed her eyes and took another gulp of wine. As her eyes opened, she examined a tear in one of her wings. She reached for the wine again. "Griffin O'Shea, I hate you."

At least, she wanted to. Riona had never been the kind to risk her life for someone else. She didn't do favors or protect anyone other than herself.

And yet, she was here with blood sticking to her black leather shirt—it wasn't hers—and tears in her wings.

Toby said something in his sleep, and Riona froze. She'd thought the kid was dying, that she'd failed to save him in time. Exhausted, she crawled toward the bed and poured water onto a corner of the fur blanket before brushing it against Toby's heated face.

She leaned closer, her eyes widening as she saw tendrils of white magic swirl beneath his skin.

As she stared, it seemed to stop writhing. The first strands rose from his body, and she shrank back, watching the magic swim into the air, ignoring her altogether.

"She did it." Toby smiled. "Tia released the memories."

That was what the white ropes of magic were?

At this moment, people across the realms were remembering the ones they'd trapped here.

Commotion sounded outside, the sound of many footsteps and a rabble of fae.

Riona fortified herself with a long drink of wine. She

struggled to her feet, keeping the jug in her grasp as she reached for her sword. Pain radiated down her wings and into her back as she tried to lift it.

It seemed she wouldn't go out with a show of skilled swordplay. Riona ripped a knife from its scabbard. Her other hand weakened, and she dropped the wine, watching as ceramic pieces shattered at her feet. Casting one more look at Toby, she ducked out of the hut.

She stumbled across the village, knife at the ready as her injured wings hugged her body.

A large group of fae—both dark and light—rested outside the village. Riona hid, watching them for a sign of Egan. But there was none.

"What are you doing?" Gulliver's whisper came from behind her, making her jump.

"Gullie." She panted.

He grinned, but his smile dropped quickly. "You're hurt."

She shrugged. "Nothing I can't handle. We need to be quiet. These warriors could belong to Egan." Though, she'd never seen his warriors with farm implements and rusted swords for their weapons.

A laugh burst out of Gulliver. "Riona, these are the people of Myrkur, the ones who didn't join Egan. Villagers, healers."

"What are you saying?"

"That we still have friends in the realm." He gestured toward the man she now recognized sitting in the center of their camp with a group of his soldiers. Hector. As soon as she talked to him, Toby would be safe, and she could return to his bedside.

Shauna smiled at her as she approached. "Hello, Riona." She got to her feet. "What's wrong?"

"I'm okay. But Toby ... Griffin's ... nephew. He needs help. Do you have any healers with you?"

"Show me where he is." Shauna slipped into a tent and returned with a sack of supplies. "Nessa and I went back for Toby, but he was already gone." There was hope in her voice.

Riona nodded. "He's asleep, but he'll be glad to be with you." She slid her gaze over the lines of men, women, and even some children stretching as far as she could see.

Magic wound through Riona, tugging at her the way she'd grown used to. Egan was looking for her.

"What's your plan with this army?" Riona matched Shauna's pace.

"There's no concrete plan." Her brow furrowed. "Griffin told us the other kingdoms were coming and that they would fight for us. Now, with the barrier down, we deserve the chance to fight for our kingdom rather than relying only on help from others."

Riona nodded because she understood. These people might not have much. They lived under constant threat from Egan. And this, here, was fighting back.

Riona tried to ignore the pain lancing through her from the damaged wing, but she couldn't hide her wince.

"I'll give you something for the pain once I see Toby." Shauna didn't look at her. "And you will take it. Because we need you at full strength, Riona."

Riona only nodded as she led Shauna into the room where Toby slept. She paced back and forth while Shauna checked the kid over before finally stepping back.

"I don't know what's wrong with him." Fear laced her voice. "I think all we can do is wait and see."

That wasn't good enough for Riona, but she didn't know what else to do.

Shauna fished something out of her bag and handed it to Riona. "Oiche bark. Chew on this for the pain. It'll help your wings heal. I'll assign a watch on you and Toby. I'm assuming you prefer to stay here with him."

"I'm not leaving him." Not an option.

Shauna nodded like she'd expected that. "Let me know when he wakes."

When she left, Riona let herself relax onto the floor as she chewed on the oiche bark. The effect was almost instant. Relief wound through her, pushing away the pain. Before long, she felt herself nodding off.

Movement made Riona jerk awake. She was on a horse.

How?

With a groan, she lifted her head to see a troop of soldiers wearing Egan's colors.

"She's awake," one of them yelled.

Another appeared in her vision, a young man with tiny horns. "Morning, my lady. It's good to see you awake."

"What's happening? Where are we?" None of this made sense.

"On the way to his Majesty's camp. We aren't moving out quite yet as he has another priority, so they'll still be there. The King will be right pleased with you, my lady. I always told people there was a reason you were his favorite. And look here! You found one of them kids he's looking for."

After that, it didn't take long for Riona to figure out what was going on. She looked to a horse-drawn cart beside her mount. Toby lay in the cart, his eyes wide. She wished she could reassure him, but that wouldn't save their lives.

"How did you get us out?"

The soldier who'd spoken before puffed out his chest. "We knew they were holding someone, so we slipped past their camp and killed their guards easily enough. The young one with the tail though ... he was a funny wee one."

Riona's chest squeezed. Not Gulliver.

"We only knocked that one out."

Relief flooded Riona.

Egan's magic looped around her again, pulling her toward him.

And this time, she had no choice but to obey.

Egan's lips curled up the moment he saw Riona stumble into his camp with a damaged wing. It would heal soon enough, but Riona hated anyone seeing her with a vulnerability. His smile fell, and she couldn't help but wonder if the concern on his face was genuine.

The army stood, ready to march from the only kingdom they'd ever known, something she was surprised hadn't happened yet. Dark Fae marched with their own kind. Riona averted her eyes as she walked through lines of ogres beating clubs on the ground in excitement.

Still, Egan hadn't given the order to march.

She walked past Slyph standing in narrow lines. Once the battle started, they would leap into the air, raining havoc from up above. Each had a bow in one hand and a quiver of arrows strapped to their backs.

What was Egan waiting for?

Next were the Asrai, in their land form. Their eyes held the power of the ocean as they wielded long, thin swords.

Riona couldn't keep track of the different species of Dark Fae who'd answered their king's call.

She stumbled, pain lacing through her. She kept moving. Egan didn't near her, instead standing perfectly still, watching her approach.

His power pulled at her, not letting her stop.

Riona could only watch as one of Egan's ogres stomped across the ground at the barrier, a boy dangling from his hands.

Toby's eyes widened as he yelled.

A strange fear awoke in Riona. She'd never counted on anyone, never had a fae she loved, one she wanted to make proud.

"Now," she whispered to herself. "I do."

It was those words that kept her going, those words that brought her to join this army of cruelty and despair. They didn't belong trapped in Myrkur, but they didn't belong outside it either, not in the rolling Fargelsian hills. Not in the beautiful danger of the Eldurian deserts.

And certainly not in the frozen tundra of Iskalt.

As she looked at the fae she passed, she wondered how many of them were here simply because they didn't know where else to be. They didn't have a side. No one fought for them. At least serving in Egan's army paid them a wage and provided their meals.

Riona lifted her chin as she reached Egan. "Are you going to let the boy live?" Her voice was cold, devoid of emotion.

Egan looked to the ogre who shrugged and tossed Toby's body onto the ground like a sack of grain. He groaned, and Riona released a breath, relieved he was still making any sound at all.

"May I?" Riona pointed to Toby.

Egan nodded.

Dropping to her knees, Riona pushed his hair out of his eyes. "We're going to be okay, Toby." She sat back on her heels. Looking up, she caught Egan's curious expression.

"Riona." He sighed. "My Riona. Have you chosen a side at last?"

She nodded, pushing to her feet as she said the words that betrayed every thought, every feeling she'd had over the last few months. "I have, sire. If it would please you, I would like to remain by your side."

He smiled. "Good answer." He pointed to her wing. "You are injured."

Riona crossed her arms over her chest, knowing she had to do this. For Toby. For Griff. "My injury is nothing, Majesty."

"Good. Good. My army is prepared for battle, Riona."

"Prepared, sire?" She'd assumed the army would march as soon as the barrier came down, yet here it stood. And she wouldn't be asked to fight?

A smile slid across Egan's face. "There is a prize greater than the three fae realms, my dear. One that holds untold power. The lady Enis has told me of the magic we can possess. But there is an army on our border, and until young Toby here can learn his family's portal magic, our people must fight to give us time."

"Portal magic?" She took a step back from him, her eyes going wide.

He nodded. "I will find the ultimate power, the only thing greater than this book."

"And what is that, sire?"

"Its source."

Enis appeared at Toby's side, giving Riona no chance to ponder the king's true wishes. "The boy ... is he ready?"

Egan nodded. "Take him. We don't have much time. I'm counting on his power. It is the only use I have for him to remain alive."

Enis pulled Toby to his feet and wrapped an arm around him. "We won't fail you."

"See that you don't." Egan turned away from them. "Riona, you will join your Slyph brethren to attack from the skies, but your job is to report back to me. Do not let yourself perish. Retreat when you can and return here. Our army must battle this night, but you and I have until sun up before our battle truly begins."

Riona didn't trust Enis with Toby, but she didn't have much choice. Hardening her heart for the coming battle, she only nodded.

This time, she'd make sure no one questioned her loyalty. She'd stay just long enough to get Griffin's son to safety.

Stepping in line with the other Slyph had a surreal quality to it. Yet, they'd never considered her one of them for the other half of her blood. Her heritage set her apart.

Riona had always been an "other" to each group of fae, even among the Tuatha Da Dannan, the land fae, she was *other*.

But not to Griffin.

Around her, fae jumped into the air, hovering above the army. Even if Egan was distracted for the moment, they had to be ready if the armies of the three kingdoms came for them.

Gritting her teeth against the pain, Riona leaped upward, letting the flap of her wings carry her higher still. Up here, the pain faded away, and everything became clear. She adjusted for the injured wing and spiraled up.

She would do whatever was necessary to save Toby and bring an end to this army.

"We will defeat our enemies!" Egan screamed. "Here and in the worlds beyond."

Slyph readied their bows, preparing for the deadly accuracy the Light Fae wouldn't be able to match.

Riona's thoughts turned to Griffin and Tia, hoping they were safe. Because this army … it was a force of destruction.

And now, she must go to war against her allies, against the fae she'd fallen in love with.

Because, not all love is forever. Some faded away like the morning dew.

And others, the kind a father had for his children, was eternal. She spent most of the last year fighting with Griffin, and it seemed that would never change. But she refused to let this world break him, shattering his heart.

She refused to let him mourn his son, a son he couldn't claim.

As long as Toby remained with this army, so would she.

But she'd watch and listen and plan.

She'd find a way to break Egan's hold on her. And then, she'd fight harder than she ever had.

This time … oh, this time … Riona smiled. She had something worth fighting for.

CHAPTER THIRTY

Griffin

The ground trembled beneath Griffin's feet, and a cloud of dust rose into the sky, obscuring the rising moon.

"It sounds like a stampede." Brea stared down the mountain pathway into the Northern Vatlands. They waited for Egan's army along the open tundra of the Iskalt snow plains, hoping to trap the Dark Fae army against the vast mountain ridge.

"It *is* a stampede." Griffin didn't take his eyes off the narrow mountain pass where they would get their first glimpse of Egan's army any minute. Even now they could hear the grunts and snorts of Egan's foot soldiers and the grating sound of ogre's laughing. "I did tell you about the ogres, didn't I?"

"Ogres?" Myles took a step back behind the line of fae rulers. "For real?"

"For real." Griffin sighed. "But keep your eyes on the sky. The Slyph will arrive in the first wave along with the ogres."

"Myles, are you sure you won't go stay with Tia?" Neeve reached for her human husband's hand. "I know you're dying to see this, but I don't want you actually dying."

"Please, Myles," Brea pleaded with her best friend. Her fragile friend with no magic to speak of.

A rumbling filled the sky like rolling thunder.

"That'll be the Slyph." Griffin craned his neck to watch the sky.

"Okay, that's my cue to go babysit my niece who can protect me from whatever that is." Myles kissed his wife and squeezed Brea's shoulder. "Be safe, guys. I can't lose any of you. But I'm no help here."

"Go." Neeve gave him a shove, murmuring Gelsi protective spells under her breath.

"Get ready!" Lochlan shouted to the sea of Iskalt soldiers in formation behind them. His horse paced along their ranks. He would ride with his people against the ogres, while Brea commanded their magic wielders against the Slyph, and Neeve would lead the spellcasters of the Fargelsian army to help both.

Egan's brute strength was no match for their collective magic and their united front.

"Mother of God," Brea whispered as an army of Slyph shot across the sky, swooping low to rain down their arrows upon the Light Fae. Griffin's magic gathered in his palms and he threw a protective barrier into the sky. Most of their enemy's arrows bounced off magical shields like his.

"Magic, Brea!" Griffin shouted. "Use your magic, woman." Most of the Light Fae had reacted like Brea, too stunned to do anything more than shield themselves from the arrows.

"Right." Brea shook off her shock, shouting orders to the Iskalt magic wielders. She didn't have Iskaltian magic, but she knew enough about it to lead them. Her Eldurian magic was of no use at night, but her Gelsi magic was strong. "*Skjöldur!*" She called on her Gelsi shield magic to protect everyone around her.

"*Svero.*" Her magic lashed out like a sword against the lunging Slyph coming at them from the sky.

Griffin's violet magic exploded from his hands, crashing into the chaos.

"What's happening?" Brea cried out, sending out spells to make the Slyph fall from the sky, but they didn't.

None of their magic was working against the Dark Fae. Only their shield magic protected them from their enemy's arrows.

"I thought you said they didn't have magic," Neeve shouted over the roar of wings beating against the sky.

Griffin frowned, searching for a target. Casting his night magic into the sky, he watched it burst against a Slyph with leathery wings like a bat. His magic engulfed the Dark Fae, but it didn't touch him. Instead the magic seemed to bounce off him and returned to Griffin. It would have killed him if not for the shields.

"Gullie's tail." Brea's voice rose above the din of war. "Gullie's tail!" She turned toward Griffin. "I've seen this before." She scrunched up her face as if trying to sift through memories that still didn't feel quite right.

"Get there faster, Brea!" Griffin reached for his bow and knocked an arrow, joining Neeve and her soldiers as they launched their arrows into the sky. Most of them found purchase where their magic hadn't.

"Toby came to get me that day Tia tried to fix Gulliver's

tail. I saw it when I first walked into the room. Tia's magic seemed to bounce right off of Gullie at first, like she couldn't touch him with her magic. That's when he passed out. But they're still kids, so it ... got through somehow."

"They have defensive magic." Griffin launched another volley of arrows. It never made sense that Dark Fae had no magic at all. But, of course, they wouldn't have magic behind the barrier. But that didn't mean they never had it. "They have natural glamours that shield them from humans. It all makes sense. They can't wield magic, but they don't need it. Magic can't touch them."

"Griffin O'Shea! What is the meaning of this?" Lochlan charged right up to him, his horse nearly barreling over him.

"They have some kind of natural defense, Loch!" Brea called to her husband, putting herself between the brothers. Lochlan's scowl told them both what he thought about that. "Our magic can't wound them, Loch. We can only ... push back so they can't get through our protective wards."

"We've put up a wall to keep the ogres out, but they will barrel right through it, eventually." Lochlan glanced back at his soldiers. "I don't think our shields can outlast their brute strength much longer. Why didn't you tell us this?" Lochlan gripped his sword in his hand.

Griffin tried not to roll his eyes at his brother. "For the last three hundred years, they've been behind a wall that takes their magic along with the magic of every Light Fae who passes through the barrier. Just as our magic has been returned to us, so has theirs. We just never knew they had any to be returned."

"We need to retreat!" Neeve shouted.

"We cannot let these beasts into Iskalt." Lochlan's horse reared back.

"They are fae, Loch, not beasts," Griffin grabbed the horse's mane to still him. "Best you learn that lesson quickly, brother. We will leave up our protective magic long enough to retreat and regroup. Then we will come at them with weapons rather than magic. This is going to be a long and bloody war, brother, and I'm going to need you to fight with me, not against me."

Griffin looked to the Slyph raining arrows down from above, catching sight of a familiar set of wings as Riona turned, flying away from the battle as if called back to the master she'd always served.

The third and final book, Fae's Promise, will be here December 2nd!

ABOUT M. LYNN

Michelle MacQueen is a USA Today bestselling author of love. Yes, love. Whether it be YA romance, NA romance, or fantasy romance (Under M. Lynn), she loves to make readers swoon.

The great loves of her life to this point are two tiny blond creatures who call her "aunt" and proclaim her books to be "boring books" for their lack of pictures. Yet, somehow, she still manages to love them more than chocolate.

When she's not sharing her inexhaustible wisdom with her niece and nephew, Michelle is usually lounging in her ridiculously large bean bag chair creating worlds and characters that remind her to smile every day - even when a feisty little girl is telling her just how much she doesn't know.

See more from Michelle MacQueen and sign up to receive updates and deals!
www.michellelynnauthor.com

ALSO BY M. LYNN

QUEENS OF THE FAE

Fae's Deception

Fae's Defiance

Fae's Destruction

CRIMES OF THE FAE

Fae's Prisoner

Fae's Power

Fae's Promise

THE HIDDEN WARRIOR

Dragon Rising

Dragon Rebellion

FANTASY AND FAIRYTALES

Golden Curse

Golden Chains

Golden Crown

Glass Kingdom

Glass Princess

Noble Thief

Cursed Beauty

LEGACY OF LIGHT

A War For Magic

A War For Truth

A War For Love

ABOUT MELISSA

 Melissa A. Craven is an Amazon bestselling author of Young Adult Contemporary Fiction and YA Fantasy (her Contemporary fans will know her as Ann Maree Craven). Her books focus on strong female protagonists who aren't always perfect, but they find their inner strength along the way. Melissa's novels appeal to audiences of all ages and fans of almost any genre. She believes in stories that make you think and she loves playing with foreshadowing, leaving clues and hints for the careful reader.

Melissa draws inspiration from her background in architecture and interior design to help her with the small details in world building and scene settings. (Her degree in fine art also comes in handy.) She is a diehard introvert with a wicked sense of humor and a tendency for hermit-like behavior. (Seriously, she gets cranky if she has to put on anything other than yoga pants and t-shirts!)

Melissa enjoys editing almost as much as she enjoys writing, which makes her an absolute weirdo among her peers. Her favorite pastime is sitting on her porch when the weather is nice with her two dogs, Fynlee and Nahla, reading from her massive TBR pile and dreaming up new stories.

Visit Melissa at Melissaacraven.com for more information about her newest series and discover exclusive content.

facebook.com/emergenovel
twitter.com/melissaacraven
instagram.com/melissaacraven

ALSO BY MELISSA

Emerge: The Proving (Book 7) Coming Soon

ASCENSION OF THE NINE REALMS

(Coming Fall of 2020)

The Valkyrie (An Ascension Novel Book 1)

The Warder (An Ascension Novel Book 2)

The Berserker (An Ascension Novel Book 3)

The Druid (An Ascension Novel Book 4)

Made in the USA
Middletown, DE
11 July 2023